Awake

A Novel by

Bill McConnell

For Noah, whom God has gifted

Other Books by Bill McConnell

Non-Fiction

Professional Christian?

Fiction

Invisible Jesus

Miracle Man

Broken

Introduction

She had laid the book she was reading on the small table by her bed and was looking up at the ceiling. It was late, but time held little meaning for her. The darkness was her friend, hiding her from eyes that might discover her secret if they looked too closely. She would remain still for many hours, lying on the bed until it was safe to get up and begin the next day's routine. Her secret was hers alone, a burden and blessing she had been able to keep for over forty years. A burden because it could not be shared, and a blessing because it gave her the opportunity to live as no one else she had ever met. She suspected there were others who were like her, but it was just that, a suspicion.

She was by default a student of history, looking first through books and now computers for others who might be like her. It was too overwhelming to think there was no one else who lived like she did, separated from everyone else by the secret she carried. It was a miracle that no one had found out her secret, though over the years some had suspected. Except for the scar that ran across her forehead, the result of a nasty fall when she was child, she looked like what she was, a middle-aged woman. She had chosen a vocation where she served others, a vocation she believed was a logical choice for someone who had been given what she had come to view as a gift.

If there were others, she had never found them. She searched news websites nearly every day looking for stories that might reveal someone else who was like her, though the odds of another person being able to hide what they were from the rest of the world seemed incredibly long. She had only been able to survive through an incredible series of circumstances that bordered on the miraculous. Those circumstances determined the direction of her life, and had brought her years ago to the room and the bed she was lying on.

She took a deep breath and listened intently to see if there was any noise coming from outside her room. It was always a temptation for her to leave the room and walk silently down to where the children were sleeping. If she had her way she would be there every night; watching over them as they slept, wondering what the future held for them. There were twenty-four children in three large rooms, grouped by age and gender. She had seen hundreds come and go over the years, and remembered each one by name.

Over those years, she would walk silently through the rooms, looking at each child as they slept, certain she would one day find a child who shared what she was. It was a certainty that would not go away, even after forty years. She knew she was much nearer the end of her life than the beginning, but she had not yet given up hope. What she was had not given her a longer life span, at least not in the conventional sense. She would die one day, and it did not seem fair that she would have to live her life without having at least one person know what it was like to live differently from everyone else. Someone she could confide in and talk with about the challenges, the loneliness, the strain of hiding the accumulation of knowledge and wisdom that made her different from everyone else she had ever known.

Several hours later she was sitting up in bed with her computer in her lap, visiting various websites that might have a news story about someone who was different from everyone else; someone who might be described as a freak or a mutant; someone who could not possibly exist, someone who defied the accepted boundaries of evolutionary biology. It was early enough in the morning that if anyone happened to look into her room they would think she had merely risen early to read and not begin to guess the truth. Not finding anything out of the ordinary, she turned off her computer and rose from her bed, walking slowly out into the hallway.

Making her way down to the kitchen, she put water into the large coffee pot, and after adding the coffee, turned the machine on. While she waited for the coffee to brew, she walked to the front door of the building to retrieve the morning paper. She turned on the outside light, and then opened the door. The paper was there, sitting to the right of what looked like a picnic basket. Inside the basket was a blanket, which she slowly unwrapped. With the outside light on over the porch, she could now clearly see what was in the basket.

"Well, what do we have here?"

Part One

1

It wasn't until the baby had been home for a week that she noticed anything was wrong. The birth had been as normal as possible, even though it was her first. They had named him Francis Xavier, a name that reflected her deep devotion to the Catholic faith. Her husband at first protested, telling her the child would be the object of derision with such a different name, but she was adamant. She had despaired of ever having a child after having been married nearly a decade, and viewed her son as a gift from God. It was only by chance she found that instead of her baby being normal, as he certainly appeared to be, he was, in fact, an aberration, something she could have never imagined.

He did everything a baby should do, that wasn't the problem. He ate, he made the appropriate number of messes in his diaper each day, he would cuddle with his mother and make the right sounds. When she laid him in his crib for his naps, and then at night, he would sleep without any apparent fuss. Except that he didn't.

It wasn't until the baby was three weeks old that she became aware of the peculiarity in her son that would come close to driving her insane and out of the Catholic church.

Since bringing the baby home she had tried to keep him on tight a schedule. This reflected not only her desire to help her son but also her own personality. It would be perfectly in character to say that she was wound rather tight, and liked everything in order and in its place. Some mothers would find this challenging with a newborn, but she was up to the task. Her entire world revolved around being a wife and homemaker, and now that she had added the role of mother to her identity, her life was complete. The future looked bright those first few weeks, and as she settled into her new life with her son she felt blessed and fulfilled, thanking God each day for the little life that made her whole.

Late one night, when she could not sleep, she got out of her bed to look at him as he lay in his crib. He was still sleeping in their bedroom so she could hear him when he was fussy at night and needed to be fed. She had nursed him a few hours earlier and knew that he would be fast asleep. However, when she looked down into the crib she was startled to see him looking up at her, eyes wide open. He had not made a sound, yet there he was looking up as he lay on his back. Gently taking him out of the crib, she took him to the corner of the bedroom and sat down in a rocking chair. Rocking slowly back and forth, she closed her eyes and waited for her son to go back to sleep. After a few minutes, she opened her eyes to see if the rhythmic moving of the rocking chair had done its work.

It hadn't. The baby was looking up at her, eyes wide open, sleep nowhere in sight. She held him tighter and continued to rock, knowing that eventually he would have to fall asleep. It wasn't long before she nodded off, still holding her baby. For two hours, she sat in the chair fast asleep while the baby looked up at her from the blanket he was wrapped in. Finally, just as the sun was coming up and beginning to bring light into the room, she awoke. It took her a moment to realize where she was and what was happening. After remembering what had brought her to the chair, she looked down into the blanket. His eyes were still wide open, and as she looked down he made a noise and began to stir, indicating it was time to eat.

Her first thought was that he must have slept at the same time she was asleep, and that he had just woken up to eat. She rose from the chair and took him downstairs so she would not wake her husband, who did not have to get up for another hour. Sitting down on the couch, she offered him her breast and he eagerly began to feed. He looked up at her the entire time, his eyes fixed on hers. As she sat there waiting for him to finish, she wondered about what had happened that night. If he had been up all night, or most of the night, shouldn't he be fussy? Shouldn't he be crying or exhibiting some form of tiredness? Then she realized, for the first time, that her son never really cried, though when he was hungry he could get fussy. It also occurred to her that every time she laid him down for a nap he wasn't asleep, she just knew it was time for him to rest. She would lay him down and leave him in his crib, returning later to see if he was awake, which he invariably was.

She would have gone down this train of thought farther if her husband had not come down the stairs. When he found that she was not in the bed, he went in search of her and his son. He sat down in a chair across from her in the living room.

"Did he wake up early? How is he today?"

"I guess so. I'm not sure. I woke up in the middle of the night and went over to look at him. He was wide awake, just looking up from the crib. I rocked him for a while and then fell asleep. When I woke up he was still awake."

He noticed there was a trace of doubt in her voice, a suggestion that something might be wrong.

"Let me take a look."

He got up from his chair, and walked over to the couch. Bending down, he took the boy from her and held him close to his chest. The baby appeared to be fine, looking up at his father with wide eyes and what could be considered a smile. There appeared to be nothing wrong, and as he gave him back to his wife, he said,

"I'm sure everything is fine. Don't worry about it. If he was tired wouldn't he be fussy and crying?"

"Yes. At least I think so. But then, he doesn't seem to cry at all, does he?"

The husband sat back down in the chair and paused to think for a moment. His wife was correct, their son didn't seem to cry very much, if at all. Then he thought, how many parents would want a child that didn't cry and seemed to adapt seamlessly to life with his parents?

"Let's not worry about it for the time being. Why don't you make us breakfast and I'll hold him until its ready?"

She heard him, but the words did not register. Her thoughts were moving in another direction as she looked down at her son, and she held him tighter as her husband said again,

"Why don't you give him to me while you make breakfast."

Without speaking she got up and gave him the baby, and then walked slowly toward the kitchen. He wasn't worried about his son, but there was something in the tone of her voice and in how slowly she walked to the kitchen without speaking that concerned him. Figuring that everything would work out, and there was a reasonable explanation for his son's behavior that night, he rocked the child until his wife reappeared in the doorway and motioned for him to come into the kitchen to eat. He laid the baby in a basinet they kept in the living room and went in to have his breakfast. His wife did not join him, but walked over to the basinet and looked down at her son, waiting to see if he would go to sleep.

2

It was two weeks later that she took him to the doctor. Her husband insisted she take him, because she was getting increasingly fragile due to both loss of sleep and a persistent feeling that something was wrong with their son. Already possessed of a delicate constitution and somewhat of a perfectionist, the constant attention she was giving her son was close to driving her husband to distraction.

She would get up at all hours of the night to check and see if the baby was asleep. If you ignored the wide-open eyes and the quiet noises he made while staring up from his crib, he appeared to be sleeping. The husband reasoned that he must be sleeping because no one, not a baby or an adult, could go without sleep. Yet he could not convince his wife to leave it alone, and she was the one beginning to suffer herself from lack of sleep and the accompanying paranoia it sometimes causes in those who either can't or for some reason refuse to sleep.

Meals were late or sometimes forgotten altogether. The house, which was once the picture of cleanliness and order, also began a descent into clutter and mess. One week after the first incident, she began to take the baby to Mass each morning after he left for work. He had no idea what she hoped that might accomplish, and when he tried to talk with her about it she would only say, "God knows." The last straw, which caused him to make the doctor's appointment, was when he came home from work one evening and his wife was gently swinging a burning incense holder over the baby's basinet in the living room. She was mumbling something unintelligible, and as he gently took the incense holder from her, she said,

"It's alright. You'll see. It's alright."

They arrived a few days later to see their pediatrician. He had not seen the baby since looking him over in the hospital after he was born. The couple sat across from the doctor in obvious discomfort. The doctor began by asking,

9

"How is the little guy doing?"

It was the husband who answered, and as the doctor listened he could not help but notice that the mother was not only physically gaunt, but had a haunted look in her eyes. She would not meet his gaze, looking only at her son, who was wrapped in a blanket clutched tightly to her chest.

"Well doc, he seems to be doing fine, except that he never seems to close his eyes. It's kind of disturbing, if you know what I mean."

Looking again at the mother, the doctor knew exactly what the husband meant, though the idea that the baby never closed his eyes made no sense to him.

"What do you mean he doesn't close his eyes?"

"Just that. He never closes his eyes. At least that I've ever seen."

The doctor thought for a moment, running through his mind any condition or illness that might cause a baby to keep its eyes open. The fact that this might mean the baby didn't sleep did not yet cross his mind.

"Is there anything else you have noticed? Anything out of the ordinary?"

The wife looked up at the doctor and spoke for the first time.

"Anything else out of the ordinary? Isn't it enough that he never closes his eyes?"

She spoke the words with a quiet desperation that told the doctor she was close to the edge, physically as well as emotionally.

"Why don't you let me take a look at the little guy? Let's see what a quick examination can tell us."

The doctor got up from the stool he was sitting on and motioned to the mother to bring the baby to the exam table. He waited for a moment as she thought about what to do. She was living on little to no sleep, and obeying even simple commands was almost beyond her ability. He didn't want to take the baby from her, and looked imploringly at the father. He understood what the doctor wanted, and said to his wife,

"Why don't you give the baby to the doctor? I'm sure he can find out what's wrong."

She got up slowly from her chair and gently laid the baby on the exam table. When she continued to stare down at the child and showed no sign of letting the doctor proceed, her husband got up and gently guided her back to the chair. Before she sat down, she looked at the doctor, and said in a whisper,

"God is watching."

The words sent a shiver down the doctor's spine, not because of what she may have meant, but because for the first time she looked him directly in eye, and he could see the precariousness of her emotional state. He made a mental note to talk with the husband alone before they left and suggest she see her own doctor, or perhaps a psychiatrist. He then turned his attention to the baby.

He unwrapped him from the blanket and first poked and prodded him to see if he displayed the appropriate reactions, which he did. The doctor took his temperature, his weight and length, looked into his eyes and, finally, took a small sample of blood. He had already administered a hearing test before the baby had left the hospital, so there really wasn't anything else to do. It appeared to the doctor that the baby was perfectly normal. He wrapped the baby back in the blanket and handed him back to his mother. He didn't know what he might say that could ease the parent's minds, so he again asked,

"You've never seen this baby close his eyes? Never?"

The husband knew right then and there that the life he knew was over. There was nothing wrong with his son, except for the fact that he never closed his eyes. He had searched the Internet for hours on end to see if there was some kind of syndrome or illness that might account for this, but had always come up empty. He already knew the answer but decided to ask the doctor anyway.

"You don't know of any condition or illness that might cause a baby to never close their eyes? You've never seen anything like this I suppose?"

"No, I haven't. And no, I've never heard of a case like this. I'm sorry. He looks perfectly normal to me."

The doctor still had his doubts about whether the baby never closed his eyes, but he did have a suggestion he thought might bring some clarity to the situation.

"Why don't you do this. Buy a nanny camera and install it over the baby's crib. You can have the video recorded on your computer and send it to me. I'll take a look and maybe we can find out what's going on."

The husband agreed it was a good idea, but he already knew what it would show. Like his wife, he had dragged himself against his will into checking on his son at different hours of the night, always with the same result. As they were getting ready to leave, the doctor turned to the wife.

"Why don't you go out and make an appointment for about two weeks from now."

She left without speaking, not realizing the doctor wanted to talk to her husband without her present. When they were alone the doctor said,

"You need to take her to see her own physician. She's right on the verge of a nervous breakdown. At the very least he can prescribe her some sleeping pills. At the worst, she might need to see a psychiatrist."

"You don't believe us, do you?"

"Excuse me?"

"You don't believe that my son never closes his eyes, do you? That's why you want to videotape him at night, right?"

"At this point I don't know what to believe. Your son would be the first baby I've ever heard of who has this condition. I suppose that's possible, but I just don't see how it could be."

The husband shook hands with the doctor and left the exam room to find his wife. He knew exactly what the future held, and he was terrified. What would the doctor do when the video confirmed what they already knew? What advice would he give them then? More importantly, how was he going to stop the downward emotional spiral his wife was in? He was pretty sure he could live with the fact that his son might never close his eyes as long as everything else was normal, but he was just as sure his wife could not. He found her talking with a woman making the required appointment, and when she was finished he said,

"Let's go home now."

She responded by looking down at the baby in her arms.

"There's nothing to go home to."

There was one thing that no one had yet considered, not the parents or the doctor. They were focused on the abnormality that the baby never closed his eyes, which put the baby into a category all by himself in terms of medical history. What never occurred to either the doctor or the parents was the fact that if the baby never closed his

12

eyes it might mean the baby never slept. Of course, the reason this never occurred to them was the fact that people cannot survive without sleep. It is a proven medical fact, beyond dispute. The longest anyone had ever gone without sleep seemed to be 11 days, though after 5 days without sleep death is possible due to any number of factors. When the parents took the baby to the doctor he was just over a month old. The idea that he had not slept during that time was inconceivable, that's why it never entered the doctor's or the parent's minds. Until it did.

3

She sat quietly in the semi-dark, waiting for him to begin. She held her baby on her lap, a rosary wrapped around her fingers. It was an hour before Mass, a time when the priest was available to hear confessions. The door opened on the other side of the booth, indicating the priest had arrived. Though she could not see him, she knew he would cross himself before he asked her if she had any sins to confess. She had already repeatedly crossed herself, hoping the ritual would bring her relief or a measure of faith. It did not. When he opened the small screen that separated them, she knew it was time to speak.

"Father, forgive me for I have sinned. It has been two days since my last confession."

She paused for a moment before continuing. It was at this point she was to list her sins to the priest and then receive her penance. She had given much thought to her sins, and finally said,

"I am guilty of the sin of pride. I am guilty of failing God as a wife and mother. I know now why He has punished me."

The priest, who had heard thousands of confessions during his years in ministry, was taken aback. Though the confessional was supposed to be anonymous, he knew who sat on the other side of the booth. She came to Mass almost every day and was one of his most faithful parishioners. He was looking forward to baptizing her baby, and had wondered why she had not yet presented him to the church for the sacrament. Then there was the tone of her voice. There was a desperation present, and a touch of grief. Instead of giving her some form of penance, he broke his usual protocol.

"How has God punished you? How have you failed Him?"

"It's my child, father. He has punished me by giving me a child of the devil."

These words were spoken calmly, with a voice devoid of emotion, and the hairs on the priest's neck stood up on end. He had no idea how to respond, and frantically ran his mind through what he might say. It was obvious to him that he needed to speak with her outside of the confessional booth, but what was said in the confessional was supposed to stay in the confessional. It would be trite to just give her some form of penance when it was obvious she was in some kind of mental or spiritual crisis. He finally thought he had a way out of his dilemma.

"Your penance is to talk to your priest about the child. You are absolved of your sins if you will do this."

He waited for her response, which she gave after almost a minute of silence.

"I will, but it won't help. Nothing will."

4

Two things happened in the next three days. First, the father dutifully bought a nanny cam and attached it to the wall above his son's crib. His wife watched with an air of detachment, not asking any questions or making any comments. He figured two nights' worth of video would be enough to convince the doctor they were telling the truth about their baby. Transferring the file to a DVD, he dropped it off at the doctor's office on his way to work. He didn't bother to look at what he had recorded because his wife had spent much of those two nights sitting by the crib silently watching her son stare up at the ceiling.

The doctor had spent some time looking through pediatric journals and various articles he found on the Internet, but could find nothing even remotely related to what the parents had told him. When the DVD arrived, his heart sank because he knew that the husband would not have left it for him if it didn't conclusively prove the child never closed his eyes. He didn't have time to watch over 15 hours of video, so he brought in a nurse from a temporary agency to view the DVD. He made clear what he wanted her to do, but she still had questions.

"You want me to watch hours of video to see if a baby closes his eyes?"

"Yes. The parents claim that they have never seen him close his eyes. Not once. I don't know what to believe, so I suggested they videotape him while he slept."

"And all I'm looking for is to see if he closes his eyes. That's it?"

"Yes, and don't take it lightly. These people are convinced there's something wrong with their child even though he seems perfectly normal to me. Why don't you watch until lunch and then come and tell me what you've found?"

The four hours passed interminably, and gave the nurse a severe case of the creeps. It wasn't watching the baby that was disturbing, it was the seen and unseen presence of the mother who would sit by the crib for a time and then leave, only to reappear minutes later. When she was in the frame of the camera she sat so still the nurse could not detect any movement. It was as if she was focusing all her will on the child so that she had nothing left of herself. If the mother was at all self-conscious about being filmed, she showed no sign of it. When lunch time arrived, she went and found the doctor, who was just finishing up with a patient. He took the nurse to his office, and motioned for her to sit down.

"Well?"

"He never once closed his eyes. He would blink, like a normal baby, but he never closed his eyes that I could see. Do you want me to watch more this afternoon?"

"You might as well, but I don't think it's going to be any different. I've never heard of a baby who never closes his eyes. I don't know what to tell them."

"There's one other thing."

"What?"

"The mother gives me the creeps. She just sits there for hours on end. Watching and not moving. And when I say not moving, I mean she sits as still as a stone. She's headed for a breakdown, but I suspect you already know that."

"I've told the husband to have her see her own doctor. Whether he's done that or not, I don't know."

15

The nurse was ready to go back to viewing the tapes, when she had a final thought. It was too fanciful to be considered seriously, but after watching the baby for hours she had noticed something that the doctor had not brought up, for obvious reasons.

"You know doctor, if you watch the DVD you would swear the baby isn't sleeping at all. I know it's impossible, but that's what it looks like to me."

"A baby that doesn't sleep? No way."

The nurse got up from the chair and turned to leave. Her parting words were,

"You thought the same thing about the baby never closing its eyes, didn't you?"

"There might be some kind of physical explanation for never closing its eyes. Maybe something with the muscles around the eyes. Something like that. But never sleeping? It can't be."

The second event happened when the mother met with the priest from her church. She had made an appointment as soon as she could, hoping the church would have an answer for her, though her faith was being stretched thin. The only reason her child would not close its eyes, the only reason that made sense to her, was that God was punishing her. There was no physical reason her baby stared continually at whatever was in front of him, eyes never closing, at least that the doctor could find. That left the realm of the spiritual, a realm that held both good and evil. Since she believed God was punishing her, it was easy for her to think that He had given her over to the devil, to do with her what he pleased. There was no doubt that her physical and emotional state, brought on by sleeplessness and deprivation, contributed to her thought process.

She also knew, however, that the church taught the reality of demon possession, and the possibility of exorcism. As she waited outside the priest's office, these thoughts were swirling through her mind, leaving her open to the idea that her child was not physically but spiritually afflicted.

The priest sat at his desk on the other side of the door, wondering how he was going to deal with the woman waiting outside. Most of his counseling appointments bordered on the mundane: arranging baptisms, pre-marital counseling, occasionally helping those who had addiction or other personal problems, and those parishioners who came to see him about matters of faith or conscience. He could not recall the last time he had someone come to him in such distress; distress that seemed to be the result of her belief that somehow God was punishing her, but for what? She had said she was proud, and had failed as a mother and wife. Failed how? To the priest, she was the model of propriety and piety, one of the few "traditional" Catholic women left in his church. He knew he would have to tread carefully, and let her bring up what she had confessed to him while in the booth.

He got up from his desk, and crossed his office to open the door and let her in. When he saw her sitting in the outer office, clutching her baby tightly and slowly rocking back and forth in the chair, his heart sank. She looked like she hadn't slept in days and did not acknowledge his presence, even though he was standing right in front of her. He cleared his throat to get her attention.

"Why don't you come inside and we'll talk."

She raised her head and silently rose, a spectral image more like a ghost than a human being. The priest guided her to the chair in front of his desk, and when he was seated he began by saying,

"You don't look good. How are you feeling? Are you getting enough sleep?"

"It's my baby. He doesn't sleep. I don't know what to do. That's why I'm here."

Her words came as such a surprise that he was momentarily taken aback. What did she mean that her baby didn't sleep? This is why she came to see him?

"You mean that your baby doesn't sleep well? That he is keeping you up at night? Something like that?"

She raised her head so slowly that it seemed she was deliberately exaggerating the effect for the tension it brought to the room. Looking the priest straight in eye, she spoke with a voice that seemed to come from outside of her.

"I said my baby doesn't sleep. Ever."

He was in over his head, and he knew it. It wasn't possible that her baby wasn't sleeping, so what was she saying? And why had she come to see him instead of a doctor?

"Have you taken him to a doctor?"

"He doesn't sleep, ever. The doctor knows this but won't help me."

What she was saying was making no sense, and the priest began to think that he needed to get her to a mental health professional. There were several that he referred people to, people that he knew he could not help. Before he could turn the conversation in that direction, she said,

"Only you can help me. You need to fix my baby."

"What do you mean, fix your baby?"

Slowly, and with a conviction in her voice that brought a thought to his mind that was preposterous, barbaric and insane, she said,

"You know what I mean. You need to fix my baby."

He thought back to the words she had spoken to him in the confessional. The priest had dismissed them as the product of an emotional and distraught woman, but now he was not so sure. Child of the devil? What had she meant when she used those words?

"May I see the child?"

Without hesitation, she stood and gave him the baby, wrapped in a blue blanket, to the priest. He sat down and uncovered the blanket to get a full view of the child. The child looked perfectly normal, moving his arms about since removing the blanket had given him the space to move freely. As he held the child he tried to think how someone could think this child was anything but normal? Giving the child back to the mother, the priest thought he had a way to end the session and perhaps get the woman the real help she needed.

"Why don't I pray for you and the child? I'm sure that will help. Then I would suggest you see a friend of mine who might be able to help you in this situation."

Before he could pray, she responded by saying,

"I didn't come here for prayer."

"Well, what did you come here for?"

Holding the baby in one arm, she reached into her purse and brought out a small book. Turning to a page she had earmarked with a post-it note, she handed it to the priest. It was a red book called Rituale Romanum, written by Cardinal Jorge Arturo Medina. The priest knew what the small book contained, though he had never read it. Holding it in his hands, he refused to open it, and, hands trembling, gave it back to the mother.

"I don't do that. I won't do that, and I think you need to leave."

She rose from her chair, putting the book back in her purse. Her parting words to the priest, spoken in a whisper, were,

"If you won't, I'll find another priest else who will."

He knew she meant it, though he doubted she would find a priest who would do what she wanted. It was her mental state that concerned him. The priest knew where the husband worked, and would call him momentarily, but he needed to calm down emotionally first. His breathing was rapid and holding his hands out in front of his body, he noticed they were still shaking. Why shouldn't they be shaking, he thought? When was the last time sometime had come to him with a request to do an exorcism?

5

The next day the husband met with the doctor, though he already knew what the doctor was going to tell him. He would be wrong, and the appointment would set in motion a series of events that would lead he and his wife to move to the other side of the country. But not with their son.

They sat in the doctor's office, and the doctor did not know quite where to begin. In the last two days, he had thought about nothing but the child. He had watched several hours of the videotape just to assure himself of what the nurse was telling him. It was true that the child never once closed his eyes, and the thought that the baby never slept was beginning to take over his mind. As a physician, he was convinced that you could not sleep without closing your eyes. Open eyes allow the brain to receive stimuli that forced it to respond to what it was seeing, even if you were just a baby. There was nothing in any of the literature he had managed to find online that said you could sleep with your eyes open, nor were there any articles, research or studies that gave any physical reason why a baby's eyes would never close. He knew he had nothing to offer the father, which put him in a awkward position.

"I don't know what to tell you. I've never seen anything like this before. Your son seems perfectly normal, except for the fact that he never seems to close his eyes."

"So, what do I do? It's driving my wife nuts."

The doctor paused before answering, not believing that he was going to propose what seemed like the only logical explanation.

"Let's consider this. What if your son is different from everyone else? What if your son doesn't need to close his eyes? What if it's just the way he was made?"

The doctor stopped again, and then added the words that would change everything.

"What if your son doesn't need to sleep? What if that's just who he is?"

If the words seemed incredible to the doctor, they were lunacy to the father.

"You mean my son is a freak? That he's different from everyone else? It's impossible."

Intellectually, the doctor was forced to agree. But the videotapes did not lie. The father had spent more than enough time, as had the mother, looking at their son staring silently into space in the middle of the night to know what the doctor was saying might be true. The father's train of thought was broken when the doctor said,

"Look, let's talk about your wife for a moment. For whatever reason, your son seems to be perfectly normal, but I'm concerned about your wife. Do you think she's able to live with this?"

The husband knew the answer, but did not want to admit to the doctor that his wife was close to a nervous breakdown. She seldom slept, she barely ate, and spent most of her time watching over her son, perhaps waiting for the time when his eyes would close and he could be considered "normal". He had tried talking to her about seeing her own doctor if for no other reason than to get some sleeping pills. But she demurred, saying that only a priest could help her now.

"I don't know what to think. She won't go see her doctor, she won't eat or sleep and she's constantly fingering her rosary."

He paused for a moment as the weight of his situation again took hold of his emotions. Shaking his head, and speaking more to himself than the doctor, he said,

"This isn't going to end well, is it?"

"No, I suspect not."

The doctor would never hear from the husband again, and eventually the incident would recede from his memory due to the busyness of his life. He would be one of only a handful of people who would ever know about the absolute uniqueness of the child, and the only one who would remain untouched by that uniqueness.

6

The husband wasn't the kind of man to take things lying down. After he left the doctor's office he began to construct a plan that might save his wife, if not his son. He knew eventually his wife was going to break, either emotionally, physically or both. It was the phone call from the priest that brought a final clarity to his mind on the course he needed to pursue. After talking with the priest on the phone in his office, he made two calls, one to his boss and another to a realtor. When he was given assurances by both men that what he wanted was not only feasible, but eminently possible, he brought his computer to life and did a Google search. When he found what he was looking for, he printed out the address, and then took the sheet of paper from the printer.

He knew it would take all his persuasive powers to convince his wife that what he was planning was the best for their son. There were buttons he could push to get his way, and part of him hated what he was about to do. However, he could see no other way out for them, and he knew it was only a matter of time before his wife went over the edge.

He wasn't as religious as his wife, but he did believe in God, and had been brought up in the Catholic faith. He wondered what kind of punishment he would receive for what he was going to do. Because the government had paid for law school, he was obligated to serve four years in the Army. He was deployed twice to Iraq, usually defending soldiers who had committed some type of crime. On an off day, he was driving with a convoy when the lead vehicles were struck by several IED's. Those who weren't injured tried to help those who were wounded, but more than ten soldiers died in the attack. As he went from one injured man to another, trying to assist in any way he could, he could instinctively tell who had a chance to live and who was going to die from their wounds. That was the hardest thing he had ever done, trying to figure out who was going to live and who was going to die.

Here he was faced with the same dilemma. It wasn't a matter of who was going to live or who was going to die, but who he had a chance to save. He was convinced his wife would likely go insane, or perhaps even die, because he knew she would never be able to come to grips with whatever their son was. There was a chance they would be found out, but it was a chance he would have to take. Moving across the country, putting space between the images that would always hold memories of their son, it might work. But only if he could convince her it was God's will, otherwise he knew she would drown in grief and despair.

When he arrived home that evening, she was sitting quietly in the living room, slowly going back and forth in the rocking chair. The baby was in the basinet looking up and around, eyes wide open as usual. He sat down across from her.

"Can we talk for a minute?"

"Did you see the doctor?"

"Yes, I did. He watched the videotape for hours and knows what we told him is true. He even thinks it may be possible that he never sleeps, as impossible as that may be."

On hearing those words, she straightened up in the chair, and then leaned forward.

"I know that. It's what I told the priest. It's my fault, and he won't do anything about it."

"What's your fault? You haven't done anything wrong. No one has."

"Why did it take us years to have a baby? Why do we have a baby that doesn't sleep? I know why. I was proud, and God has seen fit to punish me. I know how to fix this, but the priest won't help me. But I'll find another priest. You'll see."

Every instinct told him it was fruitless to argue with her, but he was being drawn into her world against his will.

"What are you talking about? You're the most religious person I've ever met. How can you be proud? What do you think you're proud of that makes you think God would punish you?"

She responded slowly, breathing heavily, as if saying the words brought added condemnation.

"I tried to be the perfect wife. I tried to be the perfect Catholic. I tried to have the perfect home. I tried to marry the perfect husband. I did all of this for myself, and now it's all come back to haunt me."

She laughed aloud after she said the word "haunt", a subtle reminder that she believed there were dark forces arrayed against her and her son. Forces she needed to combat to bring her back from the brink. The husband knew that if he was going to act it needed to be right then and there; she was close to losing the ability to have any type of rational conversation.

"I can fix this."

"What do you mean, you can fix this? Do you know a priest?"

"No, but I do know a place where the baby can be safe. A place where they can help him. A place where God can protect him from the evil in this world."

He held his breath as the words penetrated her consciousness, working their way into her mind. She got up from the chair and walked to the basinet, looking down at the child.

"What place?"

"A safe place, a place that is run by Nuns. A place that looks after children, and protects them from evil."

He avoided using the word "orphanage" because he thought it might suggest she was abandoning her child instead of giving him to people who would shelter and care for him. He disliked using the word "evil", but felt it necessary to try and connect with her on an emotional level. When she continued to look at the child and not speak, he continued, saying,

"You know this is what God would want you to do. It's best for the child, they might even know a priest who could help. This is the best for our son. You've done everything you could. Now it's time to let God do the rest."

His world hung in the balance, and he knew it. If she refused, he would lose them both. If she consented, with time he might be able to bring her back to some sort of sanity, but even that could prove to be too much. After what seemed an eternity, she finally turned to him.

"You can never tell me where you are going to take him. I know that I'm weak and I'll try to find him. Promise me you'll never tell me where he is."

"Of course. I've arranged for us to move to California. My company has an office there. You'll like it, it's sunny and we can start over. You'll see."

She moved away from the basinet, not hearing a word her husband had said. Slowly walking up the stairs to her bedroom, she would remain in bed for the next two days until they were ready to fly out to Los Angeles. It was a vain hope, believing that a change of location would begin to restore or heal her from the trauma of giving up her son, a son that she believed was the result of what she was and what she had done. After just a few months living in a new house in Los Angeles, he would commit her to a mental institution, where she would spend the rest of her short life. She never again spoke about her son, the experience was walled off deep in her subconscious, in a place where only demons dwelt.

7

She took the basket into the kitchen and sat it down on a large table. Unwrapping the blanket that covered the baby, she looked down at the child and wondered what circumstance had brought him to her. As she looked through the basket she could find no note, only some diapers and a bottle presumably filled with formula. It had been years since a baby had been left at the front door, that baby had stayed at the orphanage for nearly seven years until he was adopted. It was the policy of the orphanage to have children stay for at least five years so they could be given an education, an education which included the teachings of the Catholic church. They Nuns who ran the orphanage, which was one of the few remaining in the state, felt it was part of their calling to give the children God brought to them a foundation of religious instruction on which to build their lives.

The children came to the sisters from all sorts of circumstances, usually as the result of a tragedy. There were seven sisters and three lay people who ran the orphanage, none of them getting any younger. It was an unspoken reality among them that if they did not find some younger workers, they would eventually have to close. Such was their faith in God that they believed it was His responsibility to take care of the children; they were merely the instruments He had chosen to carry out His will.

She wrapped the child back in his blanket, and gently lifted him out to get a better look. He wasn't a newborn, he looked well fed, and he did not appear to be sick. He looked up at her with a steady gaze, wiggling at the constraint of the blanket. Sitting down on a chair at the table, she took the bottle and offered it to the child. He was hungry, and greedily sucked at the nipple, all the while looking up at her as if what was happening was completely normal.

"What's this?"

She had not noticed Sister Margaret, who had entered the kitchen from the hallway that lead to the large dining room. Sister Margaret walked over to the chair where Sister Flavia was feeding the baby, and looked down at the child.

"When did this happen?"

Sister Margaret was the head of the orphanage, having lived there for nearly fifty years. She ran the institution as her personal fiefdom; no one challenged her authority because everyone knew her first thought was always for the children, and what was best for them. If she was occasionally stiff and unyielding in her demeanor and decisions, it was overlooked by the other Nuns and the staff, and especially the children, who saw past her somewhat autocratic behavior.

"It seems someone has left us a present. I found him this morning when I went out to get the paper. There was no note, no paperwork of any kind. Just a bottle. He seems perfectly normal, though we should probably have the doctor examine him."

She put it out there, and waited to see how Sister Margaret would respond. There would be no reason for the doctor to examine the child unless it was going to stay at the orphanage. Otherwise, they would call Children's Services, who would come and take the baby, undoubtedly putting him in foster care until they could sort out what to do. Sister Margaret immediately knew what Sister Flavia was proposing, and took a step back, bringing her arms to her chest and narrowing her eyes. She thought for a moment, and then said,

"We don't have room. All the beds are full. We haven't had a baby for years. You know this."

"Yes, that's true."

Sister Flavia paused for a moment, and then spoke in a voice that carried just a trace of questioning.

"We must ask why God has brought the child to us at this moment, what does He intend for us to do? Could it be for a reason that we don't understand now, but will come to understand in time? I can watch the child, and it can stay in my room."

Then Sister Flavia added as an afterthought, anticipating what Sister Margaret was going to say,

"You know that I'm much younger than you. I can watch the child and do my work."

It was a running joke between them that Sister Flavia was around ten years younger than Sister Margaret, though you would not have known it from the pace that Sister Margaret set for herself. Finally, knowing that her next words would have more weight, she said,

"After all these years without a baby, why would God do this now? Might it be the last chance we have to be with one so young? And think of what it would mean to the other children to have a baby among us."

Sister Margaret thought for a moment, silently seeking what she thought God would want for them. Finally, as she went for her first cup of coffee, she said,

"I'll call the doctor. You'll need to make a trip to the store for clothes, diapers and formula."

With that said, Sister Margaret left the kitchen with her coffee to begin the routine that seldom varied from day to day. She would spend time in her office going over the day's schedule, making sure that everything was in order and the day held no surprises. Sister Margaret loved order, routine and structure, learning from long experience that without them the orphanage would not thrive as it tried to raise, educate and provide for two dozen children. Yet her day began with a huge surprise, and as she sat at her desk she wondered if she had made the right decision. She had a soft spot in her heart for Sister Flavia, though she would not admit it to herself. Sister Flavia was different from the other Nuns, including herself, though Sister Margaret could not quite put her finger on what made her different. Sister Flavia worked harder and longer than anyone else, was more faithful in her prayers and devotions, and was certainly the most informed and educated among them. Sister

26

Margaret did not understand how she could accomplish everything she did and still be the most thoughtful and caring of them all. It didn't make sense to Sister Margaret that someone who worked that hard would never seem to struggle with the physical realities that came with getting older, and Sister Margaret did not like things that made no sense to her.

Sister Flavia was still in the kitchen, looking down at the child who had just finished the bottle of formula. She would have to leave for the store soon because the child would need to be fed again in a few hours. As she got up from the chair and went in search of something she could use as a basinet, she said to the child,

"Why would someone leave you with us? What's your story, little one?"

Sister Flavia would soon find out.

8

It was the children who were the happiest about the new arrival at the orphanage. They gathered around the basket after breakfast to look at the new addition to their extended family. Sister Margaret had made the announcement after breakfast, letting the children come into the kitchen to see the baby in groups of six. When one of them asked what the baby's name was, Sister Margaret was caught short. It was Sister Flavia who answered.

"His name will be Jacob. That's what we will call him."

After the last group had seen the child, Sister Margaret shooed the children off to the large room off the chapel that served as their school. The Sisters rotated teaching duties, using curriculum for the children that was self-directed, allowing the children to learn at their own pace and requiring more supervision from the Sisters than actual teaching. Sister Flavia had skipped breakfast to make a quick run to the store and returned just as the last group of children were leaving the kitchen. She would need to do more shopping, but had formula, diapers and a few onesies to use as needed. The clerk at Wal Mart looked puzzled at why a nun would be buying things needed for a baby, and noticing the puzzlement on the woman's face, Sister Flavia said,

"It's a long story. I hope it has a happy ending."

When she returned to the orphanage, Sister Flavia put the baby in the basket and took him to the chapel. Every Sister, either before or after their morning tasks, spent time in prayer in the chapel. She sat him down on the pew next to her, and after crossing herself and silently saying the rosary, thought about the events of the morning. Sister Flavia had been brought to the orphanage just as the baby sitting next to her, except she was five years old, and she knew why her mother had requested her child be taken there when she died of cancer. She was different from everyone else, a difference that could end any chance of a "normal" life if found out. Her mother had protected her from those who might find out about the secret that defined her short life. Though her mother did not share that secret with the Nuns she entrusted her child to, she had confidence God would continue to guard the child as she grew.

By the time she entered the orphanage at age five, Flavia knew she was different. Her mother had explained to her that no one would understand her secret, and she taught her how to live with that secret so that others would not suspect. It was nothing short of a miracle that a five-year-old would have the discipline and emotional strength to hide what she was from those around her, but she did, for the twelve long years she lived with the Sisters.

She was an orphan, and as such she qualified for full tuition at any of the state universities. It was during her time at university, where she received two degrees in three years, one in history and the other in philosophy, that she decided to become a Sister and return to the orphanage that her mother had entrusted her to. It would be the easiest place to hide what she was, and offered her the chance to give back to others what the Nuns had given to her. There would be no chance for a "normal" life out in the world, someone would find out, especially if she fell in love and married. How do you hide what you are from the person you are closest to? She was tempted to try, but after much agony and prayer decided it was not possible. She was strong, but not that strong. Instead, she gave herself unreservedly to God, and to a life she hoped would bring benefit to others and fulfillment to her.

In a large measure, those wishes were fulfilled. The community of Sisters, combined with the lay staff and especially the children, brought her a sense of belonging and purpose. Yet, life was not without its challenges. She was always on guard, knowing that if she was found out there would be no explanation that would serve to satisfy the questions that would naturally be raised. Then there was the enormity of understanding she was different from everyone else around her. The discipline and strength of character it took to lie for hours on her bed pretending to sleep she attributed to God, who she felt had a purpose for her that was only partially fulfilled when she became a Sister. There was an awareness in her that there was something else out there, and as the years passed she did not give up hope, but continued to wait for what was to come.

That first day flew by as Sister Flavia worked to manage her responsibilities and attend to the baby. It was easier than she would have thought, the baby would occasionally make noises and utter small cries when he needed to be changed or fed, but otherwise he lay quietly in the basket, unaware that his life had taken such a dramatic turn.

It wasn't until later in the afternoon that Sister Flavia thought to lay the child down for a nap, though he wasn't fussy or rubbing his eyes as babies typically do when they are tired. She took him up to her room after feeding him and changing his diaper, and then gently closed the door and walked downstairs to supervise the children's afternoon recess.

Two hours later she slowly opened the door to her room, first to listen, and then to look. Hearing nothing, she assumed the child was asleep, and left to begin the preparations for dinner. She reasoned that the events of the day had left the boy over tired, and wondered if she was in for a long night if he continued to sleep. She was right, but not in the way she thought.

Returning to her room an hour later, just before dinner was to be served, she walked quietly up to the basket to see if the child was still asleep. He wasn't, and she wondered how long he had been awake. She reached down into the basket, and took him into her arms. Talking more to herself than to the baby, she said,

"You're sure a good little one. What happened to bring you to us?"

Turning around to leave the room, she made a mental note that she would need to purchase a crib, car seat and other odds and ends the baby would need. As she left the room to go down to dinner, she said to the child,

"Let's go show you off to everyone. They're so pleased that you're here."

He was the center of attention at dinner, as would be expected. Many of the children ate their meal as fast as possible so they could take turns holding him, talking to him as if he understood every word. After dinner the children, staff and Sisters gathered in the chapel for a time of prayer and reflection. When everyone was seated and the children had quieted down, Sister Margaret lead them in the Lord's prayer, and then, broke from tradition, speaking to the assembled group about the day's events. She gestured toward Sister Flavia, who was in the back row holding the baby.

"You all know what has happened today. For reasons that only God knows, He has brought us a baby, a baby that needs love and care. We have not had a baby with us for many years, and having him here will bring many challenges and disruptions. I have thought all day whether we are equipped for this responsibility."

She paused to give her words added weight, and her tone was serious, as was the expression on her face. Sister Flavia had a moment of doubt, knowing the fate of the child she held in her arms was in the hands of Sister Margaret, who was the undisputed leader of the orphanage. Then Sister Margaret said,

"But I know that we are sufficient for this challenge, and that God will give us the strength to help this child find his way in life."

The children burst into applause, something that Sister Flavia had never seen before in the chapel. Sister Margaret clapped her hands together to restore order, and when the children had settled down, said,

"The children can go and finish their studies or play outside until dusk. The rest of you are dismissed to your duties."

9

It was a busy evening for everyone in the orphanage. Sister Flavia and two other sisters cleaned up after dinner and began the preparations for breakfast the next morning. The baby lay quietly on the kitchen table, on a blanket surrounded by pillows. Sister Flavia thought it best that he have some room to move, and would glance over at him while she worked. The two other Sisters, Catherine and

Maria, who was from Guatemala, would occasionally stop what they were doing to bend over and touch the child, still adjusting to the new life that was now a part of their world. Sister Maria, who was the youngest of the Sisters, while looking at the child, said to herself,

"What would have happened if I had found you this morning? Would you get to live with me, I wonder?"

She wasn't jealous of Sister Flavia, who by now everyone knew would be the child's guardian. Perhaps she was wondering about what her life would have been like if she had not been called to the Sisterhood, a life that presumably would have included children of her own. Though she was talking to herself, Sister Flavia was close enough to hear what she had said. Turning around from the sink and walking over to the table, she said to Sister Maria,

"He belongs to all of us, but only one of us should care for him. I'm certainly not his mother, but I believe God had me find him, for whatever reason that may be."

"Of course, Sister."

Sister Maria blushed, and walked out of the kitchen to bring more dishes in from the dining room. Sister Catherine watched her leave, and when she was sure they would not be overheard, said to Sister Flavia,

"Sometimes she has doubts. She didn't mean anything by it. It's just that none of us has been around a baby for some time. Just give her some time."

Sister Flavia was aware that Sister Catherine was talking, but did not hear what she was saying. Though she had spoken softly to Sister Maria, Sister Flavia was surprised by the reaction she had to the words Sister Maria had spoken to the child. It had never occurred to her that anyone else should watch over the child, or be considered his guardian. She loved all the children that lived at the orphanage, and she had even had favorites over the years. Her devotion to the Sisterhood, however, had always come first. All her emotions, will and purpose centered around her faith that expressed itself practically in devotion first to God, then to her Sisters, and, finally, to the children. She now knew that even though the child had been in her life for less than one day, her priorities were subtly changing. The child had been given to her, she had found him on the steps that same morning, she would be the one who would raise him, and if anyone said anything different.....

She stopped her train of thought immediately. A lifetime of sacrificial belief, of putting others first, of being devoted to the good of others, brought her up short. Sister Flavia had never thought in terms like these before, and she was troubled that her attachment to the child had produced these feelings. Taking the child off the table and wrapping him in the blanket, she headed for the chapel to sort through what she was feeling.

There was no one else in the chapel, and after she closed the door and crossed herself, she sat down in the front pew. Two figures dominated the wall in front of her; a life size statue of the Virgin Mary to her left, and to her right a representation of Jesus hanging on the cross. She didn't know how to phrase what she wanted to say, so instead of finding exactly the right words, she just said,

"Did You give this child to me, or to all of us? Am I the one to raise this child, or do You want something else for him?"

She asked the question because she lived in a community, a community where the needs of the many came before the needs of the individual. It was foreign for Sister Flavia to think of her needs, or her desires, before the needs of the community. The Sisters had no individual property, except for their clothes, and their vows compelled them to put the needs and desires of others ahead of their own. Yet, here she was with a fierce desire to keep the child in her care, though she realized he, too, belonged to the community. She assumed that Sister Margaret would acquiesce to her stated desire to care for the child, but she knew Sister Margaret would do what she thought best. If that included letting others share the burden of caring for the child, there was nothing Sister Flavia could do.

Losing track of time as she continued to gaze at the two figures who represented everything she believed and was committed to, she was startled when a hand gently touched her on the shoulder. Startled, she turned quickly around to see Sister Margaret standing behind her.

"May I sit with you?"

Sister Flavia motioned with her hand, and Sister Margaret sat down beside her.

"You're troubled, I can sense that. You're wondering what they think, and what they want you to do. You have feelings you have not experienced in many years, feelings you think are contrary to the vows you took."

"Something like that."

"If I didn't think the child belonged here, I would have called Children's Services and he would be gone by now. The only reason I have allowed him to stay is that I believe in some way that I don't yet see, and may never see, your destiny and that of the child are bound together. Does that help?"

"It does, thank you."

"Good. Now, don't you think it's time to get him to bed?"

They left the chapel together, Sister Margaret heading to her office and Sister Flavia upstairs to her room. As she walked she looked down at the child to see if he was, indeed, ready for bed. He was moving around in the blanket and making the occasional baby sounds, but seemed wide awake. It was nearly 9 o'clock, and except for the two hours she had left him in her room, he had been awake all day. She thought, he must be tired, so I'll change his diaper and lay him in the basket and he'll eventually fall asleep. The basket was big enough for him to sleep in, but she knew she should get him a crib the next day.

It took her just a few minutes to prepare herself for bed, preparations that she undertook solely for the pretense that she was like everyone else. She would read for an hour or so, and then lay quietly on the bed until around four in the morning, when she felt it was safe to begin looking through her computer in the search for someone who might be like her. It never occurred to her what she might do if she found the person she was looking for; her thoughts were centered only on the search.

Laying quietly in bed, she continued her reading of a biography about Napoleon. She frequently read biographies of people who claimed they needed little sleep in order to function. It was said Napoleon only needed four hours of sleep each night, which led Sister Flavia to wonder if he slept at all. Since Napoleon had died in 1821, it didn't really matter. But it did make Sister Flavia wonder.

She was just about to turn the light off when she heard the baby utter a snuffling noise, and then watched as his little hand rose just over the edge of the basket. Sitting up in the bed, she thought about what she should do. It was nearly eleven, he hadn't slept much all day, and though it had been years since there had been a baby at the orphanage, she knew that during their first months they slept hours each day. She got out of bed and looked down into the basket, which was sitting on the one table in her room. He was certainly awake, looking up at her, eyes wide open. She had fed and changed him before laying him down in the basket, was there something she had forgotten to do that would put him to sleep?

The one thought she had was that it might help if she rocked him, so she quietly put on a robe, and wrapping him in his blanket, took him downstairs to the only rocking chair in the building. It was dark in the common room, and as she sat down and began to rock slowly back and forth, she could feel him moving in her arms. He was quiet as he wiggled under the constraints of the blanket, but after several hours of rocking he seemed no nearer to sleep than he had when she laid him in the blanket hours earlier in her room. Giving in to the inevitable, she took him back to her room and laid him on the bed, her mind trying to come to grips with what was happening. She would have been more worried except for the fact that the baby seemed to be perfectly fine. He was eating, he was soiling his diapers, and he reacted to whatever stimuli was put in front of him. The day had been quite fateful for him, but he didn't have the ability to understand any of the day's events. Sister Flavia knew that an adult might run off nervous energy or adrenaline if something so life changing happened to them, but he was just a baby.

Then it happened, and her life would never be the same. The child was lying on the bed, next to the biography of Napoleon. Looking down at the child, it hit her like a thunderbolt, and she gasped and took a step back from the bed. The thoughts came flooding into her mind so quickly that she became dizzy at the implications of what was running violently through her consciousness.

She was not alone after all, and the enormity of the moment overwhelmed her ability to control her emotions. It had been years since Sister Flavia had shed tears, and for the next several minutes she silently sobbed into her pillow, trying not to be heard by anyone who might be walking past her room, though it was barely two in the morning.

Bringing herself back to a semblance of control by slowly breathing and beginning to think of everything this new reality portended, she paused to thank God for answering this most personal of prayers. She knew she was being given a responsibility greater than any she could have ever imagined, and asked Him that she would be equal for the task. Then she had a thought.

Putting pillows around the child, she sat at the desk and turned on her computer. She guessed that whoever left the child that morning lived in the state, so she began by looking up birth records. It took her some time to find a website that listed recent births in the state. She could not refine the list to just look for male births, so she had to wade through hundreds of names. Not knowing exactly what she was looking for, she just had to trust something would jump out at her and make sense of what she was experiencing with the child.

Finally, an hour into her search, she found him. It was a name that reeked of Catholicism, a name that spoke volumes to her. There were other names that probably reflected a strong Catholic faith, but none so pronounced as the one she continued to stare at. She clicked on the name to find out who his parents were, and then wrote them down on a piece of paper. Quickly typing the results into Google, she found that the parents lived about an hour away from the orphanage in a suburb of Boston. She then typed in their address, and knew for certain she was looking at the parents of the child lying on her bed with eyes wide open. The house was up for sale, and looking at another website it was apparent that the parents had lived there for nearly a decade. Sister Flavia then typed the husband's name into Google, and found that he was an attorney for a large firm in Boston.

She had no doubt that once they discovered the nature of their son, it was something they could not live with. Sister Flavia would never know the whole story, but what she could imagine broke her heart. So now she knew what she believed was the whole story of little Francis Xavier. The parents, probably the mother, discovered sometime in those early days that the child never slept. They may have taken him to a doctor, who would say that such a thing was impossible. Sister Flavia guessed that the thought of raising a child who would be different from every other person he would ever know was too much for the parents. They could have dropped him off at any fire station or state run orphanage, but instead chose a Catholic orphanage, which spoke volumes to her. If the child had been left in the care of another group they would have no doubt uncovered what both the parents and Sister Flavia had discovered, namely, that for some reason the baby did not sleep. She could imagine the publicity, the medical tests and, finally, the freak show that would follow the child for the rest of his life. It was in hope that the child might receive protection from that kind of life that had probably been the reason he was left at the only Catholic orphanage in the state.

Which immediately raised the question in her mind, would she be able to hide what he was from those in her community? Then an even more disturbing question was forced upon her consciousness. Should she tell Sister Margaret about the child? Would it be a sin to conceal from the leader of her community such a profound reality? A reality that if found out might endanger the way of life the community had fought so long and hard to maintain. Finally, if she revealed what the child was, would she have to reveal what she was, and answer for maintaining a secret identity from those she had vowed to share her life with?

They were questions without easy answers, and she knew that no matter which direction God led her, there were going to be difficulties she could hardly imagine. Hiding who she was took planning, discipline and, she believed, divine intervention. There were times over the years when she felt sure Sister Margaret knew; times when she would look at her with a knowing glance, yet say nothing. Then there were times when Sister Margaret would make an offhand remark, saying something like, "You're up earlier than usual this morning, Sister." Or, "I don't know how you manage to know everything that goes on in the world and get all your work done," a reference to the fact that Sister Flavia would be on her computer when she was sure everyone else was asleep, looking for any bit of news or research on arcane scientific websites that might lead her to someone like her.

That thought caused her to look again at the child, whose eyes were wide open and staring up at the middle-aged woman who was now her guardian and protector. Her thoughts turned again to the parents, who had left their son with those they hoped would help him find his way in life. What happened to them, she thought? How would they live with what they had done, even if they thought it was best for the child? Would they find strength in their faith, or would this drive them from the arms of the church? She could not imagine the pain of guilt, confusion, despair and loss they must be feeling, especially the mother. Sister Flavia had never had her own children, but she keenly felt the loss when children from the orphanage left to make their way in the outside world. Children that she had poured much of her life into were suddenly gone, and though some would return to visit, most got on with their lives.

The early morning light was just beginning to replace the darkness outside when she had a thought. She knew where the father worked, and though he seemed to have left the state, she might be able to contact him and give assurance that his son would be safe with the Sisters. Opening her computer for last time that morning, she quickly found the phone number for his law firm in Boston. She would wait until later that morning, and then make the call. It was getting close to the time she would need to leave her room and begin the preparations for breakfast. Until then she would hold the child in her arms, pondering the future that lay before them.

Part Two

1

Jacob lay on his bed in the boy's room, waiting until he could begin to read. He shared the room with seven other boys, all of whom were fast asleep. It was not safe to read until after midnight, when everyone in the community was most likely asleep. Except for Sister Flavia, who he knew would be lying quietly on her bed either praying or thinking through the events of the day. She had long ago given up looking for anyone else that was like them, or so she said. Jacob suspected that occasionally she would be drawn to her computer to scan through the news or research journals that might reveal another person who would never once close their eyes, and sleep, dream or wake up to a new day.

When the clock by the side of his bed finally read midnight, he pulled the book out from under his covers and, adjusting his pillow to support his head, began to read. He used a small flashlight for light and slowly began to turn the pages as he worked his way through his third book that week. It wasn't one of his favorites, but Sister Flavia told him he needed to broaden his interests and not just read books on computer programming, science and technology. She had told him it was a classic, and that it would benefit him to understand more than just how things worked. It was just as important, she said, to know how people worked; what moved people, what gave people purpose, what motivated people and, finally, why people acted the way they did. Jacob found it hard to say "no" to Sister Flavia, so he kept reading The Count of Monte Cristo, though he already knew how it was going to end.

He quickly turned the flashlight off when he heard a noise at the end of the room. Turning over to see what was happening, he saw that Johnny was having another nightmare, something that was becoming more frequent. Jacob sat up in his bed to see what was going to happen, for sometimes Johnny would end up throwing off his covers as he seemed to fight with someone in his dreams. Johnny had been at the orphanage just a few months, and was only five years old, five years younger than Jacob. Sister Flavia had hinted that

Johnny had a difficult childhood, and was brought to the orphanage because his parents were not good people. Jacob knew that if Johnny continued to toss it would bring one of the Sisters into the room, so Jacob got out of his bed and walked quickly to Johnny's bed, just in time to shake him gently awake before the nightmare got the best of him.

"Johnny, it's Jacob. You're having a bad dream, it's okay."

Johnny was sobbing quietly, the terror of his dream overcoming his emotions and leaving him frightened and feeling alone in the world. Jacob patted him gently on the shoulder, trying to help him calm down and go back to sleep. Not for the first time did Jacob wonder what it was like to dream, to have a world that existed only in your mind, a world that was there one minute and then gone when you woke up.

"Jacob, what's happening? Is he having another nightmare?"

Jacob had not noticed when Sister Margaret entered the room. She lived in a small room between the two areas that housed the boys and the girls. Sister Margaret always left her door open so she could hear whatever might be happening in the two rooms, though as she neared her eightieth birthday her hearing was not what it used to be.

"Yes, Sister. I heard him and thought I could help."

She sat on the bed next to the small boy, wrapping her arms around him.

"Johnny, you're safe. You're just having a bad dream. Why don't you lay down and try to go back to sleep? Jacob, you can go back to your bed."

Jacob noticed that Sister Margaret did not tell him to go back to sleep, and wondered, as he had many times in the past, if she knew his secret. Sister Flavia had cautioned Jacob to not underestimate her, she knew everything that went on in the orphanage, and if they weren't careful she could uncover their secret, if she hadn't already.

"Yes, Sister."

He walked back to his bed and lay down so that he could watch what was happening with Johnny and Sister Margaret. It was dark in the room, but he could see Sister Margaret sitting on the bed, talking quietly to Johnny, and gently running her hand up and down his back to reassure him of her presence. Twenty minutes later

Johnny was asleep, and Sister Margaret, instead of going back to her room, walked down toward Jacob's bed. Jacob closed his eyes and pretended to be asleep, waiting for her to leave the room. She stopped at the foot of his bed, and looked down at him.

"Goodnight Jacob. You can go back to reading your book now."

She spoke the words softly, so he did not hear what she said. Turning quickly, she went back to her room, hoping that Johnny would have a peaceful night's rest. Jacob would wait for an hour, and then resume reading. He would finish the book just before dawn, knowing that he would have to tell Sister Flavia his impression of the book when they were alone sometime later in the day. Jacob smiled at the thought, knowing that she would now let him read a book of his own choosing. His favorite subject, if it could be called that, was the esoteric world of computer programming. He had his own computer, but was limited to using it for only two hours a day. The Sisters thought Jacob's intellect bordered on being a genius, but tried to keep him with the other students as much as possible, though that was becoming increasingly difficult. The truth was Jacob's IQ wasn't that much higher than any of the other children's, but because he spent hours each night reading, over his short life he had amassed a fountain of knowledge of knowledge that few adults would ever possess.

It had not been an easy road, and Jacob knew he owed everything to Sister Flavia. In his younger years she had protected him, hiding what he was from everyone, including Sister Margaret. She had explained to Jacob that Sister Margaret had enough to occupy her, and did not need the added worry of what to do with a child that never slept. When Jacob was two, she had her first discussion with him about how he was different. He didn't understand everything, but knew the other children slept at night while he did not. There were close calls during those early years, and Sister Flavia always suspected Sister Margaret knew, but for some reason kept that knowledge to herself. When he was four, he went to live with the other boys, and had to learn how to lie quietly on his bed while everyone else slept. Sister Flavia had taught him to read during that year, and when he was five she let him read in his bed when he was sure everyone was asleep. There were times when one of the Sisters caught him reading, and took his book away, and asked him what he thought he was doing. He always replied,

"I couldn't sleep."

Which, of course, was true.

He was always the first boy up, spending an hour or so before breakfast on his computer. The Sisters allowed this because Jacob never seemed to be tired or irritable during the day from rising so early. Jacob would usually read articles on different websites about either computer programming or scientific theory. When he didn't understand something, he searched around the Web for an answer, and was increasingly proficient at knowing how to navigate around the Internet to get the answers he sought for the questions that flowed from his mind.

For any other boy, his behavior and knowledge would have set him apart and possibly caused him to become socially isolated. It was here that Sister Flavia brought him a needed balance, constantly reminding him that the pursuit of knowledge alone was not sufficient to give him happiness and purpose. Jacob knew she was right, and made an effort to be what he was, a ten-year-old boy.

While Jacob was reading in the darkness of the boy's room, Sister Flavia was lying on her bed, her normally tranquil soul troubled by thoughts she could not suppress. For ten years, she had guided and protected him, and it had taken all her wisdom, patience and guile to get him this far without being discovered. She thought back to her own early years in the orphanage and how as a child, without anyone to protect or guide her, she had managed to keep her secret from everyone. Even as a child she sensed the hand of God watching over her, and seemingly blinding the eyes of the Sisters, staff and children to what she was.

She sensed no such divine intervention in Jacob's life. It was reasonable to think He was providing that safeguard through Sister Flavia, but it was also true that Jacob resisted the idea of God in a way that was becoming obvious to her. It wasn't that he was rebellious or without faith, but he was much more drawn to the physical world than to the spiritual. She had tried to guide him by giving him books that spoke of faith and God, and while he dutifully read them, she knew that his heart was not in it. There was a fine line in Jacob's life, and she knew it. If she took away the books and computer time that seemed to be taking him further away from God, it might drive him completely away from her.

There was another troubling issue that she was constantly reminded of, even as she lay in her bed looking up at the ceiling. She was getting older, and though she still managed to fulfill her devotions and tasks each day, her stamina was less, and her body protested on occasion, telling her in no uncertain terms she was much nearer the end than the beginning. Sister Flavia often wondered how much not ever needing to sleep affected the rest of her body, or was there something in her that compensated for that uniqueness? What would her death be like, she thought? Would anyone other than Jacob suspect that she was different from nearly everyone in human history? Of her eternal destiny she had no doubt, though she wondered if she would be judged differently from others because of the gift she had been given. Did she do enough, was she faithful enough, was being given basically two lives to live really a gift? Or was it a curse? If she had to hide it from everyone else, and spend endless hours lying quietly on her bed trying to discipline her thoughts to keep from going mad, and then she stopped.

It was unlike her to feel any form of self-pity or such deep introspection. She quickly asked for forgiveness, and got up from her bed, walking over to the table to get a book she had been reading. It had been many months since she had read in her room so late at night, but she thought, what was the worst that could happen? Someone might see her reading so late and ask if everything was okay, and she would answer, yes, I just could not sleep. It was what she had told Jacob to say if he was caught reading, and it had the virtue of being the truth. Her last thought before she opened her book was that she would need to take Jacob to the library in the afternoon after school. He needed new books to read, books that she was afraid would slowly take him away from her.

One final thought would wind its way through her mind before she returned to her book. She often wondered if Jacob felt the enormity of his difference, the fact that the two of them, for all they knew, shared an anomaly that was unique in human history. Sister Flavia thought that logic and the law of large numbers would dictate that for whatever reason there must be others who were like them, but a lifetime of searching left her with no reason to believe logic or the laws of probability proved anything. It was reading the books

42

that she gave him that had so far proved to be Jacob's salvation. Unlike herself, Jacob never spent hours lying in bed alone with his thoughts. He would patiently wait until the other boys were asleep, and then begin his regimen of working his way through whatever books and subjects had caught his fancy. It was difficult hiding from everyone else the number of books he read; she brought them from the library and would surreptitiously put them under the mattress of his bed during one of the mealtimes. Sister Flavia had for years been in charge of the shopping for the orphanage, so it was easy to incorporate trips to the library into her routine, though the looks she got from the librarians were often puzzling as they silently wondered why a nun would want books on programming and computer languages.

Since Jacob had entered her life she had entrusted him to God, and it was the belief that God would take care of Jacob that finally gave her a measure of peace. The future would take care of itself, and her worrying about Jacob would not change or alter what that future was going to be.

2

Three days later, on a Friday, the sisters loaded the children into the orphanage bus for an outing to the beach. It was a warm Spring day, and everyone was grateful for the opportunity to do something different, something outside of their normal routine. The ocean water would not be warm enough for swimming, but the chance to run around for hours on end and explore the state park they were going to would be a treat after the long winter. Sister Flavia sat with Jacob in the back of the bus, silently watching the landscape go by, occasionally turning her head to watch as he worked his way through a book on artificial intelligence. She knew he was never going to be a "normal" boy or adolescent, and knew that the outside world would hold dangers for him she had never experienced.

Though the weather was almost perfect, there were only a few cars in the parking lot. Sister Margaret had chosen a weekday because she knew there would be less people, meaning it would be easier to keep track of the children. She had chosen not to go on the outing, and though she would never admit it, her age was finally beginning to catch up with her. Sister Maria, being the youngest of the Sisters, was nominally in charge of the excursion. Before letting the children off the bus, she asked them to stay on the beach where they could be seen, and to pick someone to be their buddy so no one would ever be alone. Sister Flavia quickly said to Jacob,

"I'll be your buddy. I'd like to take a walk down the beach and talk with you, if that's alright?"

Jacob didn't mind, he wasn't drawn to the physical activity that the outing offered, in fact, he was hoping he could find a quiet spot and finish the book he had brought. As the two of them rose to get off the bus, Sister Flavia spoke softly to Jacob.

"Jacob, why don't you leave your book?"

Jacob was so used to having a book in his hand that it was by instinct he thought nothing about taking the book with him.

"Sure. Sorry."

"Nothing to be sorry about. We just don't get the opportunity to spend much time together alone."

Minutes later they were standing at the edge of the high tide line, looking out at the vastness of the Atlantic Ocean. Though the waves were small, Sister Flavia had to be careful the whitewater did not reach her robes, which were grazing the sand and would absorb any water that touched them. Up and down the beach the children were running along the edge of the incoming surf, shoes off, shouting as the cold water touched their feet. The three other Sisters were sitting on a log, watching the children and enjoying the warm sunshine. Knowing that they would not be overheard, Sister Flavia said to Jacob,

"Do you ever think about who you are Jacob? About the fact that you are different? Has it been hard for you? Hiding it from everyone?"

Jacob was embarrassed to talk about himself, like most children he did his best to fit in, and though he set himself apart from the other children by his profound knowledge, no one held this against him. He tried to change the direction of the conversation by replying,

"You're like me. Is it hard for you?"

"Yes, it is hard for me. Not as hard as it used to be, but yes, it has been hard. But God has helped me. I hope He is helping you as well. It will not get easier as you get older."

Jacob did not want to talk about God with Sister Flavia. It made him anxious, though he did not yet know why.

"What do you mean it will get harder as I get older?"

"One day you will leave the orphanage. It won't be for several years, but it will happen. You will no doubt go to university, and live among people who will not understand you if they find out who you are. Do you understand?"

Jacob had not yet, in his short life, had to deal with the questions Sister Flavia was asking him. When they talked at the orphanage, it was usually about his studies, what books he was reading, his relationships with the other Sisters and children, and, finally, was there any change in his body that he had noticed? She had hoped that he might be different from her, that he might one day become tired and fall asleep for the first time. It would save him from the temptations that filled his future, temptations she had never faced living in a cloistered community.

Jacob did understand, but not fully, and not in a manner that would give him an idea of what it would be like when he left the community. He knew that if he talked about God it might end her questioning.

"I guess God will help me when I leave, won't He?"

She looked at the boy standing next to her, who was only a few inches shorter than her. He was smart, telling her what she wanted to hear to try and redirect the conversation away from anything spiritual. Sister Flavia could continue to spar with him, but thought the better of it.

"He will, if you let Him. Why don't you tell me about the books you're reading as we walk down the beach?"

Jacob looked quickly up at Sister Flavia as she began to walk down the beach. He was surprised that she changed the subject, letting him talk about the books that formed such a large part of his life. Jacob spent nearly eleven hours a day reading or working on his computer, amassing knowledge on a scale that few people would ever achieve or even dream of. Following her down the beach, he answered,

"I've been reading about artificial intelligence. I don't understand everything, but what I do get is really neat. It's like in the future computers will think for us, maybe even drive cars and fly planes."

"Do you think that will be a good thing, Jacob? That computers might be able to think for us?"

Jacob thought for a moment, and then replied.

"They wouldn't make mistakes. People make mistakes. Wouldn't that be a good thing?"

"What if the people who make the computers were bad people? Don't computers do what they are programmed?"

She waited as Jacob thought about what she had said. In his world, computers were the gateway to everything that interested him. The only reason he read books at night was that the books were easier to hide than working on his computer. If he had his choice he would spend all his waking hours, which of course was his entire life, wandering through the endless offerings that were available in cyberspace. His curiosity was endless, shaped by his ability to absorb nearly everything that was put in front of him. When he didn't answer after a moment or two, she said,

"I know that you don't have anything else to do in the middle of the night except to read. I know you are drawn to the world of computers and science, but that world has its dangers. I hope you learn how to balance your life, though I know it will not be easy."

She stopped walking, and looked back to see where the other children were. They were spread out over the beach, some were braving the cold water and were in the ocean out to their knees. Others were kicking a soccer ball around, still others were sitting with the Sisters, chatting away while enjoying the sunshine. She had gone far enough with Jacob, and gently touched him on the shoulder.

"Why don't you go play with the other children? It looks like they're having fun."

He was hesitant to leave her because he knew there was more she wanted to say to him. Jacob's greatest fear was to somehow disappoint Sister Flavia, the one person that knew who and what he was, and accepted him unconditionally because she shared his identity. He was not the least introspective about who he was, not in the way she was, at least not yet. His innate curiosity and agile mind looked on his "anomaly" as a gateway to worlds that held the promise of inexhaustible knowledge. For the moment, the acquisition of knowledge, the outcome of his curiosity, was an end in itself. However, with the accumulation of knowledge comes power, power that even a ten-year old boy could become aware of.

Sister Flavia knew that eventually the walls of the orphanage would cease to be able to contain the boy. Already, the Sisters did not know how to structure lesson plans to accommodate what they saw as Jacob's prodigious intellect. They were forced to use high school lesson plans, which he easily mastered, leaving him free time to pursue his own interests in both books and online. Sister Margaret was uneasy about allowing him increasing time on the computer, but grudgingly gave in when he gave her a print out each day of his browsing and surfing history. When she was convinced that he was restricting himself solely to academic pursuits, she was satisfied. It did not occur to her that Jacob was smart enough to doctor his browsing history to produce any result he wanted, if he chose to.

As she looked at the blue water stretching to the horizon, Sister Flavia saw clearly the battle that would take place in Jacob's life in the coming years. He would go university, and would excel at whatever studies or interests he pursued. This was not her concern, at least not her main concern. For ten years, she had guided him in how to live with what he was, and there was no doubt that the structured environment of the orphanage had helped Jacob to not only survive but also to thrive, at least intellectually. She had spent her life looking out for him, and when he was delivered literally to her front door, she dedicated her life to him, believing that God had a purpose for him that transcended what He expected from everyone else. Why else would He have given Jacob this gift if not for the benefit of mankind?

Jacob, however, did not yet seem to see who he was in terms of how his life might affect anyone else. He was riding a wave that seemed to have no end, and for now he was content with that. His life had boundaries, boundaries that would disappear in the coming years. Sister Flavia had learned over the years to trust God with everything; her faith and commitment to His will were usually strong enough to overcome thoughts that threatened her peace. She wanted to entrust Jacob's future to God, but it meant she would eventually have to remove herself from his life. It was that thought that brought her fear to the surface.

She turned from looking out to sea to gaze down the beach at the children scattered along the shore. Jacob was kicking a soccer ball with some of the other children, everyone else on the beach oblivious to what he was. Not for the first time, she wondered what they would think of him if they knew how different he was. From all appearances, he was ten-year old boy who just happened to be considerably smarter than everyone else in the community. She knew they could live with that, after all, someone had to be the smartest person in the room. Jacob was still a boy, a boy who had not yet come to grips with who he was, a boy who would eventually have to find a way to live emotionally and, more importantly to Sister Flavia, spiritually, with who he was. As he grew, she understood she would have less impact on his life, and then he would be gone.

Sister Flavia was drifting toward a dark place, a corner of her mind that held her fears and doubts about the future. A lifetime of faith and devotion had held these anxieties about Jacob in check for the last ten years, and as she tried to calm her mind she closed her eyes and prayed fervently that God would guide and protect him in the coming years. Her reverie was broken when the soccer ball touched her leg. She opened her eyes and saw Jacob standing before her, panting and out of breath. He had noticed that her eyes were closed, and looking up was confused by the look on her face; a look sadness that he had only rarely seen.

"Are you alright, Sister?"

"Yes, Jacob. I was just praying. The ball startled me."

He paused for a moment, and then asked,

"What were you praying for?"

"You, Jacob. I was praying for you."

The solemnity with which she spoke the words brought him up short. Jacob had spent his entire life in close proximity to Sister Flavia, and knew her as well as anybody. He understood that she prayed for him, she probably prayed for everybody, but there was something behind her words that he did not understand. Not knowing how to respond, he moved the ball away from her with his foot and started jogging down the beach, twice looking back over his shoulder to see her staring intently at him. Her look would bother him for the rest of the day, though he did not know why. Jacob did not like it when there were things in his life that did not make sense, that was perhaps why he gravitated toward science and computers, areas of life that were guided by programs, physical laws and rules of order. The spiritual world that was the foundation of Sister Flavia's life was mysterious and puzzling to him, causing him to view it with suspicion.

Later that evening, when he was sure the other boys were asleep, Jacob quietly got out of bed and walked slowly to the kitchen to get something to eat. He would often find himself hungry late at night, and would eat some bread and jam, something he knew would not be missed. He stopped in his tracks when he rounded the corner of the boy's room. The light was on in the kitchen, and he could hear a conversation between Sister Margaret and Sister Flavia. Jacob knew it was wrong to eavesdrop on them, but continued to move slowly toward the kitchen, stopping on the other side of the wall where he could hear them talking. It was Sister Flavia whom he heard first.

"Perhaps we can find another donor. The bishop might be able to help us find others who would support our work."

"The archdiocese has problems of its own. I doubt that they will send any donor money our way, they know there are other agencies that would take care of the children. We are the last Catholic orphanage in the state, they might think our day has come and gone."

"How long will our endowment last?"

Jacob had never thought about how the orphanage paid its bills or where the money came from. He could tell from the tone of the conversation the Sisters were concerned about how they were going to survive financially. Sister Margaret answered Sister Flavia's question, and sounded extremely tired when she said,

"With the donors we have left, assuming nothing else happens, the endowment will carry us for a few more years."

There was silence as the two women contemplated the meaning of those words. Jacob was just about to go back to his bed when Sister Margaret said,

"There's another reality. One that we seldom talk about."

"And what's that?"

"None of us are getting any younger. No one has joined us since Sister Maria, and that was years ago."

Jacob never thought about the Sisters getting older. They were the constant reality in the community, they had always been there and Jacob assumed they would always be there, even after he left. It was Sister Flavia who spoke next.

"God will provide, Sister. He always has."

"Yes. Let's just hope He does so soon."

Jacob sensed the conversation was over, and moved slowly away from the wall where he had been listening. He was back in his bed moments later, thinking about what he had heard. There was nothing he could do about the Sisters getting older, but as he lay silently on his bed he thought he might be able to do something about the issue of money.

3

It took Jacob two years to figure out how to provide more money for the orphanage. It took three more to accumulate those funds and get them to the Sisters. That first night, after overhearing the conversation between Sister Margaret and Sister Flavia, instead of reading his book, Jacob brought his computer to bed. Risking being caught red-handed, he spent the night researching ways to make money. Over the coming months, as he sped around the Internet from one website to another, it became clear there was really only one way open to him, as a boy of ten, to amass a large amount of money in a few years. He had no doubt he could do it, but he would need the involvement of one other person, someone who was over eighteen, someone he could trust.

He would not need the other person for a time, until he figured out exactly how his plan would work. Once he had proved it would work, he would need to recruit someone to carry out the logistics involved. Jacob set aside all his personal pursuits and began to focus exclusively on his plan to save the only home he had ever known. To keep his work secret, he had to create a false browsing history, something which gave him a moment's pause. He had never disobeyed or hid anything from the Sisters, except for his "anomaly". However, he thought that in this case the end did justify the means. It would not be the last time Jacob would use that reasoning, though the next occurrences would be far in the future.

While Jacob was eagerly pursuing his goal of saving the orphanage, life went on as normal. Sister Margaret appeared to be slowing down as she neared eighty years old, and even Sister Flavia was finally beginning to look her age. A few children left when they turned eighteen, always replaced by new ones, each had a different story of how they came to be there. Sister Flavia took over more of the day to day operation of the community as Sister Margaret spent more of her time in spiritual exercises and devotion. With his time spent formulating his plan to provide for the Sisters, and Sister Flavia basically running the orphanage, they spent less time together. The dynamic of their relationship slowly began to change. Jacob felt it, as did Sister Flavia, but neither one spoke about what was happening. It wasn't that they didn't see each other, that would have been impossible given the structure of the community. However, as the months, and then years went by, they were there with each other, but not in the way they had been in the past. That all changed when one day a letter arrived at the orphanage, a letter that also contained a check for three million dollars.

It was Sister Flavia who opened the letter and found the cashier's check. She was in her office, the office that once belonged to Sister Margaret, going through the day's mail. The letter came in a plain envelope with nothing to distinguish who it was from. There was a return address, but upon checking it would turn out to be a private post office in Los Angeles, California. The letter was not signed, and merely said, "I know you can use this." Far from being overjoyed, the letter and the check left Sister Flavia troubled, though she did not know why. She called the bank in California that issued the check, and found out the check was good. Before she could ask, the banker told her he was not at liberty to tell her the identity of the Good Samaritan. Sister Flavia thanked him and hung up the phone, more puzzled than ever. The money would enable them to keep the orphanage open for years, solving a problem that was never far from her and Sister Margaret's mind.

Sister Margaret usually spent the hour after lunch in the chapel, which is where Sister Flavia found her. Crossing herself before she sat down next to Sister Margaret in the front row, Sister Flavia softly said,

"Can you come to the office when you have time. It's important."

51

Sister Margaret slowly nodded her head, and Sister Flavia left and returned to her office, pondering the sudden turn of events that changed the future of the community she had given her life to. She knew she should be thankful, however, could such a sum come without strings or attachments that might taint the gift, or the giver? What connection did the orphanage have to California? There was none that she could think of, and no one knew that the orphanage was in financial trouble.

The arrival of Sister Margaret interrupted her thoughts, and Sister Flavia waited to speak until Sister Margaret was seated in the chair across from her desk. Without any preamble, Sister Flavia handed the letter and the check to Sister Margaret. Looking them over, she handed them back to Sister Flavia.

"You called to make sure the check is good?"

"Yes. It is. It's quite a bit of money. I don't suppose you have any idea who might have sent it?"

"None. We've never received a donation anywhere near this large, at least since I've been here."

"This would seem to solve our financial problem. It does trouble me that we don't know where the money came from or who gave it. Am I wrong to be troubled, Sister?"

"No, you're not. But we don't know the story behind every gift and donation we have received over the years, do we? It's just the size of the gift that causes you concern?"

"Yes. But my concern should not stand in the way of God's provision. I'll take it to the bank with your permission."

"You don't need to ask my permission. You're been in charge for several years now, you know that."

It was the first time Sister Margaret had openly stated what they both knew. Sister Flavia was in charge, though everyone still looked to Sister Margaret as the leader of the community.

"Why don't you take Jacob with you. It would do him good to get out, even if just for a little while."

"I'll do that."

Sister Flavia found Jacob at his computer in the large common room. He was allowed unlimited time on the computer because he had passed all the state tests necessary for his high school diploma. She knew that his time at the community was coming to an end, they were already talking about having him attend university in the fall. Jacob wanted to go to Harvard, which was only an hour's drive from the orphanage. She knew he would have no trouble being accepted. As an orphan with a prodigious intellect and having graduated high school two years early, he was a prime candidate for a school like Harvard.

"Jacob, I'm going to the bank. I thought you might like to come with me."

He immediately minimized his computer screen, and got up from the table.

"Sure. Let me sign off and I'll meet you out front."

She wanted to ask him what he was looking at, and why he so quickly hid it from her, but thought the better of it. Sister Flavia turned and left the room, going out the back door to bring the van around to the front. The van had seen better days, and she thought it might be prudent to purchase another vehicle. Jacob was waiting for her as she brought the van around the driveway to the front of the building. He opened the passenger door, sat down, and then she pulled out onto the highway that ran in front of the orphanage. After a moment's silence, Jacob said,

"Why are we going to the bank?"

After living at the orphanage for fifteen years, Jacob knew how things worked. The Sisters, especially Sister Margaret, loved routine. Going to the bank was always combined with a trip to either the store or perhaps the post office.

"I need to make a deposit. We received a special gift today. It's a large amount of money, so Sister Margaret thought it best if we took it to the bank as soon as possible."

"Does this mean we won't run out of money?"

Jacob was more than brilliant, a walking encyclopedia, and had devised and carried out a complicated plan to raise millions of dollars. He was not, however, as skilled in his interactions with people. Sister Flavia immediately turned to him.

"What do you mean "run out of money"? Has anyone said anything to you about our financial condition?"

Jacob was caught, and he knew it. Of course, no one had said anything to him about the community's finances. He thought quickly, and then said,

"I just thought because the gift was large it might be because there was a large problem."

Sister Flavia had known Jacob his entire life, and realized he was not telling the truth. He was looking out the window at the passing landscape, hoping she would not press him further. It was not to be. She pulled the van off the highway into the parking lot of a small church, and after shutting off the engine, said,

"What have you done, Jacob?"

It was not in him to tell Sister Flavia another lie, but he found it just as difficult to tell her the truth. He had never felt he had done anything wrong in finding a way to provide for the community. However, he did it in secret, which he knew would upset the Sisters. He thought, better to just get it over with.

"I figured out a way to make money for the orphanage. It took me a few years, and then a few more to make it work."

"This money comes from you? Jacob, I have a check for three million dollars, and you're saying you're responsible for this?"

Jacob turned in his seat, and looked at Sister Flavia. He wanted to see her face and get a feel for what she was thinking. Her voice was filled with questioning, not believing that a boy, even a boy who lived in a world few if any other boys inhabited, could accomplish something so dramatic. For a brief moment, he felt a surge of pride, but it would soon vanish.

"Yes. I wanted to help the orphanage. I knew you needed the money, so I figured out a way to get it."

"How did you know we needed the money? Did someone tell you?"

"I overheard you and Sister Margaret talking one night. It was a long time ago. I wanted to do something to help."

Sister Flavia remembered the conversation, even though it happened years ago.

"You started this years ago? You've been working on this for years? What exactly did you do to make three million dollars?"

Jacob knew there was no way Sister Flavia would understand the complexity of what he had done, and thought for a moment before he began his explanation.

"I basically found a way to buy and sell stocks based on an algorithm I wrote that looked at how they performed in terms of what's happening in the world."

He could see she was lost, so he continued.

"I wrote a computer program that scanned about 100 websites that dealt with news, current events, things like that. I had the program look for certain words, words like: inflation, upheaval, downsizing, turmoil, gold, instability, fluidity, disruption, prices, commodities. Words that described what was happening in the world related to business. Then the program compared what happened to stocks in the Fortune 500 that same day. It took time to refine the algorithm, but eventually the program could predict what was going to happen to those stocks in the next day or so by what words were used. Not perfectly, but good enough so that you could make money."

It was at that moment Sister Flavia knew Jacob was someone she would never completely understand. If he could devise and carry out a plan to raise three million dollars while still a boy, what else could he do? Then she had a thought.

"How could you do this by yourself? You're not old enough to buy and sell stocks. How did you do this, Jacob?"

It had been hard enough telling her about what he had done, now he would have to tell her the whole truth.

"I had to find someone to help me."

"Who, Jacob? Who do you know outside of the orphanage that would do this for you?"

"My father. I found my father."

4

It should not have surprised her, but it did all the same. After all, she had found him, and Jacob's ability to accomplish things was apparently limitless.

"How much contact have you had with him?"

She didn't ask the obvious question, the unspoken reality they both shared. The question that related to why he had left Jacob at the orphanage years ago. If Jacob and his father had talked about it, Jacob would have to bring it up.

"I sent him an email, and then we talked once on Skype. I had to convince him that my program would work. He looked at the stocks I sent him each week for a few months, and then he agreed to help. I emailed him a couple times a week so I could tell him which stocks to buy."

There were so many questions Sister Flavia wanted to ask, yet she was hesitant to cause Jacob any pain. After all, his father had abandoned him to the Sisters when he was only a baby.

"How do you feel about your father, Jacob? You're trusting him with large amounts of money. Have you thought about that?"

"I didn't really have a choice. I knew how hard it must have been for him to leave me here, so I thought he might help because he might feel guilty for what he had done."

It was the most introspective Jacob had ever been with her. Sister Flavia was surprised that Jacob was perceptive enough to understand how his father might feel about his lost son. She still continued to think of him as a boy, though that image was now shattered by the check that had come in the mail.

"Do you think he wants to see you? Did he say anything about that?"

"No. He has a new family. They don't know about me."

Jacob spoke without emotion, leaving Sister Flavia wondering if she should ask what was left unspoken. She thought, in for a penny, in for a pound.

"What do you mean, he has a new family? You mean he has other children?"

"Yes, he has a new family. My mother died many years ago."

"I'm sorry, Jacob."

"That's okay. I never knew her anyway. You're my family."

She didn't like it that Jacob could speak so matter-of-factly about his mother. It was true that he had never known his parents, but the thought that she died relatively young should have elicited some type of emotional response. What Sister Flavia did not know was that Jacob had spent many hours lying in his bed at night thinking about his mother. When his father had told him of her death, he knew that in some way he might be responsible. She could not live with who he was, he understood that, and had agreed to give him away while only a baby. What this did to her Jacob could only imagine. He knew intellectually he was not responsible for what he was, but still could not shake the feeling that if he was "normal" he would be living with his parents, and not writing sophisticated computer programs that could make millions of dollars in a relatively short time.

There was silence in the van, each person's thoughts running in a different direction. Jacob just wanted the conversation to be over, happy that the money had arrived from his father, knowing that he had saved the orphanage. Sister Flavia's thoughts ran in a completely different direction. Now that the shock of what Jacob had done had passed, the implications were beginning to flood her mind. Did Jacob realize the power he possessed? The ability to devise a way to make millions of dollars surely put him in a category of people that must be incredibly small. What would happen when he left her and went to university? Would the values that the Sisters had tried to give him guide and protect him? Or, would he become something unrecognizable to them? A man, like so many others, driven by the pursuit of money.

She was just about to speak when something else occurred to her. Jacob's difference, not ever needing to sleep, could this alone account for who he was and what he had done? The boy had read thousands of books in his short life, and spend countless other hours on his computer, but others much older had undoubtedly done the same. Was there something else about him that was different, something she did not share? Sister Flavia was suddenly extremely tired, her aged body was drained from all the emotions and questions she had experienced in such a short time. When he saw the color drain from her face, Jacob quickly said,

"Sister, are you alright? You don't look so good."

"No, Jacob. I'm not alright. Let's just sit here a moment so I can rest."

Jacob knew in some way that it was too much for her, all the revelations of the last few minutes. The last thing he ever wanted to do was to hurt Sister Flavia, and he silently reproached himself for the errant words that had brought it all to light. He promised himself that he would be more careful in the future. If anything he might do had the possibility of upsetting Sister Flavia, he would hide it from her, no matter how wrong it might feel. This would have far reaching consequences later, but for now the future was hidden from them.

When Sister Flavia felt well enough to drive, they pulled out onto the highway and continued to the bank. Jacob waited in the car while Sister Flavia deposited the check into the community's account. He hoped they could return to the orphanage without talking anymore about the money, and especially his father. Jacob had already moved on from the stock scheme he had worked out to save the orphanage. It had never occurred to him to make any more money than he thought the orphanage would need for the foreseeable future. He did not need money for himself, and it did not enter his mind that his father might be tempted by the amounts of money that Jacob was providing for the orphanage. Nor did it occur to Jacob that his father might be profiting himself from the information Jacob was sending him every week. He was, and it would have profound implications for Jacob years later.

5

Sister Flavia had a restless night, which was unusual for her. She usually spent the hours before 4 a.m. lying in her bed going over the day's events, praying or meditating on something she had read or thought about during the day. However, this day had proved so tumultuous and dramatic that she could not get her mind under control. There were so many implications arising from the revelation that Jacob had worked out a way to make millions of dollars that she felt overwhelmed and adrift emotionally and spiritually. Why had Jacob kept his plan a secret from her? What could be the reason he would not tell her what he was doing? Did he fear she would stop him? If God was using Jacob to provide for the orphanage, should she just be thankful and move on? If God was indeed using Jacob, did this mean that He would protect Jacob from the temptation to make more money just because he could? Jacob was in many ways still a boy, yet Sister Flavia knew that part of his life was quickly coming to an end. He would enter Harvard in the fall, and who knew what temptations would await him at a "secular" university? She knew she should trust God to protect him, but her fear for his soul was threatening to overwhelm her faith. There was an answer out there somewhere, but it would not come to her as she waited for the morning. Sister Flavia could not think of an answer, but one thing became clear to her. She would have to talk with Sister Margaret about what she had learned that day. Perhaps she would know what to do, because Sister Flavia had no idea how to help Jacob avoid a future that might cause him irreparable harm.

It wasn't until later in the day that the two Sisters were able to speak together. Sister Flavia asked if Sister Margaret could meet with her in the office Sister Flavia now occupied. When she arrived just after 3 p.m. Sister Flavia asked her to close the door behind her.

"You look tired Sister, are you feeling well?"

Sister Margaret seldom referred to her advanced age, even to Sister Flavia, who was her closest friend.

"I don't mind growing old. I do mind not being able to contribute as I used to. But I suspect that's not why you wanted to talk."

"No, but your well-being is of concern to me. You know that."

"My well-being is fine. My body is not."

Sister Flavia knew that part of the conversation was over, and quickly said,

"I need to talk with you about Jacob."

Sister Margaret straightened up in her chair, giving Sister Flavia her full attention.

"What about Jacob?"

"It's about the money we received yesterday. Jacob made the money over the last several years when he found out we were going to run out of money."

Sister Margaret relaxed, and let out a long sigh. She closed her eyes as she thought about what she had just been told.

"It does not surprise me. How did you find out?"

"He let it slip that he knew about our financial difficulties. When I asked him how he knew we were in difficulty, he told me that he overheard us talking about it years ago. He wanted to help."

"I suspect this has something to do with his computer. Did he do anything illegal?"

"I don't think so. It's complicated, but somehow he figured out how to buy and sell stocks for a profit. And before you ask how a boy could buy and sell stocks, he found out who his father is and where he lived. He used him to buy and sell the stocks. That's about it."

Sister Margaret was silent as she pondered the mysterious ways of God. The orphanage now had funds to keep it functioning long after both she and Sister Flavia were gone. God had used a boy to get those funds; a boy who was sent to them years ago, perhaps for that very purpose. What other plans did He have for the boy? Jacob would be leaving them soon, and the protection and guidance they had provided for him would leave with him. Did he realize the ability he possessed to do good or to do evil? Money was a powerful force in human life, sooner or later it would occur to Jacob that he could have and do anything he wanted. She knew how most men would respond to such power; she had no idea what Jacob would do when he came to that realization. Sister Margaret knew these thoughts must have occurred to Sister Flavia as well.

"You're worried about what is going to happen to him when he leaves?"

"I am worried, yes. I lay awake at night thinking about it. I try to have faith that God will protect him, but it is difficult."

"Yes, I can imagine it is difficult for you to sleep. Jacob as well."

Sister Flavia felt a cold chill come over her, and she thought, does she know? She was suspended in time, trying to think back over forty-five years of living at the community. Had she given herself away at some point? If so, why had Sister Margaret never said anything? And what about Jacob? She had been so careful with him. If anyone else had discovered who he was they would surely have said something. If Sister Margaret had carried the knowledge of who she and Jacob were all these years, why would she reveal it now? Was she tipping her hand, or was it just an innocent remark? There was only one way to find out.

"What do you mean, Sister?"

Sister Margaret would keep the secret she had carried for the rest of her life, which was slowly running out. She would not add to Sister Flavia's burden, so she let it go and changed the conversation by saying,

"What about the father? What must he think about a son who can make millions of dollars?"

"I don't know, but he doesn't seem to want to have any contact with Jacob. This has all happened so fast. We should find a way to help Jacob use his gift for good. Don't you agree?"

Sister Margaret had walked right up to the edge of revealing she knew everything, but again stopped just short of disclosure.

"Yes. It would be good to talk to him. You should do it as soon as possible."

Sister Flavia held her breath to see how Sister Margaret would respond. If Sister Margaret wanted to be involved in that conversation, Sister Flavia would not be able to talk about the reality she and Jacob shared, the reality that made it possible for Jacob to make those millions of dollars. Sister Margaret, however, rose from her chair and said,

"Let me know how it turns out."

6

It was not until three days later that she found the time to talk with Jacob. It was a beautiful Spring day and she suggested they take some of the younger children to a nearby park where they could play. Sister Flavia and Jacob sat on a bench under an elm tree watching as the children scampered around the playground equipment. Sister Flavia was the first to speak.

"I would like to talk about what happened the other day, if that's all right with you."

Jacob knew this conversation was coming, and again regretted the slip of the tongue that revealed he was responsible for saving the orphanage. He was embarrassed by the attention it had brought, his intent was to stay anonymous and move on to other areas of interest. He had not thought about the implications of what he had done. Sister Flavia had, and wanted to explore those implications with him.

"If you want."

"I talked with Sister Margaret about what you did, Jacob. It did not surprise her that you were able to do something like that. She believes, as I do, that one of the reasons God brought you to us was to provide for us in the future. Which you have certainly done."

Jacob had lived in a community that was built on faith; a community where God was the center of everything they did. Jacob was grateful for the care and concern the Sisters and staff had for the children, and though he had lived there for his entire life, he was reluctant to talk about God.

"It's no big deal. Really."

"Jacob, it is a big deal. It must have occurred to you that there aren't many people who could do what you have done."

It had occurred to Jacob, but he tried not to think about it. It only reminded him of how different he was from everyone else. A difference that, as he grew older, made him feel more isolated and apart. Though he was unaware of it, the emotional toll of hiding his "anomaly" was finally catching up to him. In response to Sister Flavia, Jacob merely shrugged his shoulders and would not meet her gaze. Sister Flavia continued.

"Sister Margaret believes that what you have is a gift. God gives us gifts we can use for good or for evil. In providing for the community, you have used your gift for good. We would like to help you find ways to continue to use your gift for good. Does that make sense to you, Jacob?"

"Why does it have to be a gift? Why can't it be just what it is, a computer program that made a lot of money?"

"You have read much history, Jacob. You know that money is one of the most powerful forces in life. Sometimes people do terrible things to get more of it. You must know this?"

"You're worried about my father, aren't you?"

"I try not to worry about things, Jacob. Worry is always about what may happen in the future, and I have always tried to trust the future to God. But I am not always as strong in my faith as I would like. Your father knows that you have found a way to make millions of dollars. This would tempt many people."

"He doesn't need any more money. He's already rich. Besides, I'm the only one who has the program."

Sister Flavia knew that just because someone was rich did not mean they might not desire more. Jacob assumed because his father was rich the idea of accumulating even more money would not interest him. In this Jacob would be proved wrong, but he would not find out how wrong he was for several years. After a moment's pause, Jacob said,

"I don't think I'll be hearing from him again, anyway."

"Why would you think that?"

"He wrote an email that said after he sent the check he didn't want to have any more contact. I guess he's pretty busy with his work."

Left unsaid was the fact that Jacob had been abandoned once again by his father. Jacob had once told Sister Flavia that he considered her his family, but she knew there must be a part of him that wanted to connect with his father. Sister Flavia had worked with orphans her entire life, and knew that most children never got over the trauma of being abandoned. Jacob had buried himself in his books and computers, but somewhere in his soul she knew he was wounded in the same way she was wounded. Her wounds had been softened by her faith, Jacob's might still be raw, though they seemed to be buried deep in his soul.

"Have you thought about what your life will be like when you leave us this fall?"

Sister Flavia knew it was time to change the direction of the conversation, and Jacob turned to face her when he answered. His face brightened when he said,

"I won't have to hide anymore. I'll have my own room and can do what I want."

He stopped quickly, realizing his words might be misunderstood.

"I didn't mean what it sounds like. I meant I won't have to be so careful all the time."

"I know, Jacob. Remember, I have been at this much longer than you have. It's not easy, but God has helped me. It has also helped living in the community. I think it will be much harder for you living on the outside. You will have to be very careful."

Sister Flavia had thought long and hard about letting Jacob go to university two years early. However, it was obvious to her that the orphanage was not the place for him anymore. With his insatiable curiosity and vast accumulation of knowledge, he lived in his own world at the community. When she approached Harvard about allowing him to take whatever tests they wanted to gauge his readiness, at least academically, the university was initially skeptical. They relented when Jacob sent them a corrected version of a paper one of their professors had written on the slow disintegration of the ozone layer over Antarctica. Jacob had found the paper on one of the scientific websites he frequented, and noticed that the professor's calculations were slightly off.

Sister Flavia wanted to talk more with Jacob about how God had helped her deal with the difference they both shared, but knew she had to tread carefully. They had not talked about the "anomaly", as Jacob called it, for many years. It was the unspoken reality they both shared, cutting them off from the rest of humanity, or so they believed.

"I know you think differently about what we are than I do, Jacob. It has given you the opportunity to know more about the world than almost anyone else. Your life will open up to you in ways you cannot imagine when you leave us. I know that it is difficult for you to talk about spiritual things, but I want you to again think about why God made you the way He did. If you can find His purpose for your life, it will help you."

It wasn't that Jacob didn't think about spiritual things, it's just that when he did it always came back to what he was, which always made him feel uneasy. Why him? The math of who he was at first disturbed him, and then left him with a sense of loneliness, as if he were adrift on an endless sea. Like Sister Flavia, he had searched for years to find someone else who shared the "anomaly", but always came up empty-handed. If they were the only two people in human history who required no sleep......, it was here that Jacob always turned away and moved onto something else that did not force him to deal with the immensity of who he was. When he didn't respond, Sister Flavia was just about to speak, and then Jacob said,

"What's your purpose Sister? You're just like me, why are you here?"

She paused for a moment.

"You. You're my purpose, Jacob."

7

Jacob sat across from his guidance counselor, waiting for her to speak. He had been at Harvard for a semester, and had breezed through his classes. They would not allow him to take more than 16 hours, all of which were in General Education. It was a requirement of Harvard that students take a set of general courses outside of their chosen major. Jacob knew that he could double his course load and still ace all his classes. He waited patiently for the counselor to finish reading his file, hoping he would be able to persuade her to let him increase the number of classes he took after the Christmas break.

It was almost a miracle he was able to get a room to himself. Most freshman had a roommate, a situation that would have been intolerable for Jacob. His room was tucked away in Massachusetts Hall, and wasn't actually a dorm room. It was a space that measured only 10' x 12', and for years had been the janitor's closet. Eventually the room became too small for even that purpose, and it was decided to offer it as a single dorm room. Because of its small size, few students wanted to live there. Jacob, however, growing up in an orphanage where he shared his living space with other boys, did not see the space as small. He saw it as private, a necessity for someone who worked through the night.

"It seems that you are adapting well to Harvard, Jacob. Though looking at the scores you posted on your admissions tests, I'm not surprised."

She put his file down on her desk, regarding him for a moment. Harvard had its share of young applicants, but something about Jacob was different. His IQ was high, but nowhere near genius. Most of the younger applicants to the university had extremely high IQ's, and had been considered prodigies their entire life. He came from a Catholic orphanage, hardly an institution likely to turn out someone like Jacob. He was unremarkable in appearance, of average height and weight, and unlike many of the other prodigies, did not carry himself with any sort of privilege or self-confidence. In fact, except for his grades, he was totally unremarkable. And the fact that he scored a perfect SAT.

What she did not know, and could not see from any of the information she had on Jacob, was that though he was not a genius, his mind worked differently from almost anyone else. First, Jacob knew how to study. He seemed to understand instinctively what was important and what was not. He saw patterns and rhythms in what he read and in the classes he took, and looked at his studies and classes as puzzles to solve. Plus, he read extremely fast, and retained much of what passed in front of his eyes.

"Have you made any friends since you have been here? I know that you're living in the only single room in Massachusetts Hall. Is that working out for you?"

"I spend most of my time studying. I think because I'm younger than everyone else most of the other students leave me alone. I like the privacy."

She already knew Jacob was a loner. Like every other student, Jacob had a Peer Guidance Counselor whose job it was to keep track of how Jacob was fitting into student life. The Guidance Counselor's report told her that Jacob went to all his classes, usually ate alone in the cafeteria, and was generally invisible to everyone else in the Hall. This would normally concern her, but since Jacob was excelling academically, she decided to wait and see if Jacob integrated more fully into the life of the school.

"I see that you are petitioning to increase your class load for next semester. Do you think that's wise?"

She did not question that Jacob could handle more classes. It concerned her that more classes might further isolate him, and keep him from fully experiencing student life. What Jacob had noticed about student life, however, was that it seemed to center around alcohol and sex. Because he was awake at all hours, he was aware of the partying that happened in the Hall. It was not uncommon for him to go to the communal bathroom late at night and hear carousing coming from behind closed doors or someone being sick in the bathroom. Being raised by the Sisters, Jacob carried with him a reservoir of morality that precluded him from engaging in that type of behavior. He knew where she was going with her question, so he decided to tackle it head on.

"You're worried that I'm becoming isolated and suffering socially. I understand that. But I didn't come to Harvard to fit into student life. I came here to get an education and then get on with my life. You do know what goes on in the Hall? There's lots of drinking and sex, especially among freshman. You might think that would appeal to me since I was raised in a Catholic orphanage. That I would have all these inhibitions to get rid of. I'm not super religious, but the Sisters did a good job of teaching me right and wrong."

There is no doubt that he had grown up in those first months at the university. He would have never spoken like that to the Sisters, his respect for their authority was absolute. His view of the Guidance Counselor was utilitarian; she was someone who could help him get what he needed. He wanted more classes, so he used an argument he felt would get him what he needed. Jacob was not thinking in terms of manipulating her, he seemed to know intuitively what to say to move her in his direction. It would seem that the thousands of hours he had spent reading biographies at the instigation of Sister Flavia had left its mark; Jacob understood instinctively what to say to the Guidance Counselor to get his way. It wasn't until he left the orphanage that he had the opportunity to use in practice what he had absorbed from his hours reading late in the night.

Jacob was the first student to sit in front of her and use the words "right and wrong" in her memory. Most students found the lack of moral restraint and accountability at major universities an invitation to explore behaviors that were constrained by either their parents or structures in high school that kept such behaviors somewhat in check. She knew that students in every dorm participated in drinking and casual sex, even though Peer Counselors and Resident Advisers were supposed to keep those behaviors under control. Jacob's comments were irrefutable, so she decided not to address them. If he wanted to concentrate on his studies, so much the better. She did, however, want to assign a mentor to work with Jacob. If he wanted to increase his class load, she wanted to make sure he could handle the extra work, and not wear himself out in his first year.

"What kind of classes would interest you?"

He had won, and he knew it. Jacob had thought long and hard about what he would major in at Harvard. On his application and in his interview before he was accepted, Jacob thought he wanted to pursue a degree in computer science. It made sense, since he already knew as much as those who taught the courses he would be taking. However, in that first semester his thoughts turned once again to the world of business. Though he had devised a strategy to make millions of dollars in the stock market, it wasn't the money that interested him. It was solving the puzzle that enabled him to make the money that intrigued him. Computers were bound by the programs people wrote, those programs had boundaries put there by programmers, boundaries that limited the variables that intrigued Jacob.

Business, however, had variables that changed every day. He had used his computer to figure out some of those variables, but he knew there were an infinite number of variables available to him in the world of commerce and economics. At this point in his life,

Jacob was all about the challenge of doing something unique. Plus, lurking in a part of him that he was not aware of, was the possibility of achieving something no one else had ever done. He had not fleshed out what that might be, but the desire was there nonetheless. Perhaps this had to do with being an orphan, and saying to the world, "Here I am. I'm Somebody!" Regardless of his motive, his direction was set, and he replied to the counselor,

"I'd like to start taking business classes. My goal would be to end up with two degrees. One in business and one in computer science. I think I could do this in three years, if you approve."

It was an audacious plan, and as she thought about his request she knew that if he succeeded it be a coup for her personally. To earn two degrees in three years was an achievement that would bring the graduate opportunities that were denied to mere mortals. It wasn't that Harvard lacked for outstanding students, but prodigies were hard to come by. If she attached herself to Jacob's star she knew she would be rewarded as well. Finally, she said to him,

"We'll try it for a semester. But I'd like to assign a grad student to oversee your work. Just to make sure you're not in over your head. Would you agree to that?"

He knew he didn't need anyone to oversee his work. If he went to class six hours a day that still left him eighteen hours to get his work done. With his immense capacity for study unencumbered by the need for rest, he would devour the courses in short order. Jacob didn't want the added attention that a grad student overseeing him would bring, but he figured he could somehow work around the inconvenience. In this he would be proved wrong.

"Sure. Whatever you think is best."

They spent the next half-hour going over a class schedule that would have overwhelmed any other freshman. Jacob left her office knowing he would graduate Harvard before he was of legal age, though the thought of what he would do after had not yet crossed his mind.

8

That first semester was difficult for Sister Flavia. She had watched over Jacob for fifteen years, and now suddenly he was gone. He had promised to email her several times a week, and he generally followed through. His descriptions of life on campus were embellished to make it seem like he was fitting in more than he was. Jacob didn't lie to her, and his only motive was to keep her from worrying, but he did stretch the truth. It was not lost on her that he always mentioned how much more work he could do at the university than at the community. Because he had his own room, he did not have to worry about someone discovering his secret. She could read between the lines, however, and doubted that Jacob had made any real attempts to integrate into student life.

Sister Flavia knew this was probably for the best. If he concentrated on his studies it would minimize the chances of him getting into trouble. She knew what college life was like from her own experience years ago. Yet, the reality was that at some point Jacob would have to find a way to interact with people without revealing what he was. It had been easier for her, choosing to live with the Sisters provided structures that helped her hide in plain sight. Jacob was out in the real world, a world that would take him apart physically and emotionally if it found out who and what he was.

Her own world had grown smaller since he had departed, and she was finding it difficult to do the daily tasks of overseeing the community. She was feeling her age more keenly, something she had observed in Sister Margaret years earlier. It was time, she knew, to begin transitioning the leadership of the community to one of the younger Sisters. There had been new additions to the community, two Sisters had joined them from an orphanage that had closed in another state. In addition, the orphanage had received four new children in the last few months. This had been made possible due to the money Jacob had provided, money that enabled them to refurbish rooms that had been unused due to repairs they had not been able to afford.

Sister Margaret continued to decline, she spent most of her time in her room reading or in the chapel praying or meditating. She had removed herself from the life of the community, though she would occasionally join the children for dinner. Sister Flavia tried to spend part of each day with her, usually in the morning when Sister Margaret had more strength. They would talk about the children, the day's schedule, the division of responsibility among the staff and the other Sisters, and sometimes about Jacob. When Sister Flavia could see that Sister Margaret was getting tired, she would help her back to her room, and get on with the day's responsibilities.

It was after Thanksgiving, when the weather had turned cold, that Sister Flavia was summoned to Sister Margaret's room. It was late in the afternoon, a time when Sister Margaret was usually in the chapel. Sister Flavia knocked lightly, and then entered the small room. Sister Margaret was lying in bed, propped up by several pillows, a book by her side. She looked tired and drawn, and Sister Flavia thought she might be in pain by the look on her face. She brought the one chair in the room by the bed, and said,

"How are you Sister? You wanted to see me?"

"I am fine, though somewhat tired. I wanted to talk with you about Jacob. The times we will be able to talk together are coming to an end, I believe."

They had talked before about Sister Margaret's declining health, so she was not surprised by the admission that Sister Margaret was feeling her life was ending. Death held no fear for the Sisters, they had prepared for it their entire life.

"What about Jacob?"

"How is he doing at university? Is he fitting in?"

"It seems that he spends most of his time studying, which is both good and bad, I think."

"You worry about him, I expect."

"Yes, Sister. It's a new world for him. One with many temptations. I pray for him constantly."

"He is much like you, isn't he?"

"In what way Sister?"

Sister Flavia did not know where the conversation was going, and wondered again why Sister Margaret had wanted to speak with her.

"You have been like a mother to him. Guarding and protecting him all these years. It has been your purpose. I have known that."

Her words echoed exactly what Sister Flavia had told Jacob when he left for university, and she had a moment of doubt. When she did not immediately respond, Sister Margaret said,

"I know it has been hard for both of you. I know God has protected you, but I am afraid for Jacob."

Sister Flavia's mind went back over the years, trying to think where she might have revealed the secret she and Jacob shared. She was so careful, and thought she had taken every precaution. If Sister Margaret knew, why had she never said anything? She was lost in thought when Sister Margaret softly said,

"You could have told me. It might have helped."

Sister Flavia put her hands to her face, and for the first time in her life let her guard completely down. She wept until she had no more tears, a lifetime of reserve gone with the realization that Sister Margaret had loved and accepted her knowing exactly what she was. When she finally brought herself back under a semblance of control, she said,

"I'm sorry. I believed this was mine to carry alone. When Jacob arrived, everything became about protecting and guarding him. I should have trusted you. I'm so sorry."

Sister Margaret could only imagine what life had been like for her friend. It was difficult enough taking the vows of Sisterhood; you took vows of poverty and chastity, dedicating your life in service to God and others. When you left the community to go outside, even your clothing set your apart from everyone else. To add an aberration to such a life was asking for commitment and devotion Sister Margaret could hardly conceive of.

Sister Flavia would never learn how Sister Margaret found out about her and Jacob. It wasn't important, so she refrained from asking. What was important, and the reason that Sister Margaret had wanted to speak with her, was that she was dying. It had been obvious to everyone at the community that Sister Margaret was in failing health, but no one expected that the end was near. She explained to Sister Flavia that her doctor, who had just been out to see her the previous day, confirmed that the congestive heart failure she had been living with for years was worsening, and because Sister Margaret was adamant about not going to the hospital, there really wasn't anything he could do except provide comfort care for her. The doctor was sending a nurse to the community the next day to make her as comfortable as possible. Before that happened, Sister Margaret wanted a final, private conversation with Sister Flavia.

"It's time you began to turn over your duties to the younger Sisters. Our time is ending, it's their time now. Jacob will need you, he thinks he can survive on his own, but I believe he is wrong. He has much knowledge, but little wisdom."

"He's still a boy, there's still time for him."

"He is a young man out in the world, not a boy. We don't yet know if what we tried to teach him found a place in his heart. You cannot force him to live by what he knows to be true, but it is possible to guide him. You will have to be cautious in how you relate to him. Too much, and you could drive him away. Too soft, and you may have no influence all. But I believe God will guide you."

It always came back to faith with Sister Margaret. Sister Flavia had never seen her waver in her belief that God was always present, the unseen hand behind everything that happened in the community. She trusted the children to God, the running of the orphanage, the daily challenges they faced, and, finally, at the end of her life, her eternal destiny. Sister Flavia wanted to believe that God would take care of Jacob, but with him living on the outside, she wasn't sure how much influence she could provide.

"How do I guide him when I hardly see him?"

"Something will happen when he will need to decide for himself which path he will follow. You will need to be there for him at that time."

Sister Margaret was correct, there would be a point in Jacob's life that he would be forced to decide what he believed and how he would spend his life. Sister Margaret, however, would not live to see it, nor would Sister Flavia.

9

Jacob spent Christmas at the orphanage, and was there when Sister Margaret passed away. There was a wake at the community that was attended by Sisters and priests who had known her over her long life. It was part celebration, and part mourning. One of the priests served Mass in the chapel, and then the Sisters and staff who worked at the orphanage held a private service at the gravesite. Sister Margaret was buried in a local cemetery, close to the community she served for over fifty years. Jacob was allowed to attend, standing close to Sister Flavia in the fading afternoon light. It was cold, and there was snow on the ground from a storm that had come through the area earlier in the week.

When the service was concluded, the group moved away from the grave toward the parking lot where the community van was parked. Sister Flavia had not been able to have any private time with Jacob since he had returned for the holiday, she was too busy attending to Sister Margaret in her last days, and then planning for her wake and service. Just before they arrived at the van, she turned to Jacob.

"Why don't we walk back? It's not far, and we haven't had much time to talk."

"Sure. If you want."

There was hesitation in his voice, and she heard it. Jacob knew he had to return to the orphanage for the holidays, knowing also that Sister Flavia would want to talk with him about his first semester at the university. In actuality, there wasn't much to tell. He spent all his time studying, just as he did at the orphanage. Sister Flavia, however, wanted to talk about something completely different.

"Before Sister Margaret died, she told me she knew about us. How she found out I don't know, and I never asked her. I thought you should know."

Jacob didn't know what to make of what Sister Flavia had said. There was one thought that came immediately to him, the same thought that occurred to Sister Flavia.

"Why didn't she say anything to you?"

"My guess is that she didn't want us to worry about how we might feel if we realized someone knew our secret."

They walked along the road back to the community, and for a moment neither of them spoke. Then Sister Flavia said,

"We took great care to protect our privacy, Jacob. And yet Sister Margaret found out. I want you to realize how careful you must be. In some way, I believe Sister Margaret thought our gift was given by God, and it was not her place to intrude on something she may have viewed as sacred."

She stopped walking, and turned to face Jacob.

"Others would not view what we are so charitably, I'm afraid."

73

"Are you sure? Maybe people would think we're special and let us do things they can't do because they have to sleep."

It was the first time Jacob had proposed a different view on the "anomaly", a view that was at odds with what Sister Flavia had always believed. He was young, she thought, and young people tended to be idealistic and wanted to think the best of everyone. She resumed walking, thinking how to respond. After a moment, she replied.

"Think about what you know of history. How have people who are different been treated? People like Jews, people who are mentally ill, people who are handicapped, African-Americans, little people, homosexuals, and even at times people of religious faith. Though I believe most people mean well, there are many who would take advantage of those who are different. Jacob, there is no one more different than us."

He heard what she said, and in one way it made sense to him. But on a deeper, more personal level, he knew it sentenced to him to a life of isolation and loneliness. Jacob was not quite ready to accept her version of reality.

"I don't want to be different than everyone else. It's easy for you living in the community. I don't live in the community anymore. I live in the real world."

It didn't come out the way he wanted, but it did show that after only a few months of living outside of the community he was feeling hemmed in by having to hide who he was. Sister Margaret had hinted that it might take a crisis to help Jacob determine the path he would follow, and to find his place in the world. Sister Flavia sensed he wasn't ready to listen to a long explanation about how he needed to trust God and have faith that He would guide Jacob as his life unfolded. However, she thought he needed to hear something that related to the faith he had been brought up in.

"Except for when I went to college, I've never lived in the world outside of the community, you're right about that. I don't know what you feel. But you must know that I believe God has given you this gift for a reason. I also believe He will reveal what that purpose is when you are ready to hear it."

"What if it's not a gift? What if it's a curse?"

His words took her completely by surprise, and once again she stopped by the side of the road, thinking how to reply. He was embarrassed by what he said, and wished he could take the words back. Jacob knew they contradicted what Sister Flavia had always believed about the "anomaly". They did, however, reflect his experience living outside of the community, and how he looked at his future.

"I don't believe God curses people, Jacob. Why would you say that?"

"I don't know. I don't like being different, that's all."

"What if God made you different for a reason? What if you knew what that reason was? Would that make a difference?"

Jacob's own relationship with God was complicated. He believed God existed, you could hardly grow up in Catholic orphanage without having some sort of faith, but he was mystified at the notion that God would somehow be involved with him personally. If he was honest with himself, he would have to admit that he was somewhat frightened of God, a feeling common to many within the Catholic church. He felt God was always looking over his shoulder, silently watching to see if Jacob would somehow fall short of what He expected from him. Which put Jacob in a classic Catch-22 quandary; how could Jacob please God when he didn't know what God wanted him to do? Sister Flavia's question made him uneasy, and he turned the query back on her.

"Do you know what that reason is?"

"No, Jacob, I don't. But I believe that He will show you what your purpose is when you are ready."

"When will that be?"

Sister Flavia understood the conversation was heading into a loop she could not get out of. She had no concrete answers for Jacob, which is what he wanted. It wasn't a level playing field, she thought. Her life was built on faith; a faith that would patiently wait for God to reveal what His plans were for her. She had waited decades hoping to find someone like her, and then that person was literally dropped off at her doorstep. Jacob's purpose was out there, of that she was confident. She was not confident, however, that he would have the patience to wait until that purpose was revealed. Standing on the side of the road in the cold, she was suddenly tired, and realized they needed to return to the orphanage, which was still about a mile away.

"Let's go, Jacob. I'm sure you must be cold. The others will be waiting for us."

It was typical for Sister Flavia not mention her own discomfort, and be concerned only for Jacob. They resumed walking, and twenty minutes later were back at the community. Jacob went to the common room to visit with the children while Sister Flavia went to the chapel. The enormity of losing Sister Margaret was just beginning to affect her. She had been busy attending to all the things that needed to be done when someone passes, but now, sitting alone in the chapel, she felt the loss keenly. Sister Flavia felt adrift, she had lost her mentor and confidant, and now she felt she might lose Jacob as well. She wanted to believe he would eventually come around, but it was a belief that would have to rest on her trust that God knew what He was doing. Looking up at the figure of Jesus on the cross, trying not to doubt, she thought of the prayer uttered by a man who had similar doubts. That man had spoken the words to Jesus when he brought his son to Him to be healed. Jesus said He would heal the boy if the father believed. The man realized he had some faith, but did he have enough to accomplish the impossible? She crossed herself, and then uttered the words,

"Lord, I believe. Help my unbelief."

10

Jacob returned to Harvard two days later. The school did not officially open for another week, but he wanted to get a head start on his new classes. He was able to get some of the books he needed from an off-campus bookstore, and in three days had read four of them. The school was virtually deserted, and since the cafeteria was closed, he had to eat at restaurants close to the campus. It was the first time in his life that he was truly independent; he had no classes to attend, he could come and go as he wished, and though he still spent most of his time in his room, he would occasionally go out in the early evening and walk through the town of Cambridge. He did not realize it, but his time at the community during the holidays, and the death of Sister Margaret, were affecting him in ways he did not understand.

He didn't mind the cold as he walked, it helped clear his mind so he was able to think. Jacob knew that when school started back up he would be spending all his time on his studies. He was not an introspective person, but could not shake the conversation he had on the road with Sister Flavia. There wasn't anything he would not do for her, but there was part of him that knew she did not understand what his life was like. How could she? She had lived most of her life cut off from the world, living in a community that was based on common values and beliefs. Jacob was out of that world now, and would most likely never return.

His dilemma was one faced by nearly every college student who came from a religious background. Would the years spent at a public university, or in some cases even a religious school, drive the faith out of students who had been raised in some form of religious instruction? Jacob's years at the orphanage had been submerged in Catholicism, with the hope that when he left the community he would decide for himself to continue in the faith. Jacob, however, was different from other students who came to Harvard with religious backgrounds. His devotion to Sister Flavia was inextricably linked to her beliefs. If he chose to reject or modify what he had been taught, he felt he would be rejecting her as well. The thought of doing anything that would disappoint her left him with a profound sadness. He did not want to be a hypocrite, he knew that would also upset her. As he continued to walk through the town as the day turned into night, he realized he could not come up with a solution to the problem, which is how he viewed every circumstance in his life. The fact that his "problem" lay in the realm of the spiritual did not occur to him. He turned around, and began to walk back to the campus, knowing there was a restaurant he would pass where he could have dinner. For the next hour, the thoughts that had consumed him while he walked receded into the background. He ate his meal while reading a textbook from one of his upcoming classes. When he was done, he hurried back to his room to finish the book and move on to another. Jacob didn't bother closing his door since he was the only one on the floor. When morning came it was snowing, and as he left the Hall to get some breakfast, he would have been surprised to know that Sister Flavia was in the chapel praying for him. Her prayers would eventually be answered, but not in a way that she could foresee.

11

The grad student who was to supervise Jacob showed up at his room one evening a week after classes had resumed. Jacob had been, as usual, consumed by his studies. There was a soft knock on his door, startling him, and he nearly jumped out of his chair. It was after nine o'clock, and no one had ever knocked on his door that late. He got up, and slowly opened the door. Standing in front of him was a young man, and Jacob immediately knew who he was and why he was there.

"You're my supervisor."

"That's right. You want to let me in?"

Jacob opened the door wider, and moved back out of the way.

The young man came in and looked around at the small room. It was tidy and clean, and the grad student could not believe how small it was.

"Did you upset somebody to end up in here?"

"I don't know what you mean."

"The room. It's kind of small."

"Oh. I don't mind. I like the privacy."

"I see you just have the one chair."

Jacob looked around the room, not understanding the intent of the remark.

"It's all I need."

"Why don't you sit on the bed and I'll take the chair. Is that okay?"

"Sure."

A lifetime of being on guard had not helped Jacob's social skills. Making conversation did not come easily to him, something that was obvious to the grad student. When they were both seated, the grad student said,

"My name is Noah. I guess you know that I've been assigned to make sure you don't fall apart with all the extra classes you're taking."

"I won't fall apart. It won't be a problem."

"Still, they're paying me to watch over you. You're something special, though you wouldn't know it by the size of this room."

"What do you mean I'm something special?"

"You're sixteen years old, and you're taking a double load of classes. That doesn't happen very often. Even at Harvard."

Jacob had never thought in those terms, and he wasn't happy when he thought about the extra attention he was receiving. There was an uncomfortable pause in the conversation.

"So, let me ask, how are you doing after a week of taking a double load? Are you making all your classes, falling behind on any assignments?"

"Yes and no. I really don't think it's any big deal. I know you have a job to do, but if I have any difficulties I'll let you know."

Noah was not going to be put off that easily. He took the assignment because he knew it would benefit his standing with his professors in the Business School. They were intrigued by Jacob, and wanted Noah to shepherd him through his undergraduate work until he could apply to the Business School. There was another more important reason that Noah wanted to work with Jacob. Noah had read Jacob's file, and the first thing he noticed was Jacob's IQ. It was high, but nowhere near as high as one might have thought. Students who gained early admission to Harvard were usually prodigies, or even geniuses. Except for his SAT scores, which were perfect, there were no markers that indicated Jacob should be who he was. He decided to dig a little deeper.

"You were raised in an orphanage, right?"

"Yes."

"What was that like? Being raised by Nuns?"

Jacob didn't know where the conversation was going, and wished Noah would leave.

"They took care of me. They gave me a home. They're good people."

"They must be pretty good teachers, for you to end up at Harvard."

"They made sure I did my studies, and encouraged me to read a lot of books."

Noah believed the last part because there were books in stacks leaning against the walls of the small room. It was obvious

Jacob spent most of his time studying, though Noah found it hard to believe he could go to class all day and get all his work done in the evening, let alone read anything that wasn't directly associated with his classes.

"Do you take anything to stay awake? What with all the work you have from your classes?"

It was common for students to take drugs to help them stay awake, especially during finals. Noah had used them before, as had many of his friends. The most common drugs were Adderall and Ritalin, which were easy enough to find if you knew the right person. Jacob, of course, had no need for any type of drug to stay awake. He understood why Noah would ask the question.

"I don't need much sleep. I never have. I guess it comes from living with a lot of other kids. We didn't have a lot of privacy, so the only time I could study alone was late at night."

It wasn't exactly a lie, but it was meant to deceive. Jacob looked at Noah to see if he would accept the explanation. Noah knew there was the odd individual who could get by on just a few hours of sleep, so he let it go. There was one other question he wanted to ask Jacob before he left.

"Why did you decide to major in business? It seems odd. I get the computer science part, kids your age grow up attached to their devices, but I don't get the interest in business."

At last there was something that Jacob could talk about without being defensive. He visibly brightened.

"Business has no boundaries; the variables are almost endless. It's like a giant puzzle that's waiting to be solved."

When Jacob finished, Noah added,

"And of course, there's the money. A lot of people study business and economics to make money. You're not opposed to making money?"

"Money's just a by-product of finding successful ways to succeed in business. It doesn't interest me as much as the processes and strategies used to make it."

Noah laughed when Jacob said he wasn't interested in money. Noah was interested in making lots of money, which is why he had chosen Harvard in the first place. He could have gone to any Ivy League school, but knew that a graduate degree, and then perhaps a doctorate, would guarantee him a lifetime of financial reward.

"Well, it sure interests me. I guess the Nuns did a number on you if you don't care about money."

Jacob let the remark go, not wanting to extend the conversation any longer than possible. However, he would remember what Noah said, and smiled when he thought that if Noah knew he had made millions of dollars in the stock market he would look at Jacob in a completely different manner.

"I really need to get back to work."

Noah got up to leave, and said as he left the room,

"I'll check in with you next week. Let me know if you need anything."

With that he was gone, and Jacob went back to writing his paper. Jacob forgot about the conversation almost immediately, but as Noah walked back across the campus to his room, he thought about what Jacob had said about business being a puzzle. Jacob was a puzzle, and Noah would make it his mission to solve that puzzle in the coming months.

12

One month later Noah met with Jacob's Guidance Counselor. He had written a report that detailed how Jacob was progressing in his classes as well as Noah's overall impression of the boy. She leafed through the four pages, and then sat them on her desk.

"So, he's not falling behind? In fact, he seems to be thriving. Is that about right?"

"Yes, but there are some warning signs. I didn't put them in the report because I wasn't sure who was going to read it."

She understood what Noah was saying; there was no reason to highlight anything negative when Jacob was meeting all his academic requirements.

"What warning signs are you talking about?"

"Well, he doesn't seem to have any friends. When he's not in class he spends his time either in the library or in his room. I guess that makes sense considering his class load, but it's not normal for freshman to be that isolated. Most of them can't wait to do things that were off limits at home."

"Maybe it has something to do with his Catholic background? I mean he did spend fifteen years being raised by Nuns."

"I don't think so. He doesn't strike me as religious. Plus, he spends Sundays studying. If he was religious you would think he might go to church."

"What else?"

Noah was hesitant to bring up the most obvious thing he had discovered about Jacob. If she discovered what Noah knew without him telling her, it might jeopardize Noah's position. He decided to mention it, but soften the reality of what he knew.

"He doesn't seem to sleep much. People in the Hall tell me that the light in his room is on at all hours. He told me that himself, so I don't know if we should be concerned. He shows up at all his classes and gets his work done. Every time I see him he seems fine. Just thought I should mention it."

The Guidance Counselor thought back to her days at the university. She had pulled all night study sessions, especially during exam time. There was one reason he might be staying up all night, she thought, and it wasn't something that she wanted to think about.

"Do you think he might be taking drugs? I know lots of kids use drugs to stay awake, but he doesn't strike me as someone who uses drugs. Plus, he's on a pretty tight stipend. I don't know where he would get the money."

She was referring to the fact that Jacob's tuition, room and board were paid by the state. Drugs were expensive, and if Jacob was taking any she could not think where the money might be coming from.

"I asked him that, and he kind of shrugged it off. I don't figure him for drugs."

"Okay, let's leave it at that. Why don't you see if you can get him in a study group? I know that some of his business classes have study groups going. It might help him socially. Otherwise, let's leave him alone and see what happens."

Noah nodded in response, but there was no way he was going to leave Jacob alone. Jacob was an anomaly, and Noah didn't like anomalies. Jacob should not be able to accomplish what he was pulling off, not with his background and his slightly above average IQ. Noah was smart, disciplined and focused, and he knew there was no way he could manage what Jacob was doing. Noah contemplated the will and determination needed to take a double load at such a young age, and knew he was overlooking something. If he had known what the outcome would be of his search for what he thought he was missing about Jacob, he would have given up and stayed as far away from him as he could.

13

Jacob resented going to the study group, but he figured he needed to do what he was told lest he draw any unwanted attention to himself. He was trying to stay on Noah's good side, calling him every week and letting him know he was attending all his classes and keeping up with his homework. Jacob needn't have bothered. Noah had people from both the Hall and his classes keeping tabs on him, though Noah did not tell them why. The study group met Thursday night, focusing on upcoming assignments, though the conversation often drifted into other areas of interest. There were seven students in the group, and they regarded Jacob with interest since he was taking a double load.

Jacob would not speak unless he was asked a direct question, and then tried to keep his responses as short as possible. He had never been in a group of his peers before, and everyone sensed the awkwardness. The class they were all taking, The Legal and Ethical Environment of Business, was a required first year class, and Jacob had breezed through the syllabus and already read the textbook. It did not interest him because it didn't provide a practical basis for navigating through the intricacies of the free market system. The class focused on developing a foundation of what was right, and what you could get away with within the confines of the legal system. Underlying everything was the assumption that making money was the goal of business, a goal that at this point in this life did not interest Jacob in the least. He already knew how to make money.

There was one thing in the class that did interest him, however. Four of the students were girls, and it was the first time in his short life that Jacob was in close proximity to girls without the Sisters hovering nearby. In the orphanage there were girls, but life there was so structured that there was little possibility of developing any kind of relationship with one, even if Jacob had wanted to. Jacob was about to turn 17, and though most of his thoughts and energy were directed toward his studies, he was, after all, a teenage boy who was at times was subject to the influence of his hormones.

Thursday night they were talking about a chapter that focused on the differences between what was legal and what was ethical. Many times in business there were circumstances where the law had not caught up to the reality of what happened in the marketplace. This was especially true in terms of technology. Computer programmers were always writing new software that pushed the legal envelope into unexplored areas of the law.

Jacob was only marginally listening to the conversation, his attention drawn to the girl sitting across from him. Her name was Nikki, and she was somewhat like him; uneasy participating in the conversation, most of the time looking down at her notes. When she did talk, she got right to the point, and then looked to see how her comments were received. He noticed she occasionally looked in his direction, and he often wondered what she was thinking.

"Jacob, what do you think?"

Jacob had been listening as the group expressed their opinions on whether it was wrong to use information you developed for your employer for your personal use.

"Is there a policy in place that covers proprietary information? If there is, you can't use it personally. If not, I still wouldn't use anything that I was paid to develop."

The group leader, who had asked the question, had a different opinion.

"You don't believe in "gray" areas?"

"You're back to the difference between legal and ethical. We've talked about that already."

"I thought you might have a different perspective being raised in a Catholic orphanage."

This had come up before in the group, and Jacob had managed to deflect the question. He knew they looked at him differently; he was young, he was taking a double load, and he was an orphan.

"You mean do I believe in right and wrong? You assume that because I was raised by Nuns I must have absorbed everything they believed."

He let his answer hang in the air, purposely not answering the question, hoping the group leader might move on to someone else. It was not to be.

"Something like that. We don't get many religious students here at Harvard. At least that I have met. And you didn't answer my question."

Jacob looked around the group, who were waiting to see what he would say. The last thing he wanted to do was to draw attention to himself, but he knew that unless he definitively answered the question it would just keep coming back at him in one form or another.

"Of course I believe in right and wrong. Everyone believes in right and wrong, it's just that the definition of what's right and wrong varies from person to person. The Sisters taught me that God expects us to do what is right, even when it's difficult. They spend their lives doing what they believe is right, and I think the world would be a better place if more people acted like they do."

It was the first time Jacob, or anyone else for that matter, had ever brought God into the conversation. Jacob had a reason for bringing up God; it wasn't that he was proselytizing, he just wanted to stand up for the Sisters. He suspected the group viewed them as anachronistic; holdovers from another time and place. There was a pause, and then he was surprised when the girl across from him said,

"I'm with Jacob in this. If you don't have a firm basis of what's right and wrong, how are you going to function in the business world? You'll always end up doing what's expedient."

The group leader wasn't quite ready to move on.

"But we're talking about the difference between what's legal and what's ethical. If something isn't illegal doesn't that mean ethics don't apply?"

Jacob was thinking about answering, but before he could get the words out, the girl responded.

"Slavery was legal. Women weren't allowed to vote for years. That was legal. Abortion was once illegal, now it's legal. In the "gray" areas you were talking about, if you don't have a foundation for what you believe is right and wrong, you can justify wrong by saying it's legal."

Time was running out, and the leader brought the meeting to a close. It didn't go exactly as he planned; the talk of God came out of nowhere and left him unsure how to answer. He reminded the group to read the next two chapters in the textbook, and then they were done. Jacob was always the first to leave, but before he could get up out of his seat the girl who supported him was standing in front of his chair.

"Do you want to go down to the café and get a cup of coffee?"

Jacob had never been in a situation like this before in his life, and for a moment could not respond. However, his desire overcame his shyness, and he answered with just one word.

"Sure."

14

Jacob didn't drink coffee, so he settled for a soda. They found a quiet corner of the café, located in the student commons, and sat across from each other on two overstuffed chairs. It was late, and there were only a few other people in the large room. Nikki was the first to speak. "You're usually pretty quiet. I liked what you had to say tonight."

"Thanks. I'm still trying to figure out the purpose of the group. It's pretty unfocused; I think I could find a better use of my time."

Jacob was somewhat awkward in conversation, he usually said what was on his mind despite the fact that he might be misunderstood or mildly offensive.

"You don't have to attend, you could drop out if you wanted."

"My advisor thinks it will help me socially. I don't get out much. But I guess that's pretty obvious."

"There aren't many kids who come to Harvard at sixteen. Fewer who take a double load. I can see why you don't get out much."

"The Sisters taught me how to study and to use my time. It's not that big a deal."

What Jacob said was technically the truth, stretched to the breaking point. Sister Flavia had taught him how to study, but that included how to study all night without getting caught. He hated having to skirt around the edges of the truth, especially when he had just been involved in a conversation about right and wrong. The long arm of the Sisters had followed Jacob to Harvard, and it would never really let go of him.

"You probably don't realize it, but you're a pretty big deal around the campus. They call you the "whiz kid." It's been awhile since a freshman has taken a double load, especially one so young."

Jacob had spent so much of his life learning, studying and filling his mind with information that he had no sense of being anything special. The Sisters had for years taught him he was to put God first, and then others, so he had no idea how the other students looked at him. He was so careful to guard his secret that he completely missed the fact he was a celebrity, his status enhanced by his total devotion to his classes.

"I'll be seventeen next week. That's the normal age for freshman. I'm only a year ahead."

He was caught up in trying to impress Nikki, and he didn't even know it. Even though she was several years older, he was lost in the attention she was giving him. Jacob knew nothing about her, so he asked,

"Why did you come to Harvard? I mean, I'm sure you could have gone to other schools."

"My father and grandfather went here. I didn't really have a choice in the matter, not that I mind. When I'm done, they'll expect me to go into the family business."

"What's that?"

"They manage pension funds for large corporations. My grandfather started it back in the sixties. If my parents had a boy I probably could have done something different. I'm kind of stuck."

"Buying and selling stocks doesn't appeal to you?"

"Not really. I don't like being responsible for other people's money. Why are you interested in business? Especially if you aren't interested in money."

She knew immediately she had said the wrong thing. Jacob had never told her he wasn't interested in money, he had only revealed that to Noah. Jacob, however, didn't react to her statement.

"Business is like a puzzle. I like solving puzzles. Money is just a by-product."

"That's a different point of view, for sure. I better be getting back to my room. I still have some work to do for tomorrow."

Nikki got up from her seat, and before she left, said,

"Let's do something for your birthday."

"Sure. I'll see you later."

Jacob followed her with his eyes as she crossed the large room and disappeared down the stairs that lead to the outside. There was only one person he had told that he didn't care about money. He distinctly remembered the conversation with Noah, and wondered why Noah would have told Nikki what they had talked about. Jacob was young, both in years and in experience, but he could clearly see what was right before him. Why Noah would be using Nikki to ingratiate herself with him, he did not understand. Not yet, anyway.

15

Two weeks later Nikki was again in the café, but this time she was meeting with Noah instead of Jacob. Waiting for him to arrive, she thought again about why she had agreed to pretend to take an interest in Jacob. She had initially thought Noah was interested in her, as she was interested in him, but it quickly became obvious that all Noah was interested in was information about Jacob. Nikki could not figure out why Noah needed to find out anything about Jacob. Jacob seemed to be exactly what he was; an overachieving prodigy whose life revolved around his studies.

She had met with Jacob twice during those two weeks, once to take him out to dinner for his birthday, and once after their Thursday night study group. Nikki could tell it was difficult for him being with her, he did not know how to have a conversation without it coming back in some way to his schoolwork. Despite her efforts to elicit information about his personal life, he would say little beyond what she already knew; he was raised by the Nuns in an orphanage, he read lots of books growing up, and had a special relationship with one of the Nuns. He constantly deflected any questions about how he was able to manage his course load, saying only that he had a good memory and the Sisters had taught him discipline and the value of a good education.

Noah was not happy with her progress. He had wanted Nikki to see if Jacob would take an interest in her personally, despite the difference in their ages. She tried, though it was distasteful, but Jacob didn't seem to see her as anything other than a friend. Nikki wanted out, but her feelings for Noah, though unrequited at the moment, brought her to the café. He was late arriving, and after he sat down across from her, he quickly asked her what she had learned about Jacob.

"I don't think I know any more than you do. He's a smart kid, a loner, and it seems all he cares about is his classes. What did you think I was going to find?"

"I don't know. That's the problem. If I knew what I was looking for I'd tell you to focus on that."

Nikki took a chance and asked Noah why he cared about what Jacob did with his time, and why it mattered to him.

"He's hiding something, and that bothers me. There's no way he should be able to take that many classes, do all the work and get straight A's. Plus, he got a perfect score on the SAT. You know how many kids get perfect scores on their SAT's every year? Less than 500. Certainly not a kid raised in a Catholic orphanage."

Noah had forgotten that Nikki was sitting across from him, and was talking to himself. What Nikki did not know was that Noah was consumed by self-doubt, a residue of trying to please his father, a corporate attorney who expected his son to be the best at whatever he did or attempted. The reality was that Noah was usually the best at whatever he did, though it never seemed to be enough to meet his father's expectations. He lived perpetually in the shadow of his father's disappointment, and it had lead him to do things that he would later regret. Things that Jacob would be forced to discover.

Nikki wanted to end the conversation, and find a way to extricate herself from the web that Noah wanted to spin. Despite the fact that she wanted to keep meeting with Noah to see if there was any hope of a relationship between them, she knew there wasn't any more she was going to get from spending time with Jacob.

"I don't think there's anything else I can do for you. If you want me to keep meeting with him I will, but I think he's just what he seems; a kid who's smarter than the rest of us."

Noah wasn't really listening, he had already come to that conclusion. For reasons that he would never really understand, Noah just could not let it go. Noah understood he wasn't the smartest person at Harvard, but to watch Jacob seemingly breeze through a double load of classes, it was too much, a puzzle he needed to figure out. There was one idea that occurred to him, though it was intrusive and possibly illegal. If he went through with it, he would have no more need of Nikki.

"You're probably right, let's dial it back for the time being."

He was out of his seat before she could reply, heading back to his room to spend some time seeing how much his plan might cost, though money was not an object. An hour later he had purchased what he needed from an electronics store on the Internet, now all that was necessary was some time alone in Jacob's room. Jacob never missed his classes, so he knew he would have the hour or so needed to put his plan in motion. What he would find he had no idea, but whatever it was it happened in that room, of that he was sure. Noah was right, and it would prove to be his undoing.

16

Noah had watched hours of video, and he still could not believe what he was seeing. He had attached the miniature video camera to the light that hung in the middle of Jacob's room. It was nearly invisible, and Noah made sure to change the light bulb so that it would not go out any time soon. The camera sent the video to a receiver he hid in a storage room on the floor below. Noah retrieved the video from the receiver after three days, uploading it to a flash drive. He watched it in the privacy of his room, slowly becoming aware of how Jacob managed his class load, though he found it almost impossible to believe what he was seeing.

Jacob never slept, he either sat at his desk working on his computer or in the chair reading a book. Noah never saw him take any drugs, which made what he was seeing even more disturbing. He had spent enough time with Jacob to know that he never seemed tired, never seemed irritable, and was not skipping class to sleep during the day. Noah knew that it was impossible to live without sleep, but the evidence was being played out before him on his computer screen. If it was true that Jacob did not need to sleep, it explained everything, yet it brought up so many questions that it made Noah dizzy.

He understood why Jacob would not tell anyone his secret. Jacob would become the object of unprecedented scrutiny. Noah did a quick Google search and found that there had never been a case of someone who apparently did not need to sleep. The biggest question that was running through Noah's mind, a question that revealed the ambiguity of his ethical core, was this: what was he going to do with what he had discovered? There was still part of him that doubted what he was seeing, and he knew only a conversation with Jacob would give him the absolute certainty he needed. He would wait until his scheduled meeting with Jacob to disclose to him what he had found, hoping he could think of a way to exploit what he had learned.

Two days later they were sitting in Jacob's room, going over each of his classes. Noah watched Jacob with a new intensity, trying to see if there was any physical difference he had previously missed. There wasn't, Jacob looked like what he was, a seventeen-year old student. When they were finished with his classes, Noah finally brought it out into the open.

"How are you sleeping? With your class load I imagine you don't sleep much."

"I've told you before that I don't need much sleep. I'm fine."

Noah didn't expect any other type of answer, so he dug a little deeper.

"I don't know anybody else who could take this kind of load and still get straight A's. You're one in a million. Or maybe one in a billion."

Jacob knew where Noah was going, and decided to get it over with. He had work to do, and wanted to get this conversation over as soon as possible.

"I'm not the only one, if that's where you're going. There are two of us. There may be more, but I doubt it. It's kind of a hard thing to hide."

Noah had not expected Jacob to just come right out and admit what he was, and was caught off guard. He had the video evidence, but now it seemed he wouldn't need to bring it up. There was silence for a moment as Noah thought how to respond. Jacob didn't wait for him to speak.

"I found the camera the day you put it in. It probably didn't occur to you that I might have a security system, what with the room being so small. I leave my computer camera on while I'm gone, saving the video to the Cloud. I could have pretended to sleep, but I didn't think you were going to give up. I'm sorry."

"What are you sorry for? You're the one who's a freak. How can you not ever need to sleep? Do you know what I could do with that information? Do you know what people would pay to have this kind of story? Your life would never be the same. You know that."

Jacob reached into his backpack and took out a sheaf of papers. He handed them to Noah, and waited while Noah looked over what Jacob had given him. He turned white, and his hands began to shake. Jacob was sorry for him, but Noah had made his bed, and now he was going to have to lie in it. When he could talk, Noah said,

"How did you get this?"

"You mean how did I break into your computer? It wasn't hard. You're smart, but not that smart. I don't think the school would be happy with what you've been doing, do you?"

Jacob had Noah's whole future in his hands, and Noah knew it. He would be kicked out of Harvard if Jacob revealed to the school what he knew, and Noah didn't even want to think about what his father would do to him. Noah was trying to think of a way out of the situation that had suddenly threatened his entire future, but could think of nothing.

"What do you want?"

"I've already removed the video from your computer. If you have it on a flash, I'll need that, too. I'm sorry."

Jacob was sorry, and was conflicted about the position he had put Noah in. A short lifetime of living under the rule of the Sisters had left him with a conscience that recoiled from what he had done. He didn't necessarily believe what the Sisters believed, but he would never be free from the moral influence they had over him. Which would turn out to be a good thing.

Noah would never be the same. The thought that a seventeen-year old mutant (which is how he thought of Jacob) had his fate in his hands was too much for him to bear. After delivering the flash drive to Jacob, he spent hours trying to find a way to turn the tables on Jacob. It was a vain quest, and eventually Noah would be driven mad by the thought that he could not tell the world who and what Jacob was, and how he managed to succeed beyond all expectations at Harvard. He was able to finish the last two months of that semester, but did not return to finish his master's degree in the Fall. His behavior became increasingly erratic, and when he was finally admitted to a psychiatric hospital later that year, he would talk incessantly about a boy who never needed to sleep. Knowing that such a thing was impossible, his doctors dismissed it as the ravings of someone who, for reasons they would never figure out, had developed a severe case of paranoia.

17

The last two months of the semester were anything but pleasant for Jacob. It wasn't that he was having any difficulty with his classes; if anything, he was finding it easier as time went on to both get to class and do the required work. Jacob looked at situations in life as puzzles to be solved, and taking a double load with the required extra work, even for a boy who didn't need to sleep, was just another puzzle to solve. As he neared the end of his first year, it was becoming obvious to the higher ups in Harvard's administration that Jacob was not only a prodigy, but someone they might use to bring even more attention to one of America's most prestigious universities.

Though every minute of his day was either spent in class or studying, Jacob could not free his mind from Noah. When he discovered the camera in his room, he immediately knew that Noah suspected something. Jacob remembered the caution that Sister Flavia had given him: that it would be much harder to hide what he was out in the real world. He could have tried to deceive Noah by pretending to sleep, but he not only needed the time to do his schoolwork and the other interests that absorbed him, he knew that Noah would not give up hounding him. Jacob would never understand the reasons Noah was obsessed with him, but in the long run they really didn't matter. He had to dispose of Noah, that's all there was to it.

Jacob knew from reading hundreds of biographies that everyone has something they are hiding. Some secret that was kept locked away from the world. His only hope was that whatever secret Noah had it would be enough to use against him. It didn't take Jacob long to break into Noah's computer, even though Noah had a sophisticated firewall that would have defeated most hackers. What Jacob found after searching through Noah's files would be enough to get him not only thrown out of school, but probably follow him when and if he ever applied for a job. Jacob was impressed by Noah's computer skills; the fact that he could hack into every one of his teacher's computers and download upcoming tests without leaving any trace of intrusion attested to his ability as a hacker of exceptional ability.

It was here that Jacob faced his first test of ethical and moral consequence. He sat looking at his computer screen, suspended in time, trying to figure out what to do with the information he now possessed. In one sense, he had already made that decision when he decided to break into Noah's computer, but as of yet, he had done nothing with that information. All he wanted was for Noah to go away and leave him alone, there was no reason Jacob would have to make public the information he had if Noah did what he wanted. In his mind it was a simple equation: Jacob presented the evidence to Noah, Noah would not share what he knew about Jacob, and life would go on as before. However, Jacob did not realize, as he would later, that people cannot be put into such simple equations. Noah had a lifetime of experience, relationships, upbringing, motives and background that all fed into who he was and how he related to the new prodigy on the block. Jacob brought none of that baggage into his thinking, unless it was the idea of self-preservation.

There was one concept lurking in the back of his consciousness as he got ready to print out what would ultimately be Noah's downfall. A lifetime of living with Sister Flavia, and the ethics she had tried to instill in him, would not go quietly from the recesses of his mind. There were ways to justify what he was about to do, reasons that in his mind were unassailable. If Noah exposed who he was, then his life was over. Noah could blackmail him, though Jacob had nothing of value he could give to Noah in exchange for his silence. Would he even be able to trust Noah if he had anything to give him? Jacob doubted it, and he could not risk it in any case. The one thought that he did not act on, a thought that might have given him another perspective on the situation, was that he should call Sister Flavia and ask her what he should do.

The reality, he knew, was that she would somehow bring God into the situation. This thought alone should have told Jacob that he was about to do something wrong, but he convinced himself that he could figure this out on his own. It was not lost on his subconscious that he was in his first year at Harvard, taking a double class load and getting straight A's. He must be smart enough to solve what in his view was another puzzle, albeit one with moral and ethical overtones. Convinced that what he was about to do was the only logical way of his dilemma, he had printed out the documents using a printer in the library, away from the prying eyes of Noah's camera. And that was that.

With one week left in the semester, Jacob was offered an internship for the summer by one of his professors. He would analyze data that was going to form the basis for a book the professor was going to write. It was simple enough work for someone like Jacob, but it would allow him to stay at the university. When he told Sister Flavia of his plans, she was disappointed that he would not be coming back to the orphanage for the summer. She had hoped he might work with the older students, but the reality was the orphanage was no longer his home. He had agreed to spend a week with her after school was out, and then he would return to his internship. Jacob would not mention anything about Noah, and Sister Flavia would sense there was something bothering him, but it never came up in any of their conversations. The memory of what he had done would haunt him during the next year and a half, until another event more profound and life changing surfaced, something that would change the course of Jacob's life.

18

The next year and a half flew by; a blur of classes, tests, and endless hours studying. His eighteenth birthday came and went, and he spent the summer again working for one of his professors, this time doing more sophisticated research on computer methodology and biomechanics. It was thought that his research might form the basis for Jacob's doctorate, which everyone assumed he would pursue after getting his master's degree. He was scheduled to complete the work needed for his bachelor degrees at the end of his fifth semester, right before the holiday break. There was no reason to think that Jacob's life would not continue on in this same manner, until his academic career ended and he then decided what was the next step in the arcing trajectory that was his life.

Harvard had not been shy about promoting it's rising star, and though Jacob resented the intrusion into his busy schedule, there was part of him that found the attention gratifying. He had already been featured in several news stories in the local media: the orphan who made good at Harvard. The administration had talked with Jacob about what he would do after earning his doctorate; they wanted him to consider a position at the school, assuring him that he could pursue any course of research that interested him. Jacob did not say no, but in his heart he knew a career in academia would not satisfy the need he had to solve the puzzles that existed out in the real world of commerce, capital and business. As his stature at the university grew, so did his personal life. Although he still spent most of his time in class or studying, at the suggestion of his Guidance Counselor, he began to work with two other gifted students who had entered the university a year after him. It matured him, and brought out parts of his personality that had long been hidden.

Sister Flavia had to be content to watch from a distance as Jacob's visits became less frequent. He had promised to spend the holiday break with her, celebrating the completion of his undergraduate program. Her life at the community had continued in much the same manner as before, with one exception. She was in the process of turning the leadership of the community over to Sister Maria, just at Sister Margaret had turned it over to her. Not only was Sister Flavia getting older, but she did not have the energy and stamina to oversee the needs of the children, staff and Sisters. There was a reason for her decline, which she had confided to Sister Maria, and which she would have to tell Jacob when he came back for the holidays. It was a conversation she was dreading, because she had no idea how he was going to react.

It wasn't until the third day that she was able to talk with him privately. He spent much of his time installing a new computer system for the students, one that had multiple monitors, network capability and unlimited storage capacity in the Cloud. Jacob then spent a day teaching the children the basics in how to use the new computers. He also, at the insistence of Sister Maria, installed filters that would block any Internet searches of questionable material. Sister Flavia watched all of this with a growing nostalgia, an emotion that she rarely let herself experience. The Sisters were all about living in the present, with an eye toward the future. Thinking or dwelling on the past served little purpose for those who lives were consumed with devotion to God and service to others.

She suggested they have lunch together, and told Jacob she would like to drive out to the ocean, even though it meant they would have to eat in the van due to the cold. It was the first time in over a year that they had been alone together. She parked the van on an overlook that had a view of the town of Newburyport to the north and a nature preserve to the south. As she took their lunch out of a grocery bag, she said,

"I'm glad that we were able to find some time to spend together. I know how busy you have been. The children are so happy with the new computers. Thank you for taking the time to put all of that together for them."

Jacob shrugged his shoulders in reply, a vague sense of guilt coming over him. He knew he could have come back more frequently to the orphanage, but his class load and studies had become the focal point of his life.

There was no easy way to tell him, so she gave him a sandwich, looked out over the ocean.

"I've been sick for a while. I thought you should know."

Jacob hadn't noticed anything different in her since his return to the community days earlier. Her words immediately got his attention.

"What's wrong with you? You don't look sick."

"I don't look sick, but I am. I don't have the energy I used to, and it's becoming difficult for me to walk more than a few steps at a time without stopping to catch my breath."

Jacob had not noticed these symptoms since he had been back, he was too consumed with working on installing the new computer system.

"Have you seen the doctor? What does he say?"

The orphanage had a doctor that both the students, staff and Sisters used, one who did not charge for his services.

"Yes. I have congestive heart failure. It seems that my arteries are blocked. There's really nothing that can be done. I wanted you to know."

"Of course there are things that can be done. You need to see another doctor, a specialist. I can find you one. Someone at the university will know who the best cardiologist is in the state. I'll call when we get back."

It was one puzzle that Jacob would not be able to solve, much to his everlasting regret. Sister Flavia watched as his mind went into gear, thinking how he was going to save the person who meant the most to him. She sighed, and said,

"Jacob, there's nothing that can be done. Even if I was a good risk for some kind of surgery, which I'm not, there is too much damage to be repaired. I've already seen a specialist, so you don't need to make any calls."

"How can your heart be damaged? You've never done anything wrong. You shouldn't be in this position."

"None of us lives forever, Jacob. I have always wondered if our "anomaly", as you call it, might give us a longer life span. I guess the answer to that question is "no"".

She said those words with a smile, hoping to alleviate some of the tension in the air. Jacob would not meet her gaze, he was looking out at the ocean, trying to come to grips with what she was telling him. He was already thinking about when he could get on his computer and begin a search that would enable Sister Flavia's life to continue.

"I need to get back to school. I need to get to my computer."

Sister Flavia knew what he meant, and knew it was best to let him return to the university. She understood that it was his way of dealing with the situation, although she hoped he would eventually come around to the inevitability of her condition. There was one other thing she needed to say to him before they left to return to the community.

"I believe this is God's plan for me, Jacob. I know that may be hard for you to understand, but I don't want you to worry. I'm so proud of what you have become, I hope you know that."

Jacob was still looking out the windshield at the blue expanse of sea before them. He heard what she said, but was already formulating a plan of action. He would put off entering the master's program until he had found a remedy for her, no matter how long it took. Finally, he turned to her, and said,

"Let's go. I have work to do."

19

Jacob would never put any type of plan into action to save Sister Flavia. He returned to the university the next day and made an appointment to see her doctor. Jacob had known the doctor his entire life, and sat patiently in his office while the doctor explained to Jacob that there was nothing to be done for Sister Flavia. He had referred her to a specialist who determined that the only hope she had was a heart transplant, a procedure that with her age and condition she did not qualify for. When he had finished, Jacob asked if there were perhaps any experimental or alternative types of treatment. The doctor was patient with him, knowing the special relationship that existed between Jacob and Sister Flavia. Assuring Jacob that the only thing he could do was to make Sister Flavia comfortable by limiting her activity, and then putting her on bed rest when walking was too difficult, he then added,

"She's at peace with this, Jacob. You should know that."

Then Jacob said something the doctor found strange, and inexplicable.

"If money were not an issue, is there something that could be done?"

"What do you mean?"

"I mean if I had a million dollars, is there someone who could help her. For that amount of money?"

The words came out awkwardly, as if Jacob didn't want to say them. The doctor thought for a moment.

"I don't think so. There's too much damage, and besides, I don't think she wants any extraordinary measures taken. She made

99

that pretty clear to me. She knows that her time has come, and she's at peace with that."

It was the second time he had used the word "peace", and though Sister Flavia might be at peace with her condition, Jacob certainly wasn't. She was the only parent he had ever known, and though the thought did not break out into his consciousness, the thought of being an orphan again was lying there in the back of his mind.

It was the ultimate puzzle, and it seemed that he was powerless to do anything about it. He left the doctor's office and walked to the bus station where he waited to catch the next coach back to Boston. Jacob had not asked the doctor how much longer Sister Flavia was likely to live, but he got the impression her death was not imminent. As he sat in the small lobby waiting for his bus to arrive, Jacob had a rare moment of introspection. He had been out on his own for two years, yet Sister Flavia had always hovered in the background. When he had to turn the tables on Noah, the one thought that would not leave him was what Sister Flavia would think about what he was doing. She had saved him when he was just a baby, and though he was endowed with considerable gifts and an almost limitless capacity for knowledge, he knew he could not save her. He understood intellectually that everyone was going to die, but the reality that was forcing its way into his life was leaving him feeling frustrated and empty.

There was one other avenue open to him, but it was so far out of the realm of his personal experience that he did now know where or how to begin. When he arrived at the university later that afternoon, he walked across the commons to a building that he usually passed by at least once a day. The chapel was seldom used by the students for its intended purpose, God having long since been banished from the campus.

Jacob entered the large building, which had at one time been an actual church, and sat down in the last pew. It was symbolic of his complicated relationship with God that he would sit as far away from the front of the chapel as he could. He almost got up and left before doing what he came to do, but then thought better of it. The last thing he wanted to do was to get God mad at him.

He had learned how to pray growing up in the orphanage, but those were rote prayers that everyone had to memorize. Jacob had no experience of praying to God in a personal or spontaneous manner, and hardly knew where to begin. Getting more uncomfortable by the minute, he finally gave up and said in a low voice,

"I know everyone has to die. I get that. But she's not that old, and she has given her entire life to You. If You are what she says You are, then I know that you can fix her heart. That doesn't seem like too much to ask since you made her the way she is. It seems only fair that You could do this for her. I know that she doesn't care about what happens, but I do."

Jacob felt odd adding the last part, because he knew that he had kept God at a distance most of his life. If God was going to do this, he knew it wouldn't be because of his faith, but in spite of it. His only hope was that God would somehow take pity on Sister Flavia and reward her for her life of faith and service. When he had finished, he left the chapel and went back to his room and lay on his bed for hours, looking up at the ceiling, wondering what it be like if he could fall asleep and have a brief time of forgetfulness.

20

Jacob was wrong when he had thought that Sister Flavia's death was not imminent. She died two days into the new year, being found lying in her bed by Sister Maria when she brought breakfast that morning. Jacob came out to the community the next day, and spent some time alone in the chapel with Sister Flavia. As becoming her station in life as a Nun, her casket was made of pine and unadorned, not even having handles. There would be a service the next day, and then she would be laid to rest alongside Sister Margaret in the local cemetery.

He was unprepared for her death, even though he had known it was a possibility. He was, in fact, on the morning of her death, still researching various treatments and therapies that might at least extend her life. Jacob had made several calls to the university's medical school, hoping to find someone who could steer him in a promising direction. Sitting in the chapel, surrounded by all the trappings of Catholicism in which he found no comfort, Jacob thought back over his life. Sister Flavia had been the one constant, the unseen presence that was with him as he lay on his bed all those years in the orphanage reading and learning for hours on end. She followed him in spirit to Harvard, and though he was more or less on his own, there wasn't a day that went by when he didn't think of her.

It wasn't the fact that she was the mother he never knew, that she guided and protected him all those years in the orphanage, it was the reality that she was the only other person he would ever meet who was like him. There were two others who knew what he was, his father and Noah, but only Sister Flavia knew the secret and shared the burden of being different from everyone else. Though they seldom spoke about their "anomaly", it bound them together in ways they did not completely understand but certainly felt when they were together.

Jacob was due to start his Master's program in three days, but Sister Flavia's death had caused him to rethink what he was doing with his life. He already had two undergraduate degrees, was being hailed as a prodigy and a rising star of the university, and yet it had not brought him any sense of purpose or peace. He wasn't aware of what was happening to him, but he was in the midst of trying to solve the biggest puzzle of his life. Sister Flavia had many times talked to him about his purpose in life, and that someday he would find out what it was. She was gone now, and he now knew that purpose would not be found in academic achievement. He had done that, and his mind and heart were at loose ends. What were more degrees and accolades going to bring him? He would become famous, but famous for what? Though he did not recognize it, Sister Flavia's values and beliefs were tightening their grip around his heart. She lay in a pine box, but the ripples of her life were spreading out before him. A lifetime of putting others first, of investing in children who had been abandoned, of serving everyone but herself, was staring Jacob right in the face, and it slowly dawned on him that if he could not save her, he could become her. Because of the "anomaly", he had an almost limitless capacity to affect the lives of others. He had saved the community when it was running out of money, he knew there were others he could save, all he needed was money. The acquisition of money, of course, was no problem for Jacob. He had not thought about the program for several years, but he was sure it would still work. Taking one last look at the casket, Jacob got up and started to walk out of the chapel. Jacob stopped in his tracks when he saw him standing just inside the doors of the chapel. He walked slowly up the aisle toward Jacob, and said, "Hello, son."

21

They had never met in person, only by email and the one time on Skype. He looked older than Jacob remembered, and was obviously nervous. He motioned to one of the pews, and said,

"Can we talk for a minute?"

Jacob sat down, unsure how to act, and looked toward the front of the chapel at the silent pine casket. He had no idea what to say, so they both just sat there in silence. Jacob didn't mind the silence, he had spent countless hours in silence; reading, studying or working on his computer. It was his father who spoke first.

"I'm sorry about Sister Flavia. I know how close you two must have been."

It was polite conversation, a way to begin a dialogue that was almost twenty years overdue. It wasn't why he came to see Jacob, but he had to start somewhere. Jacob was slowly getting over the shock of seeing his father, and was ready to talk.

"Why did you come? You didn't even know her. How did you even find out she had died?"

"I didn't know that she had died. That part is just a coincidence. I came to see you."

Jacob could not think of any reason why his father would come to see him; they had no relationship to speak of, and except for his help years ago in providing for the orphanage, his father had never taken any initiative to see Jacob. His father had a new wife and children, he had obviously moved on after Jacob's mother had died. The only contact they had ever had had been instigated by Jacob years ago when he needed his father's help. If not for that, Jacob doubted they would have ever met.

The reason his father had come to see him suddenly became clear to him, and he wondered why he didn't see it right off. Jacob had grown in the two years he attended Harvard. He saw life as pieces he needed to fit together, whether it was his class load, homework assignments, dealing with his professors, and especially when he had to figure out how to get Noah out of his life. Given enough time and information, Jacob could usually find an answer to any dilemma, circumstance or problem that faced him. In this case, it took him about three minutes to figure out why his father had come 3,000 miles to see him.

It had not occurred to him when he had originally asked his father for help that he might try to personally benefit from the information Jacob was giving him. He was much younger then, and was concentrating much of his time and energy in coming up with the algorithm that provided the mechanism to make money for the orphanage. It was not lost on Jacob that he had just come to the conclusion that his purpose in life might be to use his program for the benefit of others, and now his father was probably sitting next to him for the exact opposite reason. He needed to find out if he was right, so he broke the silence.

"You're here about money, aren't you?"

It was apparent from his father's body language that Jacob's guess was correct. His father looked around the chapel to make sure there was no one else who could overhear their conversation. He would not make eye contact with Jacob, and spoke in a hushed voice that Jacob could barely hear.

"Yes, this is about money. One of my partners is retiring, and I want to buy his share of the business. I don't have enough money of my own. I was hoping that you could get your program up and running and loan me what I need to buy him out."

"How much money do you need?"

"About two million dollars. I know it would take you time to make that much. I won't need it for six months."

"You knew what I used the money for the first time. What makes you think I care about helping you make money? It's not who I am."

"I understand that. But I am your father, the only family you have. I thought that might make a difference. And, I helped you when you needed help. I thought that might count for something."

"What did you do with the money you made the first time?"

"What are you talking about?"

"I'm sure that when you saw the program worked, you bought the same stocks. You would have been a fool not too. What happened to the money?"

104

His father wasn't prepared for how smart and intuitive Jacob had become. He had never told Jacob he was going to personally enrich himself using Jacob's stock tips, though it should have been obvious.

"I invested it in two shopping malls. The money isn't liquid, and the bank won't loan me the amount of money I need."

He neglected to tell Jacob that the investment in the malls was turning out to be a bad one, and that there was a possibility he might lose everything he had put into the venture.

"I didn't write the program so you could become rich. I can't help you."

"I'm the only family you have, Jacob. You won't help me?"

Jacob pointed to the casket at the front of the chapel.

"She was my family. I'm sorry."

With that, Jacob rose quickly and was out the door before his father could say anything in response. He would miss the service the next day for Sister Flavia, and the Sisters and children would wonder why he did not attend. After collecting his computer and some clothes, Jacob took the keys to the van and drove it to the bus station, asking the clerk to call the orphanage and tell them it was there. Jacob spent a few days in Boston, where he got a copy of his birth certificate. He thought about where he might go, and finally made up his mind to go south. Meeting with his father had been the spark needed to push Jacob out on his own, and once he made up his mind to do something, there was no stopping him.

Part Three

1

He spent the first two years in Miami. The first thing he did when he arrived was apply for a Social Security card. He had never needed one until now as all his expenses at Harvard were paid by the university. His internships gave him credits to use at the school instead of paying him in cash. He had a small amount of money that Sister Flavia had given him during the holidays, money she must have thought he might need at some point in the near future. He figured it would last just long enough to carry out the plan he had worked out on the bus ride down from Boston.

With his birth certificate and Social Security card, he could now get a Florida identification card from the Department of Motor Vehicles. With his Social Security card in hand, Jacob had no problem getting a job at Best Buy after demonstrating to the store manager that he could easily hack into the store's computer system. For good measure, he also worked at the local Staples after similarly impressing that store's manager when he could easily answer every question he was asked about both the OS and Windows operating system. Even though he was working two full-time jobs, Jacob had time to get to know the city where he would spend two years.

He rented a small apartment in Little Havana, and immediately began to learn Spanish. When he left Miami he would be fluent, something that would benefit him in the future. Jacob kept mostly to himself, working long hours in his apartment to get his program back up to speed. When he had saved five thousand dollars, he opened accounts at five different trading companies, figuring that by spreading out his investments he might not draw any unwanted attention.

For the first time in his life Jacob did not feel the pressure to study, read or work on his computer. Though most of his time was spent working at one of his two jobs, he had plenty of time to explore the city of Miami, and learn how to live on his own. He was still socially awkward, the result of having to hide what he was from everyone around him. Because he had to deal with customers at his work, he was learning to interact with people, and was slowly coming out of his shell. It helped that he lived completely alone, with no one caring if his light was on all night or if he left his apartment each morning at five to walk along the beach, which was less than a mile from his apartment.

It was during one of those walks, early in the morning, that he found the church. Its doors were open, and as he looked inside he saw that there were a few older people kneeling in the pews, beginning their day with an act of worship. It was a small church, not much bigger than the chapel at the orphanage. Jacob had not been in a church for months, and though he had made the commitment to give his time and energy in the service of others, that promise had not worked its way completely from his head to his heart. Against his better judgment, he walked through the open doors and sat down in the last pew, not quite sure what he was going to do.

That was settled for him when the priest walked into the front of the church from a side entrance, and raising his hands in blessing, said a prayer for the few parishioners gathered there. The people knew what to do next, and slowly made their way to the front to take the Mass from the priest, who gave them both the bread and the wine from the small table he was standing behind. When each person was done, they walked down the aisle and out into the street. It only took a few minutes, and then Jacob found himself alone in the church. He was just about to get up when the priest came out from behind the table and slowly made his way toward Jacob. When he reached the last row where Jacob was sitting, he extended his hand.

"I don't believe I've seen you here before. My name is Father Alejandro."

Jacob shook the priest's hand.

"Jacob."

The priest spoke with a heavy Spanish accent, and wasn't that much older than Jacob.

"What brings you to our little church this morning?"

"I was walking by and saw the door was open. I was raised in a Catholic orphanage in the Northeast. I haven't been to church since I came to Miami. Seemed like the thing to do."

It was the most personal information he had given almost anyone since his arrival in the city, and he wondered why he had been so forthcoming.

"How long have you been in Miami? You're on your own?"

"Almost a year. I went to college for two years, and then needed to take a break."

He left out all the details about Sister Flavia's death, his father, and the two degrees he earned at Harvard.

"You must be an early riser, are you on your way to work?"

"No. I was walking down to the beach. I don't work until later this morning."

Jacob rose from the pew, and slowly extended his hand to the priest.

"Thanks for talking with me. I need to get going."

"Of course."

Jacob was out the door, turning down the street toward the beach, and after a few steps looked back over his shoulder at the church. It brought back memories he would never be able to forget, not that he wanted to forget them. It took him another 20 minutes to make reach the beach, and when he found a bench that looked out over the ocean, he stopped and rested before he made his way back to his apartment. Jacob was a creature of habit, structure helped him deal with the hours he needed to fill each day. For the rest of his time in Miami, he would attend the 5 a.m. Mass at the church, gradually forming a friendship with Father Alejandro. Jacob kept the relationship on a rather superficial level, which the priest respected. Father Alejandro suspected there was something different about Jacob, but he would never find out. One day Jacob stopped coming, and would never again be seen at the church. Father Alejandro called the Best Buy where Jacob worked, and found out that he had quit unexpectedly, and left no forwarding address. The priest would hear from Jacob again, but not in person. When a cashier's check arrived two months later for $100,000, Father Alejandro would never know it was from the young man he had known for only a year, a young man he suspected had more to him than met the eye.

Jacob left Miami mainly because he was tired of living in the heat and humidity, and for the practical reason that it really didn't matter where he lived. He was fully committed to managing his growing wealth, and did not need to work in the conventional sense.

He had grown the initial $5,000 into more than $650,000, and figured it was time to start giving the money away. San Diego was large enough for him to be both anonymous, and to look for those in need of the kind of help he could offer. If his program continued to generate the same percentage of profits, he was looking at giving away millions of dollars each year, an act that he hoped would have pleased Sister Flavia.

2

He settled in the Pacific Beach area on the north side of Mission Bay, just south of La Jolla. At first, he was put off by the high rents, and considered moving south of the city toward the Mexican border. But he wanted to be near the ocean, and anyplace near the beach was going to be expensive. His one-bedroom apartment was two blocks back from the boardwalk, and because he was on the third floor, it offered a view of the ocean to the west. When the rental application asked for his occupation, Jacob simply put "entrepreneur." His landlord, skeptical that a young man like Jacob could afford even the one bedroom he was applying for, asked for some type of income statement. When Jacob showed him one of his trading accounts, there was no further discussion.

It took him about a month to get established in the city: he bought furniture, a small used car, and began the process of transferring his bank accounts in Miami to a non-profit foundation he set up in San Diego. All the profits from his trading accounts went into the non-profit, which paid Jacob a modest salary to cover his basic needs.

As in Miami, the first personal contact he made was with a priest at a Catholic church that was close to his apartment. The church had a broad cross section of people, unlike Miami, and Jacob walked in the door one Sunday and sat in the back pew. He never participated in taking the Mass, saying the prayers, or going to confession. Jacob knew the reason he went to the church, it was to keep the memory of Sister Flavia alive in his heart. It just wasn't in him to take the next step and become an active participant in the religion he had been raised in. That would come later.

The priest respected Jacob's privacy for a number of weeks, and then finally introduced himself when Jacob lingered in the back pew after the service had ended. The priest, whose name was Father Stephen, was older than Father Alejandro, and had been at the church for almost a decade. He officiated at the Mass each day at 7.30 a.m., which was attended by about twenty people. The parish, St. John's, was much bigger than the small church in Miami, and had a large group of singles ages 20-30. He sat down next to Jacob, and opened the conversation by saying,

"My name is Father Stephen. I've been meaning to introduce myself."

He extended his hand, which Jacob shook.

"Jacob."

"Well Jacob, I've noticed you at Mass each morning. Are you new to the area?"

"I moved here from Miami a few months ago. I used to attend a church there."

"Did you grow up in a Catholic family?"

"You might say that. I lived in an orphanage run by Sisters until I went to college."

Jacob immediately regretted saying that he went to college. It could easily lead Father Steve to ask him where he went to college, which meant Jacob would have to tell him about Harvard. It would open to the door to too many personal questions, which he desperately wanted to avoid. But the priest merely replied,

"What do you do for a living, if I might ask?"

"I'm a computer consultant. It's not very interesting."

The time Jacob spent in Miami were filled with two jobs, buying and selling stocks, and getting used to living on his own. He didn't really have any friends, so he hadn't really learned how to answer questions about who he was and what he did. Jacob had kept Father Alejandro at arm's length, but now living in San Diego he unconsciously wanted to find a way to live a more normal life. If that was possible.

"We have a large single's group here at the church. They usually meet every Friday night here at the church, and then have some type of event. You're welcome to come if you don't have any other plans."

Jacob knew all about the single's group, having read everything on the church's website. He was hesitant to join any type of group, yet he could not see himself living the rest of his life alone. There were risks in becoming known, but he figured he could manage those risks. After all, he thought, he had years of experience hiding who he was, certainly he could hide his anomaly from those who might become his friends. He had not forgotten about Noah, but that was a completely different environment, one that lent itself more easily to discovery. In San Diego, he was just another young person with a job, no different than anyone else.

"Thanks. I'd like that. I'll be there Friday."

3

When Jacob had slightly more than a million dollars in his bank account, he knew he had to start giving the money away. After researching the best way to distribute his funds, receive a tax deduction, and remain anonymous, Jacob set up a Donor Advised Fund and a non-profit foundation to manage it. The fund would supply Jacob with a tax receipt, and the beneficial charity would not know Jacob's identity. The foundation would make out the checks, but would need to give the proceeds to non-profit 501-C organizations to make the donations tax deductible. Because Jacob wanted his money to go to a certain type of recipient, he would need an organization that would be responsive to his wishes. It was then that he made the call to Father Stephen.

They met at a café on the boardwalk, just a few blocks from St. John's church. Jacob ate breakfast there every morning; he enjoyed looking out at the ocean after spending the night either reading or working on his computer. His program was up and running, and though he tinkered with it every so often, it continued to pick stocks that consistently outperformed the market averages. His curiosity took him in different directions during the late evening hours, and though it would not be fair to say that Jacob was bored, he was unconsciously looking for new challenges.

Father Stephen ordered coffee, and Jacob had his usual breakfast of eggs, toast and tea. The priest remarked that he needed the caffeine to get himself going in the morning, a comment that forced a smile for Jacob, who had never in his life needed any stimulant to begin a new day. In fact, it would be fair to say Jacob's life was one long day, punctuated only by periods of light and darkness.

Jacob had spent some of the previous evening thinking about how he would begin the conversation. There would be a certain awkwardness in what he wanted to ask, and he hoped the priest would be open to what he was going to propose.

"I wasn't exactly honest when I told you that I'm a computer consultant. I work with computers, but I'm actually more involved in the financial world."

It didn't really matter to Father Stephen what Jacob did, and wondered why he brought it up.

"Is this a distinction with a difference?"

"Yes and no. What I really do is buy and sell stocks. I've been pretty successful, and I'm looking to give away some of the money I make."

With that sentence, Jacob had Father Stephen's attention. Though his church was relatively affluent, every minister had to face the reality that churches depend on money that was freely given by its parishioners. He smiled, and then said,

"I believe we could help with that, if that's what you want."

"It is, but being raised in an orphanage by the Sisters, I have values that I would like to see reflected in how the money is used."

"What exactly are we talking about?"

"I know that the church believes in helping the poor and needy. So do I. But I especially feel for those whose lives have been turned upside down by tragedy, suffering or being a victim. I'm thinking of people whose lives could be restored in some measure by a gift of money."

Father Stephen considered what Jacob had said, and looked more intently at the young man sitting across from him. Jacob was only 22 years old, and though he spoke with the assurance and confidence of someone much older, he was still just a kid to the priest. He decided to get right to the point.

"How much money are we talking about?"

Jacob paused for a moment, knowing the priest would be startled by what Jacob was going to tell him.

"Potentially, millions of dollars each year. I understand that I can't determine who gets the money, and I'm not opposed to a percentage going to the church's general budget, but I would like the bulk of it to go to people that are in desperate need."

Jacob waited to see how the priest would react to the words "millions of dollars". Father Stephen was silent for a moment, and then slowly said,

"Let me see if I have understood you correctly. You want to give millions of dollars away, and use the church as the instrument to do this? Is that about right?"

"Yes. I would give it away myself, but the tax implications are enormous. I think the money would be better served by those in need, and not paid in tax to the government. And this is important. I need to do this anonymously. I've set up both a foundation and a Donor Advised fund to make this possible. The checks would come from the foundation to the church. It's all legal, and it keeps my name out of the picture."

There was a pause in the conversation as they both considered the implications of what Jacob proposed. For Jacob, it meant that he would be able to fulfill what he had come to believe was his purpose, the compassionate use of wealth, a purpose he was sure Sister Flavia would approve of. It would also be what he hoped was the beginning of an association with a group of people, St. John's church, that would set him on the road to what might be a normal life. He had lived in the shadows long enough, it was time to come out into the light.

For Father Stephen, the thought of millions of dollars pouring into his church was certainly a boon, and though he had no problem with giving the money to the needy, he could not shake this thought: how was a young man in his twenties able to become so proficient in the stock market that he could make millions of dollars? Before he could ask what was on his mind, Jacob broke the silence.

"I know you're wondering how a kid can make so much money in the market. I can't tell you how I do it, but I can tell you that my mind works differently from most people's. I see things as puzzles, and I solve them. The market is a giant puzzle, and I figured out how to read it, and how to pick stocks based on putting pieces of information together that others don't quite see. I don't want to advertise my success because I don't want the attention that success brings. The Sisters did a good job of teaching me the value of not only compassion, but keeping a low profile, so to speak. Can you understand that?"

Father Stephen did understand, but had never met anyone so young who embodied the type of values the church stood for, and actually practiced it in such a tangible way. Jacob wasn't done quite yet, and did not wait for the priest to reply.

"I've given this a lot of thought. I know it's going to be a big job giving away that kind of money. Why don't you set up a committee of people you know and trust to oversee the work? They could find people who are in need, how much money they might need, and pass the recommendation on to you."

"I assume you would like to be on that committee?"

"I was raised in a Catholic orphanage. I'm pretty familiar with the philosophy of the church on helping the poor."

"When would you want to begin?"

Jacob reached into his jacket pocket, and took out a plain white envelope. He handed it to Father Stephen, who slowly opened it. The check, from the Sister Flavia foundation, was made out to St. John's church, the sum being one million dollars.

4

Jacob was out the door of his apartment as usual at 5 a.m. He would walk down to the beach and then walk north toward La Jolla each morning to get some exercise. Most nights were spent reading or watching TV shows, something that was new for Jacob. There was no opportunity to watch TV at the orphanage, at Harvard he was busy studying, and in Miami he worked two jobs and was getting his trading activity up to speed. In San Diego, Jacob had much more free time, and was getting used to doing things that were normal for most people. When he had walked for two hours, he stopped at the same café every morning to have breakfast. After breakfast, he would attend Mass at the church. Jacob had always been a creature of habit, and now in San Diego he was in the process of ordering his life around different structures and events that would fill the 24 hours in each day.

The next event was the Friday night meeting of the St. John's church singles group. Jacob was looking forward to the affair, which indicated how much he had grown in his personal life. He was having interactions with people on a daily basis, though he had yet to make any real friends. The waitresses at the small café all knew Jacob, and would talk with him each day as he ate his breakfast. Most of them were somewhat older, though there was one girl who was about Jacob's age. When it became obvious that Jacob was going to show up every day around 7 a.m., they made sure she was the one to serve him. Jacob knew what was happening, and enjoyed the attention. He was a good looking young man, almost six feet tall, though there was still an air of reserve about him. Almost any other guy would have asked the waitress out, but Jacob was just not there yet. When it became obvious nothing was going to happen, she gradually lost interest and let the other waitresses serve him.

He showed up to the singles group that Friday night a little late so he could be as unobtrusive as possible. The meeting was held in the large fellowship hall, and there were about fifty young people spread out around the room. Jacob had hoped Father Stephen would be there, but in looking around he did not see the priest. After standing in the doorway for a few moments, he was approached by a girl whose nametag said "Amber". She shook his hand, and said,

"You must be Jacob. Father Stephen told me to look out for you. Let's get you a nametag."

Before he could answer, she took his arm and brought him fully into the room. They stopped at a table, and she wrote his name on a white nametag, which she then put on his shirt. It had happened so fast that he had not yet spoken, and finally said,

"I didn't get your name."

Her name was right there on her nametag, but Jacob felt self-conscious having not said anything to her.

"I'm Amber. I'm in charge tonight. Let's get you something to drink, and then I'll introduce you to some people."

She took him to a table that had soft drinks and a large bowl of punch.

"Watch out for the punch. I'm sure somebody has spiked it by now."

"Thanks. I'll just have a soda."

"Sure. Come with me, my friends are over here."

Amber again took him by the arm, and guided him over to a group sitting around a table. They stopped talking when Amber brought Jacob to the table.

"This is Jacob. It's his first time here. I think he's new to the area, so make him feel at home."

Amber pulled a chair out for Jacob, indicating that he was to sit. Everything had happened so fast that Jacob felt out of his element, and as he sat waited for someone to speak.

There were seven of them at the table, three girls and four young men. It looked to Jacob like he was the youngest by several years. It took only a moment for one of the girls to ask him what brought him to San Diego. Jacob thought for a moment.

"With my work I can pretty much live wherever I want. After living in Miami for two years, I decided to move here. I liked living by the ocean, I just didn't like the heat and the humidity."

His first answer prompted a second question, which was about his work. Jacob explained that he worked for a small non-profit, and did computer consulting on the side. He disliked being the center of attention, and hoped that his short answers to their questions would quickly divert the conversation away from him. It was not to be. He was asked by one of the other girls at the table where he grew up, an innocent question that she asked just to be polite. His answer would cause the conversation to go in a completely different direction.

"I grew up in a Catholic orphanage in the Northeast. It was a small community that also had a school. I stayed there until I went to college."

No one at the table had ever met anyone who had grown up in an orphanage, and several didn't even know they still existed. It put Jacob in a completely different world from everyone else, and for just a moment no one was sure how to respond. Jacob broke the silence when he said,

"I know it sounds sad, but it was probably the best thing that ever happened to me. I owe everything to them."

The door was open, and one of the guys at the table asked Jacob what happened to his parents. It was personal, to be sure, but he figured Jacob had had years to deal with the fact that he was an orphan.

Jacob, of course, knew what happened to his parents, and told the truth, but not the whole truth.

"I was left at the orphanage, outside the front door. The Sisters took me in, that's about it."

Jacob did not see it, but the girls at the table immediately felt for the lost soul among them. They were all from caring, large families, and the thought that Jacob grew up without one generated sympathy among them, something the other guys immediately sensed. One of them quickly sought to change the subject.

"Where did you go to college?"

"I went to Harvard for two years. Then I moved to Miami. I wanted to get out on my own. I worked a couple of jobs there, and then I started with the non-profit, and doing some consulting."

"It's too bad that you didn't get to finish at Harvard. A degree from there would go a long way."

Jacob didn't have an ounce of pride in him, so what he said next would be misunderstood by some at the table, who wrongly interpreted his words.

"Actually, I did finish. I got two degrees, one in computer science and one in business."

Those at the table looked at each other, not sure what had just happened. How was it possible to get two degrees in two years, especially at one of the most prestigious universities in the country? Several of them were trying to figure out how old Jacob was, it just didn't seem that he had lived long enough to get two degrees and live in Miami for two years. Let alone the time he had lived in San Diego. No one knew quite what to say, and then someone said,

"You got two degrees in two years? At Harvard?"

Jacob realized what he had done, and was thinking how to get the conversation going in another direction.

"It's not that big a deal. All I did when I was there was study. It helped growing up with the Sisters. They taught me discipline, and the importance of an education."

It was a big deal to one of the girls at the table, who had graduated from Boston University, and who knew how hard it was to not only get in to Harvard, but to do what Jacob had claimed he had done. She was a reporter for the San Diego newspaper, and made a mental note to see if Jacob's claims were true.

What Jacob had done was to set himself apart from everyone else at the table, and everyone sensed the awkwardness. They had come to the church looking to have an enjoyable evening after a week of work, many of them would use the evening to set up dates for the weekend. Jacob noticed one girl looking at him with unusual intensity, and blushed at the extra attention. He spent the rest of the evening wishing he had been more discreet, and though the conversation at the table eventually found its way back to sports, work, current events and what everyone was doing that weekend, they would not forget what they had learned about Jacob.

Jacob excused himself from the table after about half an hour, and went out into the courtyard of the church, just off the fellowship hall. There were a few other people there, talking in groups, no one interested in him as he looked out toward the ocean. He was thinking he needed to check on his trading accounts when there was a tap on his shoulder. It was the reporter, who had followed Jacob out into the courtyard.

"I'm Megan. There's a café just down the block. Want to get a cup of coffee?"

5

Jacob had literally no experience with girls. His life at the orphanage had included living among girls, but because he was so consumed with his studies, and hiding what he was, his interaction with them was limited. Plus, the Sisters subtly discouraged any sort of personal relationships developing among the students. When he went to Harvard it was much the same; his studies and workload consumed him. It was in Miami that he had his first real interactions with girls. Both at Staples and Best Buy he worked with girls, though he held most of them at arm's length. He was figuring out how to live on his own, setting up his trading accounts and reactivating his computer program, and had little time or inclination to develop any type of relationship with the opposite sex.

Which is not to say he didn't think about it. He was, after all, a young man with hormones. Jacob knew there would come a time when he would want to date, and perhaps even get married and have a family. However, in the back of his mind there was always the thought that it might not be possible for him to have that kind of life. He always assumed that he would have to hide who he was from everyone; that no one would be able to deal with the anomaly that defined him.

Megan, like Jacob, had recently moved to San Diego. Or, in her case, back to San Diego. After graduating from Boston University with a degree in journalism, she had moved back to San Diego to be close to her family. She got a job with the San Diego Union newspaper as a features writer, which meant she was usually free to write on topics that interested her. She also wrote an increasingly popular blog on different aspects of San Diego; from restaurant and movie reviews to profiles of interesting people in the city.

She chose a table that had a view of the Pacific Beach Pier, and after they ordered, Megan asked Jacob about his time at the orphanage. She was from a large Catholic family, and the church had always been a central part of her life. Megan had attended Catholic schools her entire life, and saw Jacob as someone who probably shared the values she had grown up with. She was a naturally curious person, and Jacob was one of the most intriguing people she had ever met.

"There were about 25 kids who lived there. It was pretty structured, but I don't think anybody cared because that's all we knew. The Sisters gave us a good education, and made sure we spent a lot of time outside the community. Everyone always talked about what they would do when they left, but I think most of us knew the Sisters only wanted the best for us."

Megan took a sip of her coffee, and thought about what Jacob had said.

"Many kids when they get done with Catholic school seem to go in the opposite direction as fast as they can. Most of the people at the church tonight were raised in Catholic homes, but few of them actually attend the church. Father Stephen told me that you attend church every morning. You don't seem to have drifted away."

"Not really. I've been studying most of my life, so I haven't had much time to get in trouble. In Miami, I worked two jobs to save money so I could start my own business."

He paused for a moment as he thought about Sister Flavia, whose influence would never really leave him.

"One of the Sisters was kind of like my mother. She was the one who found me, and I lived with her until I was four. Then I went down to live with the other kids. I wouldn't want to do anything that would displease her. I don't know if that's what you're talking about or not, it's just how I live."

"Do you talk to her very often? I imagine it must be hard living so far away."

Jacob was silent for a moment as he thought about the last time he had seen Sister Flavia. He would never be done grieving for her, but the immediacy of his grief had faded with time.

"She died a few years ago. I think that's one the reasons I moved to Miami and didn't stay at Harvard. The orphanage was only about an hour from Boston. I think I just needed a change of scenery."

He left out the part about his father, and the impact that had on him moving out of the Northeast and begin a new life somewhere else.

Jacob took a sip of his tea, and thought that in his first real conversation alone with a girl he was having to cover up large portions of his life. Megan sensed the sadness in Jacob after talking about Sister Flavia, and changed the subject when she asked him about his time at Harvard.

"How did you get two degrees at Harvard in two years? I'm curious because I went to BU, and I knew a lot of people who went to Harvard. You must be a genius."

"No, I'm not. The Sisters taught me the value of education and how to study. I'm pretty focused when I need to be. Plus, my brain kind of works differently from most people's. I see things as puzzles, which makes studying easier because things like homework and studying fall into patterns that I can then solve. I know it sounds silly, but that's how it works. I haven't asked what you do. I'm sorry that I've been talking about myself."

"I work for the local newspaper. I write stories about people and events in the city. I also have a blog. It's a labor of love for the moment, but I'm hoping it can work into a paying proposition soon. I'm living with my parents so I can save money. I'd like to get my own place, but as you must know it's expensive living here."

"I get that."

Money didn't matter to Jacob, he paid himself enough of a salary to cover his basic needs. He looked across the table at Megan, who was enjoying her coffee, and looking out at the illuminated pier down the beach. She had asked him to the café, taking them both away from the group at the church. Was it just a friendly gesture to a new person in the group, or something else? Jacob decided to find out. Doing something totally out of character, at least at that point in his life, he said,

"It's still early. Do you want to walk out to the end of the pier? Just to get some exercise?"

It sounded lame, but she got the point.

"Sure. I could use some exercise."

They both laughed at the transparency of Jacob's request, but in the end it accomplished the desired result. They walked to the end of the pier, and then back to the church, where the meeting was winding down. Megan was about the same age as Jacob, but with vastly more experience in interacting with people. She noticed there was both a genuineness and a reserve to him, something missing in most of the boys she had known. Megan had had one serious relationship in her life, and it had ended badly. She was cautious, and wondered if Jacob was an anomaly, a young man who was also serious about his faith. He was an anomaly, but it would be a few years before she found out about his anomaly. And it would completely change her life, but not in the way you might think.

6

It took Father Stephen a week to put together the committee that would give away the money that would flow into the church from Jacob's foundation. He chose seven people who represented a cross section of his congregation, and included both Jacob and Megan. Megan's family had attended the church for decades; her father sat on the church board. They met for the first time in the church's conference room, and after a time of small talk, the priest got right to the point.

"I want to thank you all for coming. I think that most of us know each other, except perhaps for Jacob. Jacob is new to our church, and I think with his background will be able to help us with the task at hand."

They had not been told exactly what the purpose of the committee was, only that it involved helping those in need. The group listened as Father Stephen continued.

"Our church has become the recipient of a large sum of money that the donor would like to use to help people who are in great need, or who have suffered some sort of tragedy. Your job will be to find people whose lives would be changed by a substantial gift of money."

There were some quick glances around the table, and then someone said,

"Who wouldn't benefit from a substantial gift of money?"

It was meant to be funny, and some in the room laughed. Megan noticed that Jacob, who was sitting across from her, was silent. Father Stephen responded, and said,

"Thanks Phil, but I think we all know what we're talking about."

"Doesn't the church already help the poor through Catholic Charities? Why don't we just increase the amount of money we already give?"

Father Stephen had anticipated that question.

"I think the intention of the gift is to help specific people, rather than sending it to relief organizations run by the church. Let me give you an example. On the news last night there was the story of an apartment fire. One family lost a child in the fire. It seems that the fire not only took one of their children, but left them destitute as well. This family needs help. There's no doubt that they will find relief through some organizations, like the Red Cross, but that's not the same as helping them with a fresh start in life."

The group thought about what the priest had said, and then one of the men in the room, a retired teacher, asked,

"So, you would want us to find people like this and figure how we might help them get back on their feet. Something like that?"

"Yes, people like this. Victims of auto accidents, abuse, crime, any kind of tragedy. We know that money can't solve every problem, but it can help ease people through the rough times."

"But aren't we talking about a lot of money here? I mean, it might take thousands of dollars to help some people, depending on the circumstances. How much money are we talking about?"

Most people in the room were thinking in terms of thousands of dollars, and perhaps helping one or two people a month. Father Stephen knew that they would be astounded when he told them how much they would have to work with. He looked around the room, and said,

"Right now, you have a million dollars to distribute. I'm assured that there will be more. You have a big job in front of you. We want to make sure the recipients will use the money wisely, for the need at hand, so you'll have to consider that as well. I know we can't be absolutely sure how people will spend the money, but let's try as best we can to make sure it will help them."

Jacob, who had thought about almost nothing else for the last several months, overcame his reluctance to speak.

"There may be times when we can actually pay for services, instead of giving people cash. I know there are many people who need help getting off drugs who either have no insurance or cannot afford rehab. We could pay for the treatment, rather than give cash. I saw a story in the newspaper this week about a family whose son has a rare form of cancer. They have insurance, but it won't pay for the treatment he needs because it's still experimental. We could directly pay for the treatment, if that's what we wanted to do."

Megan was the only one in the room who knew Jacob, though one of the ladies recognized him from attending Mass each day. Father Stephen thanked Jacob, and felt he needed to introduce him to the members of the group.

"Like I mentioned earlier, Jacob is new to the church. He was raised in a Catholic orphanage in the Northeast, so he has some experience with Catholic charity. I thought he would be a good addition."

Megan then joined the conversation.

"When do you want us to start?"

The committee would begin its work the next week, gathering information on people who were in the type of circumstances that Father Stephen had outlined.

Father Stephen would attend another meeting that week that would center on the money being given to St. John's. He knew the amount of money that was going to come to the church was going to get the attention of his superiors, so he had asked them for a meeting. He did not disclose what he wanted to talk about, so as they gathered at the Diocese headquarters they were not prepared when Father Stephen told them about the anonymous donor who wanted to use the church to give large sums of money to those in need. When he was done speaking, there was silence around the large table. There were four men in the room, besides Father Stephen: the archbishop, two priests on his staff, and the diocese's attorney. The Bishop was able to attend, but not knowing what the meeting was about, sent the Archbishop instead. The first question was from one of the priests, who asked the same question that came out of the committee at St. John's.

"How much money are we talking about?"

Father Stephen knew these men dealt with large amounts of money every day, the budget of the diocese was in the millions of dollars. The Diocese had to declare bankruptcy to pay off plaintiffs of alleged clergy abuse, and was always looking for money to meet its expenses. Father Stephen knew the amount of money Jacob wanted to give away would get their attention, which it did.

"I think we're potentially talking about millions of dollars. I already have a check for the first million."

The archbishop was the first to respond.

"And you say this money is to go to people in need? Not to Catholic charities, but to people in the community. Is that right?"

"Yes. Some of the money may be used by the church, but he wants the bulk of it given away."

"Why does he want to do this anonymously?"

"I think it has to do with his background. He doesn't want any attention for himself."

"But you know who he is?"

The lawyer asked the question that was on everyone's mind. Father Stephen had assured Jacob that he would respect his request for anonymity, and wondered where the lawyer was going with his question.

"Yes. I know who the donor is. But the money comes through a foundation, so there is now way anyone else would know."

"The donor set this up to protect his anonymity. It means he can get a tax break and still remain anonymous. Smart."

The lawyer was talking to himself, knowing that it would be difficult if not impossible to find out who the donor was. The archbishop raised his hand to stop the lawyer from talking, and said,

"We're talking about a lot of money here. Where does the money come from? Do you know that?"

Father Stephen knew, but wondered why the archbishop needed to know something that specific.

"Yes."

He wanted to add that he didn't see why that might matter, but thought the better of it. The archbishop continued.

"You see, we would not want to take money that might be tainted by criminality. We've done that in the past, without knowing it. Sometimes people give money to wash their consciences of sins they have committed."

"I don't think that's true in this case."

"And you're content with letting someone tell us how the money is to be used? It doesn't seem strange to you that we have no say in how the money is spent?"

Father Stephen sensed where the conversation was going, and noticed the archbishop's use of the word "we" when referring to the money. Father Stephen was a genuinely compassionate man, but he sensed that the plan that he had agreed to pursue with Jacob might fall apart before it really got going.

"The use of the money falls into the general mission of the church to help the poor and needy."

Father Stephen was deliberately keeping his answers short, trying to avoid offering an opinion that might differ from that of the archbishop. He knew where he stood in the hierarchy of the church, and that he remained at St. John's at the pleasure of the Diocese.

"You know that God has ordained the leadership of the church to decide how money is spent, and that we don't allow congregants to tell us how to use the money they give in offering. They trust us to know what is best, don't you agree?"

Father Stephen knew what the archbishop wanted him to say, but got right to the point when he said,

"I don't think he would give us the money if we spent it on anything other than giving it to those in need."

The archbishop leaned back in his chair, and brought the meeting to a close when he said,

"Then it's your job to change his mind, isn't it?"

Father Stephen was basically a good man, and like most priests cared for the members of his flock, trying to put their interests and needs ahead of his own. Jacob appeared to be a good Catholic, one who knew that the leadership of the church called the shots on nearly every aspect of church life. He didn't know if Jacob would bend on his insistence that his donations go to those in need, but he knew he had to try. The archbishop did not give him a percentage that he would be content with, but the priest knew it would have to be at least fifty percent. He had no idea how he might go about changing Jacob's mind, but then he really didn't have a choice in the matter.

7

It didn't take Megan long to find out that Jacob had indeed gone to Harvard, and earned two degrees in his two years there. She used her job as a reporter for the newspaper to speak with several of his professors, who spoke glowingly of his academic prowess. The one negative voice at the university came from his Guidance Counselor, who told her that Jacob was a loner whose only interest was his studies. When Megan asked her how this was a negative, the Guidance Counselor told her she should talk to his peer counselor, if she could find him. He had dropped out of school, and seemed to have disappeared. Megan thanked her for her time, and then began a search for Noah James Anderson.

After spending about an hour looking around the Internet, all she could find was that Noah Anderson had graduated from Harvard with a Bachelor's degree, was in the Master's program, and then dropped out of school. She found that his father was also a Harvard graduate, and managed to track him down through his company. When she called him at his office, and asked to speak with him about his son, he asked her why. She told him she was doing a feature story on someone his son had known at Harvard, and upon hearing this, he politely told her to go to hell.

Megan was used to people hanging up on her, it was part of the job, a reality that many people did not like reporters asking personal questions. However, there was something different in the tone of the father's voice that gave Megan pause. When her search for Noah stalled, she followed Jacob's trail to Miami. He had mentioned the name of the church he attended while living there, and she was able to speak with the priest. He, too, had nothing but good things to say about Jacob. The priest was sad to see Jacob leave, but understood his desire to live somewhere that wasn't as hot and humid. The priest did say, however, that Jacob seemed to be a bit of a loner, which might have resulted from working two jobs. When Megan learned that Jacob worked rather ordinary jobs at Staples and Best Buy, she was puzzled why someone with two degrees from Harvard would seemingly work way below their potential.

Megan spent those hours researching Jacob's life because her last relationship had ended badly. While she didn't consider herself in a relationship with Jacob, they saw each other at least once a week. They were both keeping an emotional distance, content for the time being to see what might happen in the coming weeks. She had come close to finding out about Jacob, but when her search for Noah stalled, his secret was safe for the time being. Not that she would have believed what Noah would have told her.

It took the committee about a month to find several people who they felt would benefit from the money given to the church. They decided at their first meeting that each person would come to the next meeting with at least one person, or family, that they believed would be a good recipient. They would explain the need, the amount of money to help with the need, and then talk amongst themselves to decide whether to give the name to Father Stephen. It took time to go through each story, and in the end, there was unanimous agreement about those people who would receive the money. It had turned out exactly the way Jacob had envisioned, and he thought that Sister Flavia would be pleased at how he was using the gift that she believed he had been given. It had taken Jacob over two years to get his plan in motion, and he sincerely believed that he was on the way to helping hundreds if not thousands of truly needy people in the coming years.

If he had been just a little wiser, he might have guessed that that amount of money would generate interest in others. Because he had been raised by people who were selfless and morally above reproach, he tended to see others in the Catholic church in the same light. Both the priests he had become friends with seemed to be genuinely humble and gracious people. Jacob knew the priesthood had its scandals, but because he was personally untouched by them, he believed that the values he held that made him give money to the church to help the truly desperate would be shared by leaders in the church.

It was after the committee's second meeting that Father Stephen asked to speak with Jacob. The priest had thought about how to approach him, and though he had an idea of how he might bend Jacob to the church's will, he was not sure of success. In the months Jacob had been attending St. John's, Father Stephen had come to realize that Jacob had more depth to him than met the eye. He never missed morning Mass, he lived modestly, and when they had occasion to talk together, Jacob was always deferential to the priest. They walked down to the small café on the boardwalk, with the priest feeling more depressed by the minute. After they ordered something to drink, Father Stephen got right to the point, not wanting to put off the inevitable.

"The meeting seemed to go well tonight. I'll be contacting everyone this week to see about getting them what they need."

Some of the recipients would receive cash, but most would be given the opportunity to choose a specific provider for the services they needed. The church would then pay the provider. Jacob responded by saying,

"I thought it went well. It's exactly what I thought it would be."

"It's hard when you're dealing with this amount of money. It's not like we can keep it a secret, what we're doing."

Jacob didn't want it kept a secret, and had a moment of doubt. He knew that the church's budget and financial reports would show the increase in charitable giving. He didn't know where the priest was going, and he said so. Father Stephen replied,

"It's sort of unusual to have this amount of money given to the church, without letting the church decide where to spend it. I don't think this has ever happened before. At least to my knowledge."

He was taking his time getting there, and Jacob still wasn't sure what he was talking about.

"We're doing what we agreed. I don't understand what you're trying to say."

"Well, because this is a large amount of money, the Diocese thinks that they should have some input on where the money is spent."

So, it was now out there, and Father Stephen waited to see how Jacob would react.

"You're talking about the Bishop. He wants to decide how to use the money?"

"Something like that."

"What did you say? About our agreement?"

"They pointed out that the church has always decided on how to spend offerings from parishioners. That the money belongs to God, and that they are God's representatives on earth. I know you believe that."

"And what would they want to do with the money?"

"I don't know Jacob. I didn't ask them."

"But they wanted you to tell me that they want to decide how its spent, and hope that I'll give it anyway even though I believe that God wants me to use it as we agreed?"

"Yes."

"What do you think I should do?"

"I don't believe they would stop us from using part of it for what you intended, but I can't say that for certain."

"You didn't answer my question. What do you think I should do?"

"I have to do what my superiors ask of me. I don't know what you should do."

"Do they know who I am?"

"No. I take my duty as a priest to protect your confidentiality seriously."

"I could just give people money through the foundation, but there isn't any way to protect my anonymity if I do that. I wanted to use the church because I thought it shared my value on helping those truly in need. Was I wrong to believe this?"

The priest was caught, and he knew it. If he said the church shared Jacob's value's, then why was it in effect going to shut down what he began? There was no way the Diocese was going to tell Jacob where it was going to spend his money, he would just have to trust them. The church gave money to the poor, but most of that money was distributed through Catholic Charities. If Jacob gave the money to Catholic Charities, he would never know who received it and what it had accomplished. Then Jacob said something that surprised the priest.

"Let's do this. Ask the Diocese what percentage of the money they will allow us to use for its original purpose. Then let's talk again."

Jacob spoke in a reasonable tone, and appeared to Father Stephen to be open to modifying his original plan. The meeting had gone better than he had hoped.

"Great. I'll get back to you as soon as I can."

Jacob nodded, and then reached into his jacket pocket. He gave Father Stephen an envelope which contained a check from the foundation for $850,000.

"See you at Mass tomorrow."

Jacob rose from the table and set off down the boardwalk. He needed time to think about what had just happened, though he had the beginnings of a plan in mind. The same feeling was coming over him when he had to figure out how to deal with Noah, and he reproached himself for what he felt he had to do. He knew what Sister Flavia would think, and he tried to push the thought of her out of his mind.

8

When Jacob wanted to find something out, he devoted nearly all his time to the effort. In this case, he went back to his apartment and began a systematic study of the San Diego Diocese. He first wanted to acquaint himself with how the church functioned, and then he would begin to explore areas of its operations that might yield him something he could use for his plan. After several hours, he began to get an idea of not only how the church operated, but who pulled the strings to get things done. Jacob had spent untold hours learning how to search the Internet, and the more time he spent looking through websites, blogs, official reports, budgets and other esoteric items, the more a picture began to form in his mind. After several days, he had uncovered what he thought might be a bribe paid to the Diocese when it built two new high schools

He found the connection between the construction of the two high schools and a series of large gifts given by the owner of the construction company. At first sight, there was nothing wrong with the donations, after all, many devoted Catholics gave large amounts to the church. In this case, however, it was the timing of the gifts that got Jacob's attention. The individual in question gave the donations immediately after beginning construction. The project was worth over $17 million dollars, and the donations totaled around $500,000. It was obvious the owner of the company could afford the donations, a cursory glance of the company's website told Jacob the company was probably worth close to $25 million dollars. If it wasn't for the timing of the donations, Jacob wouldn't have reached the conclusion that the gifts were probably a bribe, though it could never be proved. There was one way he might find out, and he thought long and hard about what he was going to do.

He decided a letter would be the best way to communicate with the company president. Jacob asked the man to meet him at the end of the Pacific Beach pier to discuss the bribe he paid to the Diocese in order to get the contracts for the two high schools. If the man showed up, Jacob figured he must be guilty. If the donations were perfectly legitimate, then the man would probably go to the police, or ignore the matter entirely. Jacob was seldom wrong when he took the time to piece something like this together. When he found the donations in the financial records of the Diocese, which by law had to be made public, in his mind the puzzle was complete. However, in this case he was hoping he was wrong. The owner of the construction company was Megan's father.

He had never met Megan's father, but he had seen pictures of the family on her phone, and had seen him at Sunday Mass. Their relationship had not progressed far enough for her to introduce him to her parents, a fact for which he was now profoundly grateful. Standing at the end of the pier, watching Megan's father nervously pace back and forth, he almost walked away. He would probably be able to figure out another way to distribute his money, but it would take time to dismantle what he already had in place. There was one other possibility, but it would involve going higher up the food chain, all the way to the Bishop. Jacob had hoped that by revealing to Megan's father that he knew about the bribe, he could get him to talk to the Bishop and leave everything in place.

His biggest dilemma, however, was what to do about his relationship with Megan. If he talked to the father about what he knew, the relationship was over. There was no way she would ever see him again if she found out Jacob knew her father had bribed the Diocese to get construction projects. He didn't know himself where the relationship was going, but he did know he wasn't ready to throw it all away when there was another alternative open to him. Jacob was certain the Bishop would see him since it was obvious by Megan's father's behavior that he had indeed bribed the Diocese. The man was still pacing nervously, occasionally looking at his watch. Jacob felt a moment of pity for him. He was living with a secret that if exposed would undoubtedly destroy the world he had so carefully built. Jacob knew what it was like to live with a secret that if revealed would completely alter your world. When the time for the meeting had come and gone, Megan's father took a last look around, and then began the long walk down the pier. Jacob was leaning against the pier's railing, and for a second their eyes met as Megan's father walked by. There was no thought in the man's mind that Jacob might be the one he was supposed to meet, he was much too young.

Jacob waited at the railing until Megan's father had left the pier, and then pulled out his phone. He was supposed to meet Megan that evening at the café on the boardwalk, but knew he would not be able to mask the conflicting emotions he would feel for the next few days. She understood, and would wait until Friday when the singles group would meet again. Jacob waited until he returned to his apartment, and then made another call. He was pretty sure that Megan's father would tell the Bishop about the letter, and the meeting that did not take place. When Jacob told the Bishop's assistant that he needed to talk with the Bishop about what was happening at St. John's church, he was immediately put through. They agreed to meet the next morning, and Jacob was careful to mention nothing about the alleged bribery.

That night Jacob spent hours laying on his couch pondering how he had got himself into such a situation. Everything he had done was to try and fulfill the purpose he felt he had been called to pursue.

His biggest mistake, he came to see, was in thinking that others would view the world in the same way he did, and value what he was trying to accomplish. Sister Flavia would certainly approve, it was her beliefs and principles he was trying to emulate. Father Stephen was certainly on board, until his superiors found out what was happening. Jacob wasn't blind to how the world worked, and knew that even high officials in the church could be corrupted. But knowing something, and experiencing something, were two different things. He wasn't sure he believed in the Catholic church, but he did believe in Sister Flavia.

There was an obvious way out of his dilemma, but it would involve taking the entire operation back into his own hands, and away from the church. He wasn't sure how this would affect his relationship with Megan, but the committee would go away, the priest would know what had happened, and it didn't seem to Jacob that everything would continue as if nothing had changed. His only hope was that the Bishop might be willing to let him continue to use the church as a vehicle to distribute his money, and Jacob fervently hoped he could reach a compromise he could live without having to use the alleged bribery as a lever.

9

The Bishop was a morning person, so they met in his office at 7.30. If the Bishop thought that Jacob would be awed by the ornateness of the surroundings and the prestige of his position, he was wrong. Jacob measured everyone he met by Sister Flavia, and nearly everyone came up short. He knew the Bishop had overseen the payment of $198 million dollars to victims of sexual abuse in the San Diego Diocese, which had essentially bankrupted the church. While not implicated himself, the Bishop had taken years to bring the matter to resolution, leaving most of the victims without any sort of closure or compensation until decades after the crimes had taken place. The alleged bribe paid by Megan's father made more sense viewed in the light of the settlement, the Diocese being desperate for money. Jacob wondered if Megan's father was only the tip of an iceberg that might include other "gifts" to the church that were actually bribes in disguise.

Jacob hated small talk, but let the Bishop prattle on about the work of the church, especially in terms of how it helped the poor. What the Bishop really wanted to talk about was how such a young man could make so much money in the stock market, but thought better of it. The Bishop was infatuated with money, and the trappings of power. Though like all priests he had taken a vow of poverty, he lived a lifestyle that was anything but austere. If the meeting turned out the way he hoped, it would not do anything to disturb the flow of money Jacob was providing. When there was a pause in the Bishop's ramblings, Jacob finally brought the conversation around to its intended purpose.

"You've talked with Father Stephen. Did he tell you I'm willing to discuss how the money is distributed?"

"Yes. He did. I want you to know that it's very unusual for someone your age to be so generous. Our desire is also to help the poor, but perhaps not in exactly the way you have proposed."

The Diocese annually gave away millions of dollars to the poor through Catholic Charities, money that the Bishop would scale back if he thought he could get away with it.

Jacob did not immediately respond, and waited for the Bishop to get to the point, which he quickly did.

"I know that you were raised in a Catholic orphanage. And that you have benefited from a Catholic education. An education that seems to have enabled you to become quite successful. You know that the money you give is not yours, but God's. You and I are stewards of that money. While we appreciate your input, I believe Father Stephen overstepped his authority when he agreed to let you use St. John's as a vehicle to give your money away."

The Bishop was trying to read Jacob as he spoke, but was getting nowhere. Jacob listened quietly, betraying no emotion as the Bishop was trying to maneuver him into a corner. The Bishop had much experience bending people to his will, and believed he was succeeding with Jacob.

"The church decides how to use the offerings of its parishioners, and though yours is a worthy purpose, if we let everyone who gives decide how their money is spent, the church could not function. I'm sure you understand this."

From his point of view, his argument was unassailable, and he waited for Jacob to the respond to the logic of his arguments.

Jacob was ready to respond, and said,

"Yes, I do understand. But you must also know that God not only reveals His will to the church hierarchy, but to lay individuals as well. My purpose in giving money to the truly desperate and needy in no way conflicts with the church's mission to help those in need. I'm willing to talk about percentages, so let's see what arrangement we might come to."

Pride is a terrible thing, especially when it flows from those in power who are not used to bending their will to the will of another. The Bishop wasn't willing to compromise because he felt he held all the cards; cards that he sincerely believed God had given him.

"We don't deal in percentages, Jacob, we deal in absolutes. The church has not changed what it believes for over a thousand years. We're the only organization in the world that can say that. Our convictions come from authority that was given to us by God through the apostles and then the Popes. We don't negotiate with our parishioners over how to spend the money they rightfully give to the church. God is not in the business of negotiating."

Jacob had anticipated the Bishop's response, rooted as it was in years of dictating to others what the will of God was for them. He conveniently overlooked the failures of his own priests that had bankrupted the Diocese, priests that had told others without any reservation how they were to live while they were busy seducing young boys and girls. The Bishop could talk about authority all he wanted; all Jacob saw was an old man trying to intimidate him by reciting doctrine that applied to everyone but him.

"Your mistake is that you think because I was raised by the Sisters and am willing to give large amounts of money to the needy, that I'm a devout Catholic. One that can be swayed by talk of church doctrine, history, and what God wants of me. I may go to Mass every day, but I don't know if Father Stephen told you that I never partake. I could have given the money through another charity, but I chose the church because it helps me keep the memory of someone who did everything for me alive. I find comfort in the forms of the church, not in what it believes. You can't threaten me with any form of authority or doctrine because they have no hold on me."

He let the Bishop absorb the import of his words, and waited for a response. The Bishop was in the unusual position of being out maneuvered by a lay person, and was momentarily at a loss for words. He managed to hide the rage he was feeling; a rage that came from seeing all that money potentially slip away from him. However, despite the fact that he felt he wanted to assign Jacob to endless purgatory, he managed to control his feelings, and thought of the larger picture. The thought of losing Jacob's money altogether tempered his feelings of indignation.

"You're not what I expected, I can tell you that. I'm willing to make an exception in your case because of your sincere desire to help those in need."

"You mean you're willing to make an exception because of the large amount of money involved."

Jacob spoke the truth, but he had stepped over a line, and he immediately knew it from the Bishop's reaction. He was a proud man, and could only be pushed so far. His face flushed, and he was about to send Jacob out of the room when Jacob quickly said,

"What I meant to say was perhaps we could talk about percentages, and find a solution we could both live with."

"The only percentage that I would be comfortable with is one hundred percent. That doesn't mean that we would not give some of the money to your committee; it means that we will say what percentages will be involved."

Jacob knew that the Bishop would understand that would not be unacceptable to him, and was momentarily at a loss. Was it time to bring up the alleged bribery as leverage? Jacob didn't see what he had to lose; the thought of having to find another way to fulfill his plan was not appealing. Before he could speak, however, the Bishop had one final card to play. He had asked Father Stephen to tell him everything he knew about Jacob, and now used the one piece of information that might sway Jacob.

"You know that Megan's family is a pillar of St. John's church. They have attended there for three generations. Her father is a friend of the Diocese, a large contributor just as you are. Megan is very devoted to him."

Jacob saw where this was going, and felt a wave of revulsion wash over him. He doubted that Father Stephen knew what he was doing when he told the Bishop about his relationship with Megan. As usual, Jacob went straight to the point.

"You're saying that Megan's father would keep me from seeing her? Something like that?"

"I think it's fair to say that he might not want his daughter involved with someone who is not fully committed to the teachings of the church. She is very devout, and would no doubt be appalled by what you are proposing, and the lack of respect you have for the traditions of the church."

Jacob was tiring of the continuing game of cat and mouse. He longed for the wisdom of Sister Flavia, though he wondered if she would be swayed by the hierarchy of the church and bow to the Bishop's wishes. Jacob never really experienced being tired, but he was weary, and the thought of continuing on with the Bishop was not in him. He rose from the chair and took a final look around the Bishop's office.

"I think I'll go talk to him myself. It's about time we got acquainted. Don't bother getting up. I'll see myself out."

Jacob walked across the room, and as he was opening the door to the outside, left the Bishop with some final words.

"You might want to read Matthew chapter twenty-three. Just a thought."

The Bishop had no idea what was in Matthew chapter twenty-three, and it took him a moment to find a Bible. When he was done reading the chapter he was irate, and before Jacob had reached the parking lot, the Bishop had called Megan's father, and in no uncertain terms told him what he should do if Jacob did come and speak with him. The Bishop could feel the money slipping out of his reach, and he was not happy.

10

It was still early in the morning, and as Jacob had not yet eaten breakfast, he drove back home and walked down to the café on the boardwalk. He was later than usual, and the waitress who served him asked him if he wanted his usual breakfast. Jacob nodded, and then looked out toward the ocean, pondering his meeting with the Bishop.

There was no way he could continue funneling money through St. John's church, that much was clear. The Bishop had not even proposed any type of compromise that would allow the church to keep some of his money, and this surprised Jacob. Jacob would have settled for a 70-30 split, though the thought of giving the Diocese that much money to do with what they wanted was not a pleasant thought. Because Jacob was at his core a logical, rational person, he often expected others to act in a similar fashion. But the Bishop had let his pride decide the issue, and was probably in the process of trying to hurt Jacob in the only way he knew how. If he couldn't have Jacob's money, then he would try to deny Jacob Megan through his influence with the father.

Which brought Jacob back to a question he had not yet fully thought through. What exactly did Megan mean to him? They had only been seeing each other casually, yet there seemed to be an unspoken agreement that there was the real possibility of something serious down the road. They shared the same values, and though Jacob's relationship to the church was different from Megan's, he attended Mass every day, which set him apart from every other young man Megan knew. She appreciated the seriousness which was a part of Jacob's character, a trait that she shared with him. The fact that he was an orphan, someone without family ties, and somewhat adrift in the world stirred the maternal instinct in her she inherited from her own mother.

Jacob never planned to live alone his whole life, and often thought what it would be like to be married and have a family. There was, of course, one giant caveat, and as he waited for his breakfast he again thought about the anomaly that was the defining characteristic of his life. He had hidden it from everyone, with the one exception of Noah, who had more or less stumbled across the secret from trying to figure out how Jacob managed to take a double load at Harvard. Since leaving Harvard, Jacob hadn't done anything out of the ordinary that anyone might notice, so he was pretty sure he could continue to hide what he was from everyone around him, including Megan.

The one contingent he had no answer for was this: if he got married someday, what would his future wife think about what he was? He knew there was no way he could hide the fact that he didn't need sleep if he lived with someone; the only question that mattered was one that he could not answer until he in a position to ask someone to marry him. Would someone live with another person who was different from everyone else in the world? It would require a degree of acceptance and commitment that Jacob thought might be impossible to find in another person. Jacob was unlike most other twenty-two year old young men. He eventually wanted to find someone he could spend his life with, no doubt the result of living alone for a number of years. Despite the fact that he considered Sister Flavia his mother, their relationship was not familial, her first loyalty and the focus of her life was her commitment to the church. Though he had never verbalized the thought to anyone, the lack of a father figure in his life had left Jacob with a need to become what he never had. He understood that being an orphan played into his desire for a form of stability that most people took for granted, and he knew he could not escape his background, not that he wanted to.

He put the thought out of his mind for the moment, and focused on the matter at hand, Megan's father. Jacob would see him at church Sunday, and thought he might ask him then for a time they could talk. But Sunday was four days away, and Jacob felt it would be best to get it over with and see what the fallout would be. Jacob never liked being without a fallback plan, and as he sat and ate his breakfast he thought about what he might do if everything fell apart. Several ideas came to him as he sat alone and watched the boardwalk come alive as more and more people strolled by enjoying the cloudless morning sky. After some time considering the various outcomes to his meeting with Megan's father, and the possible scenarios that might come from those outcomes, Jacob felt that he had at least the outlines of what he might do depending on how Megan's father reacted.

His reverie was broken when a familiar figure came strolling down the boardwalk, and noticing Jacob sitting in the café, stopped in front of his table. Father Stephen had completed the morning Mass and was taking a short break before heading back to his office in the church. He knew that Jacob had met with the Bishop that morning, though he had no idea what had transpired. His conscience had reproached him for the information he had given the Bishop about Jacob, and he wondered if the Bishop used it in the meeting. He was torn between wanting to take a seat at the table or just heading back to the church. The matter was decided when Jacob said,

"Please join me Father. Let me get you a cup of coffee."

The priest reluctantly sat down, though he could have made an excuse and gone back to his office. His curiosity was greater because of the possibility of what he might learn about the meeting between Jacob and the Bishop. Jacob waved to a waitress and motioned for her to bring the priest a cup of coffee.

"You probably noticed that I wasn't at Mass today."

"Yes, I did."

Father Stephen could have added that he knew why Jacob was absent, but he was nervous and wanted to see where Jacob would take the conversation. Jacob did not disappoint him.

"I had a meeting with the Bishop this morning, but I suspect you knew about that."

"Yes, I know that you met with him. It's a sign of respect that he took a meeting with you. He's a very busy man."

Jacob appreciated the attempt at flattery, but it fell flat, and both men knew it.

"How did the Bishop know about Megan? There really isn't anything between us, at least not yet. He seems to think her father can influence me in ways that he can't."

Jacob had just let the priest know that he felt compromised by the information Father Stephen had given the Bishop. Jacob felt for the man; the priest was constrained by his absolute duty to obey those above him. The thought that Father Stephen's obedience might collide with the needs and expectations of his parishioners was an occupational hazard that Catholic clergy had to deal with, leaving many of them in a state of moral uncertainty.

"I think the Bishop is looking for a way to find common ground between you and the church. The more information he has the easier it is for him to find a solution."

"It seemed to me to be more than that. I know when someone is threatening me. What really surprised me was that he didn't propose any type of solution. He must think I'm like every other young man and can be swayed by my hormones. I think you know I'm not quite that shallow."

Father Stephen knew that Jacob was unlike any other young man in his church; in fact, Jacob was unlike any other young man he had ever known. It wasn't just the ability to make vast amounts of money, which by itself put Jacob in a class almost by himself, but the complete lack of attachment to the money that he made. It was that part of Jacob that really separated him from the world around him. When the priest didn't respond, Jacob said,

"I'm going to talk to Megan's father today. I'm pretty sure he'll see me, especially if he's talked to the Bishop. I'm sorry that you got caught in the middle of all this. You deserve better."

Jacob left some money on the table, and then got up and walked back to this apartment. The priest was left pondering Jacob's words, not knowing that he would never see him again.

11

They met at his office later that afternoon. Megan's father had talked to the Bishop that morning, and though he didn't know everything that had transpired between them, he understood that it was important to get Jacob to submit to the authority of the church. What the Bishop wanted Jacob to submit to was unclear to Megan's father, but the Bishop made it clear that he wanted the father to make sure Jacob understood that if he wanted to continue to see Megan he would need to accede to the wishes of the church.

Megan's father was like many successful businessmen; he understood about authority and the chain of command. He ran both his family and his business with military-like precision; and no one in either place doubted who was in charge. It wasn't that he was without any redeeming qualities; he was fair and generous with his employees, and doted on his large family. His children benefited from the success of their father; they attended private Catholic schools and wanted for nothing. Which is not to say they were spoiled. They were all required to attend church, and be involved in some type of activity that their father believed would temper the affluence he provided them. Most of these activities revolved around the church; working with the less fortunate, serving food to the homeless, and occasionally going on short term mission trips to countries where they would build homes, work with orphans, and help doctors and nurses in mobile health clinics. Megan, who was the oldest, had much of her character shaped by working through the church in various capacities for most of her young life.

Jacob, however, knew that there was another side to Megan's father; the bribe that he apparently paid the church to get the contracts to build the two high schools indicated a willingness to justify behavior that most would consider objectionable, if not illegal. Jacob knew that Megan's father could easily justify the bribe; he got the contracts, which provided employment for his workers, and the church received a large gift which would benefit the Diocese. Whether Jacob could get Megan's father to see that what he had done amounted to a bribe was an open question, and there was the possibility that the conversation might not even get around to the bribe depending on what transpired between them.

His office was located in an industrial area off the I-5; and as Jacob parked his car he had a sudden rush of doubt. What was he doing, going against the church that had given him a home for most of his life? He knew the church was a flawed institution; why was he trying to force it to be something it could never be? It came back to Sister Flavia, she was the standard by which Jacob judged everyone and everything. She was a daughter of the church, so it must be possible in some way for the church to reflect who she was, what she believed, and the values she lived by. He was trying to do what he thought was right, what he believed was his purpose in life, and he was being thwarted by those who ought to share his commitment to help those in need.

Having fortified himself in knowing that what he was doing was right, Jacob got out of his car and walked into the office. The receptionist obviously knew he was coming, and greeted him warmly, telling him to have a seat in the lobby. It took only a moment for Megan's father to emerge from his office, which was located down a hallway in back of the reception area. He extended his hand to Jacob.

"It's good to meet you. Let's go back to my office."

He had the air of a man used to getting his way, which wasn't surprising given his success. The hallway was lined with pictures of things his company had built; malls, office buildings, schools and other industrial projects. He was just short of 50, tall and muscular. He motioned for Jacob to a seat in front of his desk, and began the conversation by saying,

"I'm glad we've finally got a chance to talk. Megan tells me that you go to Mass every day. That's rare in a young man. I like that you take your faith seriously."

"I do go to Mass every day. I'm still figuring out my relationship to the church."

"Why would you go to Mass everyday if you're not sure about your relationship to the church? I don't understand."

"I was raised in a Catholic orphanage. The forms of the church, including Mass, provide a certain comfort to me. Plus, they remind me of people who mean a lot to me."

"I can understand that. You must be very grateful to have received such a fine upbringing and education. I understand you have two degrees from Harvard?"

"Yes, but I don't think that's what you really want to talk about, is it?"

As usual, Jacob wanted to get to the point, and for a moment caught his host off guard. Megan's father thought for a moment.

"It's unusual for the Bishop to call me with a request like he did this morning. I don't know exactly what has transpired between you, but he seems to think I might be able to help you see how the church is the final authority in our lives, though I believe you already know this."

Jacob heard what the man had said, but was looking at pictures of his family on the wall in back of his desk. There was a prominent one of Megan, and Jacob felt a pang of regret, knowing that the outcome of this conversation might determine if he would ever see her again.

"I think you know St. John's has a committee that gives money to the truly needy and desperate. That money comes from a foundation that I set up. I wanted to use the church to distribute that money. However, the Bishop wants to decide by himself how that money is to be used. That's about it. The Bishop told me that he would use his influence with you to try and get me to bend to his wishes. Does that sound about right?"

Jacob had left out the part about Megan's father prohibiting him from seeing his daughter. He wanted that to come from Megan's father, and was willing to wait to see how he would respond.

"I think that because we're both businessmen, and both Catholics, the Bishop thought I might be able to give you my perspective."

Jacob already knew what his "perspective" was, but waited patiently as Megan's father continued.

"I owe my success to principles of my faith: hard work, fairness, knowing the difference between right and wrong, devotion to family, and most importantly, devotion to my church. I believe the church is the one institution we can have faith in during these uncertain times."

He spoke as if he had said the words many times, and while there was a certain conviction in his voice, it was delivered by rote. If he wanted to sway Jacob he would have to do better. Jacob responded by saying,

"Certainly, you're aware of the failings of the church? This Diocese has spent millions of dollars to pay for the sins of those you and the Bishop want me to follow blindly. I wanted to use the church as a vehicle to dispense money to those in need because I thought it valued helping the needy. Now I'm not so sure."

"Every institution has its failings, but it's the doctrine of the church that never changes. Part of that doctrine is that we obey our leaders, in this case the Bishop. You put your immortal soul in jeopardy if you defy the leadership of the church."

"I've known one person who truly embodied the teachings of the church, and it's her that I'm trying to emulate. I can't believe I'm in danger of perdition because I want to give large amounts of money to the needy. I'm simply trying to use the gifts I was given to help those less fortunate, not fill the coffers of the church so it can pay for the sins of its clergy."

Megan's father wasn't used to verbally sparring with people in his office, especially one as young and self-composed as Jacob. He had wanted to keep Megan out of the equation, but it was obvious he wasn't getting anywhere with Jacob.

"I value my family above everything else. Megan is my oldest daughter, and she has a special place in my heart. She is devoted to the church; her whole life revolves around her faith. I don't think she would appreciate your lack of respect for its leaders."

"The Bishop hinted that you might say something like that. I wonder what Megan would think if she knew her father had given $500,000 dollars to the church right after he was awarded $17 million dollars in contracts to build two new high schools?"

Jacob played his trump card, and immediately regretted it. Megan's father stiffened in his chair, and a sly smile came across his face.

"The Bishop said you were smart. It must have taken a lot of effort to connect the two, buried as they are in the archives of the Diocese. I can't help it if I'm a generous person and my company is good at what it does. We've done other projects for the Diocese, the gift was just that, a gift. If you can prove something different, then prove it. Who do you think Megan is going to believe?"

Everything he said was true, and Jacob again wondered why he thought he had a chance to get his way with either the Bishop or Megan's father. He knew he was right about the bribe, the man's smile and body language spoke volumes to that truth. It was over, and he now saw the future clearly. He did not know the specifics, but the general outline of what he was going to do was now set in motion.

"Thanks for your time."

He was up and out of the office before Megan's father could speak. Jacob walked out into the bright sunshine knowing he had made the right decision, but with a sadness in his heart he had not experienced since Sister Flavia had died. He was again alone in the world, and though there was uncertainty, there was the sustaining hope that he sincerely believed he was going to fulfill his purpose in life. In the end that would be enough.

He drove back to his apartment and found his passport. He packed some clothes, his computer, records that related to his trading accounts, and took a last look around. Jacob left an envelope with $5,000 on the kitchen table, and locked the door behind him. He would call the landlord later and explain he suddenly had to leave town. There would be no call to Father Stephen, or to Megan. Jacob would simply disappear, and would not reappear again in San Diego for many years.

Part Four

1

Jacob chose Ensenada because it was close to the border, and it wasn't Tijuana. Tijuana was too much a tourist town, and not the good type of tourism. Ensenada's population was over half a million, and though it was one of Mexico's more prosperous cities, the outlying parts of the city contained slums on par with anything in Central America. He got a room at a small hotel near the center of the city and began his search the day after he arrived. There was no rush, he wanted to get a sense of the city and in doing some basic research he found that there were a number of orphanages operating nearby. Most of those had websites, an acknowledgement that in the digital age there was a need to promote your ministry and show the world what you were doing. It wasn't lost on Jacob that all the websites were in English; and indication that most of the people who donated probably lived in the U.S.

The evenings were hardest for Jacob. He spent some of each evening managing his trading accounts, watching some Spanish television, anything to keep his mind from drifting north across the border. It wasn't the same as being in Miami or San Diego, he couldn't walk around the city at night. It wasn't that it was especially dangerous, but as an American he stood out as a target for the petty criminals that preyed on tourists who usually had too much to drink. On his first day in the city he got a new phone and deleted his email account; he knew that Megan or perhaps Father Stephen would be calling him when he didn't appear at church or the singles meeting. If Jacob hadn't had years of living inside of himself, he would have collapsed under the weight of his loneliness. He would lay in the small room looking up at the ceiling and wonder, not for the first time, what it would be like to sleep. Closing his eyes like any other person would do at the end of a long day, he would simply lie there, his mind coasting along in neutral, until he gave up and found something to fill the long hours before he could resume his search.

Jacob spent his mornings walking around the center of the city, trying to perfect the Spanish he had learned in Miami. He would have long conversations with street vendors, people at bus stops, traffic cops, workers at restaurants. He would attend a different church each Sunday, and try and talk to the priest after the service was over. When it seemed appropriate, he would ask if the priest knew of a Catholic orphanage in the city. It turned out there were several, but when Jacob visited them, it didn't seem like they needed the help he could offer. Finally, after several months, a waitress at a small restaurant on the outskirts of the city told him about an orphanage south of the city. She had lived there for several years after being abandoned by her mother, who was a drug addict. It was run by a priest and several Nuns, who lived on the edge of poverty themselves. It wasn't much, the waitress told him, but it was safe, and the children were happy to be there. There was a small church attached to the orphanage, and it seemed that the funds to operate the orphanage came partly from donations given by the parishioners of the church. The church and orphanage were located about ten miles outside of Ensenada in the small village of El Bajo. Needless to say, the orphanage, called El Refugio, didn't have a website.

The waitress gave him directions, and an hour later he was parked outside the small church. It was located at the south end of the village, a mile off Highway 1, the main north south highway in Baja California. He couldn't see much, the church faced the street but the orphanage was hidden behind high walls, a common feature in Mexico. The name of the orphanage was written high up on the outside wall, so he knew he was in the right place. It was Saturday, and there were people walking down the dusty street toward the main highway. He nodded as they passed by, and thought about what he would do next. Jacob hadn't planned what he would say, which was unusual, he usually knew what he would do and say in every situation, which was one of the benefits of having plenty of time in your life. A sign on the church gave the time for Sunday Mass, and Jacob decided he would return the next day and talk to the priest after the service.

He spent the rest of the morning looking around the village, parking just off the highway and walking through the small downtown area. There were some tourists, but most of the people seemed to be locals doing their Saturday shopping. Jacob had lunch from a street vendor, and asked about the orphanage. The vendor told him that it had been there as long as he could remember, taking in children who lived on the street or had been abandoned by their parents, many of whom left Mexico for work in the U.S. Some of the children were orphans, their parents victims of the drug war that seemed to effect every part of Mexico.

Jacob spent the night in El Bajo, and arrived early the next morning at the church. He parked up the street and watched as people trickled into the church. When there was five minutes until the service started, Jacob entered the church and found a seat in the rear of the sanctuary. There were about forty people in the little chapel, which had room for about twice that many. Most of the parishioners were women, which did not surprise him. In the front of the chapel there were three rows of children, perhaps 30 in all, who were sitting quietly under the watchful eyes of three Nuns who sat at the end of each row.

The priest, who had been sitting in the front row, got up and stood in back of a small table that held the elements for the Mass. Jacob guessed that he was around 50, in part because of his grey beard. He would have been surprised to find out that the priest was well over 60, but Jacob would never find out the exact age of the priest. Personal details like age, education, position; these were of no concern to the priest, who began the service with a short prayer. When he had finished, a young woman with a guitar came up from the front pew and led the congregation in several songs. Jacob noticed that no one seemed to pay him any attention, the service went on without any mention of the American in their midst. After the songs, the priest spoke for several minutes, and then without any prompting the congregation rose as one and went to the front to take the bread and the wine. The people walked silently out of the church after the Mass, and though several looked at Jacob as they passed him sitting in the last row, none made any effort to greet or talk with him. He watched as the children left the chapel through a back door, followed by the three Nuns, and then he was suddenly alone in the church with the priest.

Jacob sat quietly and waited to see what the priest would do. He was still standing behind the small table, eyes closed, hands in front of him in a gesture of prayer. After a few moments, he opened his eyes, and seeing Jacob still sitting in the back of the church, began to walk slowly down the center aisle. When he reached Jacob, he stopped, and said in Spanish,

"You don't have the look of a tourist, and you did not participate in the Mass. I wonder what brings you to our church this morning?"

"I've been on a journey for several years. My journey has brought me to your church today."

Jacob replied in Spanish, and waited for the priest's reaction. The priest sat down in the pew in front of Jacob, intrigued by the young American who sat before him.

"Tell me about this journey of yours."

"I was raised in a Catholic orphanage in the United States. I understand you have an orphanage here."

"Yes. The children you saw sitting in the front. They live here."

Jacob felt the hesitation in the priest's voice; he could imagine what he was thinking: what was this young American doing in my church telling me about some kind of journey? Jacob, as usual, decided to get right to the point, though he would not be completely forthcoming just yet.

"I promised one of the Sisters who raised me that when I found my purpose in life I would do my best to fulfill it."

"And you're thinking that your purpose in life is somehow connected to this church?"

"I don't know. I think you might have something to say about that."

"And you could not fulfill your purpose in the United States?"

"I tried. It didn't work out too well."

"It might help if you told me what you believe your purpose is in this life."

"I want to help the poor and needy. I know it sounds trite, but if you knew the Sister who raised me you would understand. She gave her life to help others."

"We are certainly poor. But God provides everything we need."

"I don't doubt that. I'm only looking for a place where I might contribute."

"And what could you contribute?"

149

Jacob did not want to talk about money, he would need to know more about the priest before he offered to help financially.

"I have two university degrees. I speak fluent Spanish. Maybe you could use me as a teacher? I have a car that you could use if you don't have one."

"I know you lived in an orphanage. But an orphanage in the United States must be much different from an orphanage here in Mexico. I wonder how long you could live here, and how you would provide for yourself. We can't pay you anything, I'm sure you know that."

"I have some money saved, and I have a business that I can do from anyplace as long as there is Internet."

The priest smiled, and said,

"We have no Internet here. Sometimes we don't even have electricity."

He was throwing up every obstacle he could think of to try and discourage Jacob. There was one other thought that occurred to him, something from his past that had brought him to the church years earlier.

"You said you tried to fulfill your purpose in the United States. If you're running away from something or someone, you won't find it here."

It wouldn't be the last time Jacob would experience the priest intuitively knowing what Jacob was thinking or guessing what had happened in his past. There wasn't any point in denying the truth.

"If you knew my story, it might seem that I'm running away. I'd prefer to believe that changing circumstances have led me here. But there is probably some truth to what you said."

The priest didn't need to talk any longer. He was a wise man; his wisdom came from years of experience dealing with people in many different settings. Looking at Jacob, who was waiting patiently to see what decision he would make, the priest knew there were many things Jacob was holding back. Yet, in his years as a priest he had never had someone come to him and offer to help in his rundown, out of the way, barely functioning orphanage.

"My name is Father Rodrigo. We have a room, it's not much, but you can have it if you want."

"I'll need to go back to Ensenada to get my things. I'll be back later today, if that's okay."

150

"Yes. I told you, we don't have Internet here, so you won't be able to use a computer."

Jacob got up to leave, and extended his hand to the priest. "Maybe I can help with that."

2

Jacob returned to El Bajo later than afternoon. He had bought some personal items in Ensenada that he thought he might need, and then drove the short distance to El Bajo. The village had been incorporated into Ensenada years previously, but still retained the feel of a typical Mexican small town. There was a large church just off the main highway next to the town plaza, and what passed for a tourist district. Jacob guessed that most of the people worked in Ensenada, which had a growing manufacturing and industrial base. Compared to much of Mexico, Ensenada was relatively prosperous, but you would not know that from the look of El Bajo.

It was where those who came from other parts of Mexico, hoping to find work in Ensenada, ended their journey. Because there were more people looking for work than there were jobs, those who found no employment lived where they could. Then there were those who were trying to get into the United States, for them El Bajo was just another stop on a journey that often led nowhere. Finally, no town or village in Mexico could escape the ravages of the drug war. Because the town was relatively near the border, it was often used to store drugs that would eventually find their way into the U.S.

The door to the church was open when Jacob arrived, and he walked into the chapel and looked around. There was nobody there, but he could hear children's voices nearby. He followed the sound of laughter and shrieking through the back of the church and came out into a large courtyard. A group of children were playing soccer while others watched from the sidelines. The courtyard was about 50 by 100 feet, and Jacob could now see the orphanage was built under one of the outside walls, along the edge of the courtyard. On the other side of the courtyard were other rooms, and, finally, the back wall went up two stories and was separated again into various rooms. The top of each wall was covered with bits of broken bottles embedded in the concrete to deter theft.

Jacob had not noticed the priest, who was sitting in shade provided by the wall. He wondered if the American was going to return, and was mildly surprised to see Jacob standing in the doorway of the church looking out at the children playing. He rose, and slowly walked across the courtyard through the soccer game, striking at the ball when he could, which brought laughter from the children. Jacob waited, and it was not lost on him that he was at the precipice of a new phase in his life. He knew himself, if he decided to stay, he would stay, it was not in him to quit. The relative poverty, the completely new culture, a new language, the lack of most physical comforts; these did not enter into his decision-making process. In the few moments it took for the priest to walk over to Jacob, he knew that Sister Flavia would approve of his decision. He wasn't blind to the fact that he was in some measure running away from circumstances he couldn't change, but he felt it was those circumstances that forced his hand. Father Rodrigo stopped in front of Jacob, quietly looking the young man over, as if to measure the sincerity of his commitment.

"Let's move your car off the street. It's not safe to leave it outside."

Jacob followed the priest back through the church and out onto the street. It turned out that the orphanage owned the lot next to the church, which was entered through a locked gate. The lot was also surrounded by a wall, and Jacob could hear the children next door playing. There were three storage sheds, a pile of wood and bricks against the back wall, and an old truck up on blocks. The gate was wide enough to allow his car entrance into the lot, and Jacob drove it in while the priest held the gate open. There was no door from the lot back to the church, so they locked the gate behind them, and then stood in the street.

"This neighborhood is relatively safe, and we have had few problems. The church is still respected by most of the people. During the day, it's safe if you need to leave for some reason, but be careful at night. We'll come back later for your things. Let me show you our community."

It was the same word that the Sisters used to describe his orphanage, and Jacob was lost for a moment in remembering his life there. When he didn't begin to follow Father Rodrigo back to the church, the priest stopped, turned to him, and said,

"Are you alright?"

"Yes. We called the orphanage I grew up in our "community". It brought back memories."

"I hope they are good ones."

Jacob wasn't introspective, and wanted to get past the moment.

"Good memories, yes."

He moved quickly to follow Father Rodrigo, and they went back into the church. Father Rodrigo took Jacob to the back of the chapel to his office, a small room that had a desk, some bookshelves and a bed.

"This is my room. I'm not often here, except to sleep."

Jacob would learn that the priest spent part of each morning in the neighborhood; visiting, giving counsel, praying for those who were sick. He would return before lunch to spend the rest of the day with the children. Evenings were for study and prayer.

"Let me take you to where the children live."

It wasn't much, just a long room divided into two sections by a rudimentary plywood wall. The wall divided the girls from the boys, and was able to be moved depending on the gender distribution. Under each bed was a box for the children's clothes, and as they walked down the room together Jacob noticed there didn't appear to be any way to heat the large room.

"You don't have heat?"

"We have blankets."

It was hard for Jacob to not mentally begin to think how he could change the place, but he knew he would need to go slow and gain the respect of the priest, and the Nuns, before he could offer them any kind of significant help.

There were two large bathrooms that connected to the children's room, they were rudimentary but clean. The Nuns lived together in the next room, close to the children, for whom they were responsible. They taught the children, supervised their play, gave them work to do every day, and led them in the daily devotion held in the chapel. The children were taught in a room on the other side of the courtyard, and in seeing what resources the orphanage had to educate the children, Jacob's heart sank. There were a few long tables, chalkboards on the wall, and though there were books on the tables, Jacob could see they were old and probably well out of date. Father Rodrigo could read Jacob's thoughts by the look on his face.

"We do the best with what we have. We make sure they can read, and give them some basic instruction in language, mathematics, and history. When they leave here they have enough of an education to hopefully find a job. Let me show you your room."

The priest took Jacob upstairs to the rooms that overlooked the courtyard. Some of the rooms were used for storage, others were empty. They stopped in front of a door, Father Rodrigo opened it, and they walked inside. It was about 10 x 8, with a single light bulb hanging down from the ceiling. There was no window to the outside, and only a bed, small table and chair. He would have to put his clothes in a box just like the children.

"If we have guests, this is the room we use for them. There is a bathroom at the end of the walkway. No one else uses it, so you will have some privacy. Use the bucket to clean yourself."

"It's fine, thanks."

They were interrupted by the sound of a bell, which was the signal for dinner.

"We'll bring the items from your car up after dinner. If it's alright with you I'll say you will be staying with us for a week or two. So we can see how you fit into the community."

"Sure."

They closed the door to the room, which Jacob noticed didn't have a lock, and headed downstairs. There was one thing about the room, however, that Jacob did not notice. The door did not quite reach the cement floor, there was a gap of about an inch, which would have profound consequences for Jacob in the months to come.

3

The kitchen and dining hall were attached to the back wall of the courtyard, a long narrow room with benches where the children sat and waited patiently. Jacob followed the priest into the kitchen where two ladies were cooking the meal. The kitchen was surprisingly large and had shelves crammed with bags of beans, rice and corn flour. Two large refrigerators and a freezer stood against the wall, while the rest of the space was taken up by a large propane powered stove. The two ladies preparing the meal were for the moment oblivious to the presence of the priest and Jacob, who stood in the doorway between the kitchen and dining room.

"These ladies are from the neighborhood. They are the only paid staff here, though what we pay them is very little. Let's go sit down and I'll introduce you to the Sisters."

There were three Nuns who lived at the community, and Jacob was surprised at how young they were. The Sisters at his orphanage had been much older, and, of course, two had died in the recent past. After Father Rodrigo had introduced them to Jacob, and they had taken their seats at a table that was at the end of the room, Jacob said,

"The Sisters at my community were much older."

He said the words mainly to himself, as a form of remembrance, and though Father Rodrigo heard, he did not respond. There was a reason the Sisters were relatively young, a reason Jacob would discover in time.

It was a simple meal; rice, beans, tortillas and some chicken. The cooks brought out large bowls of fruit after the meal, which constituted the children's dessert. When everyone was done, the priest stood and said a few words before the children were given an hour or so to play before they went to bed.

"I'm sure you have noticed we have a visitor with us today. His name is Jacob, and he is from the United States. He will be visiting with us for a few weeks, and we will see if we can find some things for him to do while he is here."

Like everything else he had seen so far in the community, the introduction of this new person into the orphanage was done simply and without a lot of fuss. Jacob merely nodded his head when the priest was finished, and then the children were dismissed. Four of them cleared the dishes and helped clean up, some played in the courtyard, while others went back into the room to either play games or finish schoolwork. Jacob and Father Rodrigo walked back to the lot to get his things, and on the way Jacob said,

"I know you don't know me, and that I just showed up here today, but I'd like to talk with you for a moment, if that's possible."

"Let's move your things to your room and then go into the chapel."

They sat in the back row of the chapel, trying to have a little privacy. Jacob was reluctant to bring up the matter of the Internet, but it was as good a place to start as any. He did not want to be perceived as throwing money at a problem, nor did he want to be the American who comes to fix everything. He would have to trust that the priest could see behind what he wanted to do to his motivation.

"In order to keep my business going, I need access to the Internet. It doesn't require much of my time, and I would work in the evening, but there are people who depend on me. There is an Internet café in town I can use, but that would not be my first choice. I would like to ask you about the possibility of bringing Internet here. It would be easier for me, and might benefit your students. I would of course cover the costs."

"Internet is of no use for the children without computers."

"Yes. That's true."

There was a pause while the priest considered what was happening. In the space of 12 hours Jacob had showed up unannounced at his church, told Father Rodrigo his journey had led him to the community, offered to help in any way he could, and was now was talking about bringing the orphanage a tool that could greatly benefit the children he was responsible for educating.

"And I'm guessing that you would provide the computers as well?"

"Yes. And teach the children how to use them."

The priest had seen God work in mysterious ways before, and was not surprised by the rapidity at which events were unfolding before him. What was of more interest to him was the young man sitting next to him in a run-down church on a dusty street in a town few people in America knew existed.

"You can start tomorrow if you like. It will give you something to do, and no doubt the children will be pleased."

Jacob nodded in response, and then rose and went to his room. He spent the night working out all the details in his mind about what he needed to do to get everything up and running. It was the first step in this new part of his journey, a journey that would last five years, and would change him forever.

4

The Captain waited quietly with his men, sitting in the dark behind some rocks that gave them a minimum of cover. The road just below them was used by smugglers to transport people to the tunnel that ran under the border just south of Nogales. It was the Americans who had found the tunnel on their side of the border. They could have easily destroyed it, but they wanted the operators of the tunnel caught, and that could only be done on the Mexican side. The Captain had been given the job because he was the least corruptible officer in the area. If he could capture the driver, the driver might be persuaded to give them the next man up the chain, and so on. There was a drone overhead watching for any movement on the road, and because it was getting close to morning, the Captain was considering giving up when his radio crackled.

The truck was about a mile away, a semi with a trailer attached. He did not expect something so big, and hoped his men would be able to accomplish their mission without using their weapons. There were only seven on his team, he had wanted to keep the number small because there was always the risk of having an informant among them. They had spiked the road, covering the jagged metal with dirt so the driver would not be able to avoid having his tires blow out. The truck's headlights appeared about a hundred yards down the road, and the Captain raised his hand to tell his men to be ready. When the tires blew, three of the men would rush the driver and the other four would deal with those in the trailer. When it was over, he would call for a bus to take care of the people in the trailer. He would personally escort the driver back to his base in Hermosillo, where he would be interrogated.

The assault went off just as planned. The truck's tires blew the moment they hit the spikes, and the truck stopped just past where the Captain and his men were waiting. There was crying and shouting coming from the trailer, and though the driver and another man in the cab of the truck tried to run off into the desert, they were quickly captured. Not a shot was fired, and the Captain was thinking this was one of the easiest operations he had conducted. Until he opened the door of the semi's trailer.

Crammed into the 30-foot trailer were sixty children, most of them in their early teens and almost all of them girls. The Captain was expecting adults, people who had paid for a chance to cross the border into the U.S. in the hope of finding work. The children were still crying and upset from the shock of stopping so rapidly, and after a few moments it dawned on the Captain what he was seeing, and it made him sick.

He knew sex trafficking was big business in Mexico, but he had never experienced the horror of seeing children on the verge of being lost in the sex trade right in front of him. His men looked at him with questioning faces, as if to say, what do we do now? The Captain told his men to unload the children, and then he called for the bus to come and take them to, where? He guessed that most of them had been sold by their parents, or taken off the streets of large cities, or perhaps been lied to about where they were going. The Captain had no idea what would happen to them, that wasn't his responsibility. His responsibility was the two men in the semi, and hours later he had them back at his base in Hermosillo. He spent hours interrogating them, but got nowhere. They had only been hired the day before to drive the trailer to the tunnel, using a map they had been given, and then told to walk the children through the tunnel to the American side. They would be met there by other men who would take the children. For this they would be paid $200 each. The U.S. Border Patrol had captured the men on the other side of the tunnel, who also said they knew nothing beyond putting the children in another semi after they fed them and given them water. They were to receive instructions by phone after that, but of course they never made the call to the number they were given, which turned out to be an untraceable burner phone.

The Captain returned to his normal job of working against the smugglers who took people across the border for money. It was dangerous work, but nothing like working against the cartels. The cartels bought every police and army officer they could on the Mexican side of the border, and always seemed to be one step ahead of the authorities. Though not as lucrative as drug smuggling, taking people across the border was big business, and the Captain knew there were dangers involved, and had taken precautions to protect himself and his family. He always wore a bullet-proof vest, and assigned two of his most trusted men to guard his family when he was on duty. However, he had unwittingly crossed a line when he interfered with the cartel who ran the largest sex trafficking operation in Mexico. The sixty children he intercepted, and the tunnel that was destroyed, represented a substantial loss, one that could not be overlooked. Someone had to pay.

The Captain was a religious man, and attended church every Sunday with his family. The cartel had followed him for several weeks to find out how they might take their revenge, and settled on an ambush as the Captain drove his family home from Sunday Mass. His SUV had bulletproof glass, but was no match for the RPG that caught the vehicle in the rear as it slowed down at a traffic circle in the middle of Hermosillo. The force of the explosion flipped the vehicle and caught it on fire. It came to rest on its side, with the driver's door facing the sky. The Captain managed to free himself and fell to the ground. He was intending to help his family when he was shot twice in the back, falling back to the ground. Moments later the SUV exploded, killing his wife and two sons. He was showered with debris, and left for dead by the attackers, who were sure they had accomplished their mission. The three men responsible sped away from the scene, the entire episode taking less than two minutes. Police and ambulances responded within minutes, though there was not much they could do. Witnesses were confused about the number of men, the make of the getaway car, and how long the attack lasted. The attackers would never be found, and there wasn't much of an investigation by either the police or the army. These type of attacks were all too common, and they had virtually no leads they could follow that might lead to the killers.

The Captain survived the attack, though he was in a coma for several weeks. His superiors made the decision to move him to another hospital in Cabo San Lucas, and let the media know he had died in the attack. They army made a show of burying him with his family, and kept the number of people who knew he was alive to an absolute minimum. When he came out of the coma, he was told about his family. He took the news apparently without emotion, and began to think about how he would avenge their deaths. However, in the months he spent recuperating from his injuries, he had a growing awareness that even if he could find those responsible, it would change nothing. The Captain was above all else a rational man who believed in right and wrong, good and evil, God and the devil. He would kill them, and then what? Like many who survive a terrible tragedy, he was filled with survivor's guilt. As he struggled to regain his health and the use of his body, what saved him was the amount of time he had to think about his life and what he believed. If he had been able to immediately hunt for those who killed his family, his life would have taken a completely different turn. However, because he had to spend hours either in rehab or lying in bed, much of the anger and revenge that consumed him slowly left, replaced by the question: what do I do now?

The one image that continued to haunt him was the trailer full of children he had saved from exploitation. He had lost his own children, might he be able to save others who had no chance at life? There was the added thought, though it never broke through his consciousness, that in saving children he would in some way, no matter how small, be hurting those who had taken his family from him. When he was able to leave the hospital, he took a medical discharge, and began looking for a place he might serve. When it became obvious that working through the church would be easiest path to help the truly desperate, he spent two years at a seminary in Guadalajara, and then was ordained a priest. They sent him to El Bajo, to a church and orphanage where the priest had died earlier that year. Twenty years later, he was still at the church, saving those he could, and becoming a fixture in the town.

Like many in the priesthood, he had moments of doubt, and wished at times he had stayed in the army, remarried, and had another family. The doubts always passed, however, and he looked upon the hundreds of children he had saved and then sent out into the world as his family. No one in the small community, neither the children or the Sisters or anyone in the town, knew about his background. He kept the identity he had been given when he was injured, and for the first few years in El Bajo he kept a low profile. As his faith became more personal over the years, he came to understand it wasn't enough to feed, clothe and educate the children; it was his responsibility to bring them under the umbrella of the church. He was largely successful; the three Nuns who served at the community had all been raised there, and had chosen to freely give back what had been given to them. From what he could glean after the children left the orphanage, most of them continued in the faith he had tried to instill in them.

Still, the orphanage got by on a shoestring budget, and depended on the gifts of local merchants, offerings by parishioners, and some assistance from the Diocese of Ensenada. The priest always believed God would provide, but sometimes God seemed to toy with him as the shelves became bare and he wondered how he was going to feed the children. Something always came through, but it was emotionally draining living on the edge for so many years. Now this young American had arrived at his doorstep offering to bring the community into the digital age, which he knew would greatly benefit the children when they left the orphanage for the real world. What else would he offer? The priest was wise enough to know that Jacob might only stay as long as whatever had driven him there preyed on his heart and soul. It might also happen that the tedium of living in relative poverty would wear on him, and one day he would be gone. Father Rodrigo decided he would accept whatever help Jacob would offer, and not be surprised if and when he left. If he had known how long Jacob would remain at the orphanage, he would have been astonished, and would have considered that a miracle.

5

Breakfast was at 7.30, after a short devotion in the chapel. The meal was some sort of hot cereal Jacob was not familiar with, and the usual tortillas. He sat with the children, and began to learn some of their names. He explained to them God had sent him to the orphanage to help in whatever way he could, and hoped he would get to know them in the coming weeks. It wasn't exactly a lie, because Jacob believed there was something providential about his arrival at El Refugio. He helped the children detailed to clean up after the meal, and then he went to find Father Rodrigo, who was not at breakfast. Jacob asked one of the Nuns where he might be. She only shook her head, and said,

"God knows."

Not wanting to leave without talking to the priest first, Jacob waited on the front steps of the church, watching people walk up and down the street. He wasn't in any hurry, and in waiting he looked

161

again at the list he had drawn up during the night. There was $9,000 in his backpack, and he might have to get more to purchase what he needed. He had not brought more cash into the country in order to stay within the requirements of Mexican law. There would be no problem getting more money in Ensenada, he even thought about opening an account there to make his financial transactions easier.

After almost an hour, he saw Father Rodrigo walking back up the street from the main Highway below. A child was holding his hand, one that Jacob recognized from dinner. They both sat down next to Jacob when they reached the church.

"I'm sorry if you had to wait. Each day I take one of the children down to the store for a piece of candy. Then we stop and pray at the homes of those from the church who are sick. It's a good way to start the day."

Jacob only nodded in response. It was something Sister Flavia might have done in similar circumstances.

"I'm going to go into Ensenada to get what we talked about. You said last night something about the electricity."

"It goes off from time to time. The infrastructure here is old and always breaking down. And sometimes I can't pay the bill on time. It happens."

"I was just curious. I'll be back later today."

The priest opened the gate, and Jacob backed out into the street. He waved goodbye and when he reached the Highway, turned north. He had seen a Home Depot in Ensenada, and would stop there first. Jacob found an 8,000 watt generator that he figured would back up the entire church and orphanage, and thought long and hard before he bought it. It was only $2500, but he didn't want to buy his way into the community. Then he thought, that's not what I'm trying to do. They could use a generator, I have the money, let's get the generator. He would have to trust that the priest could see the motives behind his act. If not, that would be the priest's problem, not his. Jacob arranged for it to be delivered in a week, enough time to find an electrician who could hook it up to the wiring in the building.

He had asked at the Home Depot where he would find a good electronics store, and minutes later pulled up in front of a large warehouse just off the main highway. Two hours later he left with six computers, and all the equipment necessary to install and network them together. He still had some money left, so he put off going to the bank until another day. Jacob was eager to begin; the time for searching was over, the time for doing had arrived.

Father Rodrigo helped him bring all the equipment into his office, where they would store it until he and Jacob figured out where to set everything up. The children were studying in the large room, and had no idea their world was about to expand. When the two men were finished, Jacob thought he better tell the priest about the generator. Father Rodrigo looked at him without speaking, he had guessed that when Jacob asked him about the electricity he had something in mind.

"It's not good for the computers, if the power suddenly goes on or off. It could hurt them. I just wanted to be careful. I think you'll need an electrician to install it. I don't think I can do it."

"I know someone."

And that was that.

6

There was only one option for Internet, and it took a week for them to come out and connect the church to their network of fiber optic cable. Jacob spent that week helping during school hours and creating a space for the computers in the large room. The children were intrigued by Jacob's presence, and gradually warmed up to him as he spent more time with them. When they learned he had been raised in an orphanage, they became even friendlier, and soon he was on his way to becoming a fixture in the community. His relationship with the three Nuns, however, was more restrained. They allowed him the freedom to work with the children during school, but there wasn't much social interaction between them, though Jacob tried to break through their reserve. When he asked Father Rodrigo how he might go about becoming their friend, the priest merely replied,

"Give them time."

The priest was almost as much an enigma as the Nuns. He would give Jacob tasks to do each day, and then disappear each morning with one of the children to spend time in the neighborhood. When the generator was delivered they spent the day together with an electrician connecting it to the power grid, but even then the priest was all business. Jacob suspected that the priest was waiting to gauge the strength of Jacob's commitment, at least that was his hope. The thought of living in a community where he didn't relate to the other adults was unsettling.

When he finally connected the computers to the Internet, his life suddenly became much busier. Father Rodrigo knew the value for the children becoming familiar with how computers worked, and the vast amount of information now available to them. He had Jacob draw up a plan on how he would teach the children, and then after approving it, Jacob suddenly had more work than he had time. Since there were only six computers he divided the children into five groups and spent 30 minutes each day with each group. He spent his evenings figuring out how best to slowly bring the children into the digital world, and gradually evolved a plan that would not only introduce the children to the world of cyberspace, but actually teach them how to navigate the Internet, just as he had at their age. It would take several months to get the children up to speed, and already Jacob was thinking of how he might teach them skills that would equip them to find work when the left the community.

Father Rodrigo was an early riser, preferring to do the business end of the community before he began his day working in the orphanage and out in the neighborhood. He was surprised one morning when he needed to go to one of the storerooms on the second floor where Jacob lived and saw light coming out from under the door. It was just after 5 a.m., and the priest knocked lightly on his door. Jacob had been looking at his trading accounts, and was startled by the noise. He opened the door to find the priest standing there, a quizzical look on his face. Father Rodrigo noticed that Jacob was wearing the same clothes from the day before, and though it was obvious he had not slept, the young man didn't look tired or sleepy.

"You are up early."

"I'm working on my business. I guess time just got away from me."

"It must be very important for you to stay up all night."

"I've never needed much sleep. It's not a big deal."

The priest nodded his head, and then asked Jacob if he would like to come with him when he went out that morning.

"Sure. What time do you leave?"

"I'll come and get you before breakfast. We can eat later."

Then he added,

"You are not too tired? After staying up all night?"

"I'll be fine."

Jacob had been at the community two weeks, and the priest had watched Jacob every moment he could. There had been no complaining, no seeming regret for leaving the States, and though he had spent a large amount of money on the computers and the generator, there was no hint that he wanted to be in charge or have any type of authority. Father Rodrigo decided he needed to begin to introduce him into the community at large. If he was really going to stay for the foreseeable future, he might as well become acquainted with the neighborhood.

Jacob waited patiently in his room for the priest, thinking about the state of his business. He had almost depleted his accounts when he gave St. John's the check for $850,000, leaving only enough to begin the cycle of buying stocks again. Though only three weeks had passed, there was already over $85,000 in the various accounts. The amount would grow quickly now that he had more money to invest. He would like to spend some of that money on things he felt would improve life at the community, but he knew he needed to be patient. The busyness of those first two weeks had left him with little time to think about his former life, not that Jacob was given to personal introspection. There was one way of knowing what was happening on the other side of the border, but he knew that if he went down that road it would only cause him pain and misery. So he resisted, at least for the present, bringing Megan's blog up on his computer. He tried to not think about the unfairness of it all; that he had to leave the one person he thought he might have had a chance to live a normal life with. For the moment, however, Sister Flavia, and the purpose he had found through her example, was stronger than the attraction he had toward Megan.

The priest knocked lightly on his door, and then they walked out the front of the church and down the street toward the highway. Father Rodrigo didn't bring a child with him as usual, and Jacob asked him why they were alone. The priest smiled, and said,

"I only bring one child at a time."

It was the first time Jacob could remember the priest smiling, and shrugged his shoulder in reply. Jacob was anything but a child, but he was certainly much younger than the priest, who could have almost been his grandfather.

They turned right at the main highway, and walked along past the shops that were just opening for the day. He motioned Jacob into a small restaurant, and they sat at a small table. Father Rodrigo apparently was known by the owner, who brought them two cups of coffee. After setting down their drinks, the man took the priest's hand and muttered something under his breath that Jacob could not make out.

"I helped his family many years ago. It's just how he shows his gratitude. He also gives us tortillas several times a week."

"Does he go to your church?"

"No, he goes to the big church across from the plaza. It's better for his business to go to that church. It's common here, if you are a businessman, to go to the church your customers attend."

Jacob thought, it's common in the U.S as well, but kept those thoughts to himself.

"Tell me about your business. It must be very important to keep you up all night."

Jacob looked out to the highway, at the trucks going both north and south. Highway 1 ran the length of Baja California, almost a thousand miles from end to end. He didn't want to lie, but he also did not want to reveal the scope of his activity. Jacob had confided to one priest the extent of his ability to create wealth, and now as a result he was sitting in a small café in an out of the way Mexican town. He did not have the capacity to feel sorry for himself, but he did feel regret, which was almost the same thing.

"I manage money for people, buying and selling stocks. I have to follow the market each day and make decisions for my clients."

What he told the priest was the truth, though Jacob knew Father Rodrigo would take from his words a picture that didn't represent the results of Jacob's "business." He did manage money, but his client at the moment was the community run by Father Rodrigo. He did buy and sell stocks, but only those stocks his program told him to. He didn't really have to follow the market, his program worked no matter what the market did. And Father Rodrigo would never guess that Jacob would generate millions of dollars in income during the next year.

166

"You're very young to have the trust of your clients. You must be good at what you do."

"I have two degrees from Harvard university. It sort of comes naturally to me."

He didn't mean to boast, and the priest did not take it that way. As they sipped their coffee, Jacob fervently hoped the conversation would go in a different direction. Which it did.

"We need to go if we're going to get back to the church in time for school."

Jacob looked at his watch and knew that the children would not be ready for school for about two hours. What would they do until then?

It turned out that they would visit several merchants in the center of town, some of whom donated food or other items to the orphanage. The priest was always welcomed, and before he left each place asked how he might pray for each man or woman. He thanked them for their generosity to the orphanage, telling each one that they would blessed for their kindness to the children. Finally, they headed back to the community, stopping along the way to visit two homes where there were sick family members.

The priest knocked on the door of the first house, and was invited in with the wave of a hand by an older woman, who then took Father Rodrigo's hand and kissed it in greeting. He introduced Jacob, and asked Jacob to wait while he went into the bedroom, where the mother of the house was lying in bed. Jacob could hear the conversation from where he was sitting in the outer room, and heard the priest pray first for her recovery, and then for peace in her heart.

When he came out of the room, he motioned for Jacob to follow him out of the house. The two men didn't speak as they walked down the street, and Jacob wondered if it would be appropriate to ask what was wrong with the woman they had visited. He figured that if Father Rodrigo had brought him along it was because he wanted him to get to know what it was the priest did, so he asked,

"What's wrong with her?"

"She is ill. She will probably die. She has been ill for some time."

"Has she been to a doctor?"

"Of course. Mexico has national health insurance. But the need is greater than the resources. She could be in the hospital if she wanted, but she wants to die at home."

They continued to walk in silence, and though there were many questions Jacob wanted to ask, he sensed the priest brought him along strictly to observe. He was wrong.

The next house was even smaller than the first, and only had three rooms. Again, the priest was greeted warmly, and this time he motioned for Jacob to follow him into the room where another woman was lying quietly on a small bed. She rose up into a sitting position on the bed when the priest entered, and like the others kissed his hand in greeting. He introduced Jacob as a new member of the community, and explained to him that she had recently had a miscarriage, and was slowly recovering. Then, out of nowhere, he asked Jacob to pray for her.

The last thing Jacob wanted to do was to make the woman uncomfortable, and trying to not show any of the bewilderment he was feeling, he closed his eyes and was about to pray when the priest took his hand and put it in the hand of the woman. Father Rodrigo nodded at Jacob, who had opened his eyes, and then Jacob looked at the woman.

"God, please help this lady to get better. And give her peace for her heart. Amen."

It wasn't lost on the priest that it was almost exactly the same prayer he had said at the first house, and he could see the embarrassment on Jacob's face. The woman, however, was grateful for his words, and thanked him, telling him he would always be welcome in her home. The two men left, turning down the street towards the church. Jacob waited for the priest to say something, but he was silent. When they reached the church, just as the children were walking from the dining room to the school, the priest said to Jacob,

"You're a good listener. Maybe we can teach you to pray while you are here."

Father Rodrigo would make good on his promise, though it would take time and patience for the priest to peel back the complicated relationship Jacob had with God.

7

After a week, it was obvious that Jacob had left San Diego. He did not show up at Mass for three days, and then missed the Friday night singles group. Megan had tried several times to call him, but each time she was told his phone number was no longer in service. When she asked Father Stephen if he knew anything, the priest answered that he knew no more than she did. Which in one sense was true, but in another, broader sense, was almost a blatant lie. The priest knew that Jacob had met with the Bishop, and then less than forty-eight hours later had disappeared. When he was told by the Bishop that there would in all likelihood be no more money coming to the church from Jacob's foundation, the priest could surmise what had happened.

In a battle of wills, Jacob had won. The Bishop, whom Father Stephen knew to be a proud and determined man, had thought that he could subvert Jacob to his will with the power and prestige of his office as well as the teachings of the church. He did not understand, as Father Stephen did, that Jacob's allegiance wasn't to teachings of the church as much to the form and function of the church. The priest would never know the part Megan's father played in the entire sordid affair. It was up to Father Stephen to tell the committee he had set up to distribute Jacob's money that it would no longer be needed. When asked why, he was only able to say that circumstances had changed, and the donor had withdrawn his donations. The only person who noticed that Jacob wasn't at the meeting was Megan, who for several weeks tried to track Jacob down using the resources she had at the newspaper.

It wasn't as if there was any spoken or even unspoken commitment between them, but she thought there might have been. She had never met anyone like him; a young man who seemed to take his faith seriously, who wasn't in a hurry to establish a relationship, and someone who had depth of experience and character beyond his years. Which made his disappearance all the more disconcerting. It was so odd that she thought about contacting the police until she spoke to Jacob's landlord. Jacob had called her several days after leaving, and told her he would not be back, and hoped he had left her enough money to cover the expense of making the apartment ready for the next tenant. Megan learned that Jacob did not tell her where he had gone, only that he had to leave suddenly. There could be no family emergency, since he was an orphan, and aside from Father Stephen, there wasn't anyone else she could talk to; no friends, co-workers, no neighbors. She had known Jacob for less than a year, but in the coming months and years she would measure every other young man she met against him, and they would all fall short. Most young women, had they been deserted by someone they were interested in, would have written him off and moved on with their lives. Megan, however, believed there was more to the story than she knew, and would continue to search for him off and on for years.

There was another person who was searching for Jacob, someone who had come to see the truth of the verse "pride goes before a fall." The Bishop had come to his senses two days later, when the reality that he had lost potentially hundreds of thousands of dollars due to his overweening sense of power and importance fully hit him. He was now willing to talk with Jacob about percentages, but when Father Stephen told him that Jacob had not attended Mass and was not answering his phone, his heart sank. When it became clear that Jacob had up and left, without leaving a trace of where he had gone, the Bishop knew he was beaten. He thought about tracking the young man down, but realized the futility of the effort. If Jacob had left that abruptly, there was little chance he would be willing to consider any type of compromise with someone he obviously despised. The Bishop would have to let it go, and he was not in the least pleased.

8

It was several months into Jacob's stay at the community that the priest had an opportunity to talk with Jacob about his life prior to coming to the orphanage. Jacob had spent those first months working primarily with the children; spending most of each afternoon helping them become familiar with not only working on the computers, but learning how to use basic programs that one day would help them perhaps find some kind of meaningful employment. He spent more time with the older children, especially those who were close to leaving the orphanage when they turned eighteen. Father Rodrigo was usually able to find them some kind of employment through his many connections, but the jobs were usually unskilled and low paying. Jacob's hope was that if he could teach basic computer skills, and perhaps some programming, they might be able to find jobs in the burgeoning tech sector either in Ensenada or Tijuana. Jacob was also able to convince Father Rodrigo that it would be beneficial to the children if they could learn English. Knowing English would make it possible to find employment in the tourist sector, which generally paid better and offered the chance for advancement.

With the priest's approval, Jacob began to teach English every afternoon for one hour. The children were willing to give up some of their play time, and Jacob proved to be a good teacher. He found a program specifically designed to teach English to young Latino children, printed up lesson plans for each student on the printer he convinced Father Rodrigo he needed for the task. As it became obvious after several months that Jacob wasn't going anywhere, first the children, and then the Nuns, began to warm up to him. The busyness was a tonic for him; Jacob was happiest when he had work to do; not only did he have plenty of work, but the work was fulfilling, and brought back memories of his own life growing up at the community.

Which is not to say that Jacob experienced happiness like "normal" people. His happiness was wrapped up in fulfilling his purpose, which was an extension of devotion to Sister Flavia. It was the priest who noticed that though Jacob was by now fully embedded in the ministry of the orphanage, there was a distance in his relationship with God. Jacob attended every chapel with the children each day, as well as the church service on Sunday. But he never participated in the Mass, and Father Rodrigo thought it was time he found out why Jacob was ready to give so much of himself in service to others, but so little of himself to God.

Jacob had let several months go by without suggesting any other improvements he thought he could provide for the community. He wanted to show the priest he wasn't only there to fix things; he needed Father Rodrigo to understand he was committed to the ministry of the orphanage for the long haul. However, his trading accounts were now bursting with money, and he felt it might be time to let the priest know he was ready to help with the more pressing physical needs of the community.

Father Rodrigo had the same thought, and after dinner one evening took Jacob aside and asked him if he would go with him to Ensenada the next day. When Jacob asked him what he needed to do in Ensenada, the priest said,

"I need to buy a truck. The one we have is not able to be fixed. Or so says the mechanic."

Jacob nodded, knowing that Father Rodrigo was signaling that he was willing to let Jacob use his money for the benefit of the community.

"Why do you need a truck?"

"There are people and businesses in Ensenada that would donate food to us if we could pick it up. People I have talked with in the last month or so."

"I have a condition. I hope it won't be a problem."

Father Rodrigo believed he knew Jacob, and wasn't concerned when Jacob talked about having a "condition".

"Yes?"

"If you're going to do this, do it right. Get a new truck, one that will last for years."

It made sense, but sometimes things that made sense did not accomplish the purpose for which they were intended.

"It would be better to buy a used truck. A new truck would bring unwanted attention. No one in this neighborhood has a new truck. Most will never own a car."

Jacob understood, and nodded his head in agreement. Then he left with some of the children to supervise them while they played games on the computer. As he let the children take turns at the computers, his mind was already racing ahead to what else he might do to help the community. He had learned from one of the Nuns that the orphanage had to turn away several children in last month; there just wasn't enough space in the community. There was, however, a vacant warehouse that joined the back wall of the orphanage, the wall where Jacob's room was located. It fronted another street, but could easily be joined to the community by knocking a hole in the wall. He had no idea how much it would cost, but it would easily be within his reach. Jacob knew how much it must bother the priest to turn away children; surely he would be open to the idea.

172

It was only a short drive to Ensenada, and once they were on the main highway, Father Rodrigo asked Jacob, who was driving his car, about his first months at the community.

"I think I'm beginning to fit in, now that I have something to contribute. I really enjoy working with the children. It reminds me of home."

The priest wanted to explore the subject of Jacob's time at the orphanage he grew up in, but before he could speak, Jacob said,

"I heard you had to turn away some children this month. It must be hard to do that."

"This happens sometimes. I try to find other places for them. Occasionally I can place them in other orphanages."

"Have you ever thought about making the community larger? I mean if it was possible?"

Father Rodrigo knew where Jacob was going, and thought for a moment before he answered.

"Even Jesus did not heal everyone He could. He didn't feed everyone He could. He did not save everyone He could. I believe God gives us what we can do, and does not judge us for not doing more."

"But what if He gives you the resources to do more? Aren't we responsible to use what we have to benefit others? Otherwise it's just money sitting in a bank somewhere."

The argument made sense, and the priest had often dreamt of what he would do if money were not an issue. It pained him to turn away children, even if they found a home in another orphanage. He knew there were children in Tijuana and Ensenada who lived on the streets, many of whom would end up in trailers heading to the United States or other parts of Mexico, lost into the dark world of sex trafficking. He had one concern, and though it might offend Jacob, he thought it best to be honest with him.

"I would not want to start something I could not finish."

"I understand that."

"I would also need to know more about your business. The way you make your money."

Sister Flavia had known about his business, but the thought of revealing how much money he made troubled him. He knew from experience how money could tempt and corrupt people. The priest sensed the conflict in Jacob.

"It seems we have to trust each other here. I have to trust that you'll not begin something and then leave us, and you need to trust that I will use the money wisely. Something like that?"

"It's more than that, but yes, something like that."

They had almost reached the truck dealership, and Father Rodrigo suggested they continue the conversation later. Three hours later they left in possession of a four door Ford F-150 pickup. Jacob called his bank, and had them wire the money to the dealership. The cost was just over $12,000, which represented less than 3% of the money Jacob had in his accounts. When they were finished, they drove the truck off the lot and left Jacob's car at the dealership. They would pick up it the next time they were in Ensenada.

They stopped at a restaurant near the harbor, one of the places that had promised to provide food for the orphanage if the priest could come and get it. They sat in the back to have a measure of privacy.

"Tell me about your business. You bought the truck like I buy candy for the children every morning."

What the priest was afraid of was that Jacob was somehow involved, or had been involved, in some type of illegal behavior. He had known men in the drug trade who had made large amounts of money, and then sought to clear their consciences by giving money to charitable causes. He doubted that Jacob fell into that category, but he needed to be sure.

"When I told you that I buy and sell stocks, and manage money for my clients, that was the truth. What I didn't make clear is that right now you are the client."

"You will understand my skepticism that it seems unlikely that such a young man could make such large sums of money. Do you know things that others do not?"

"If by that you mean am I doing anything illegal, the answer is no."

Jacob decided that if he wanted to gain the trust of the priest he needed to be more specific about his success.

"I wrote a computer program that looks at many different variables in how certain stocks relate to how the news is reported. It took me several years, with lots of mistakes along the way. Most people would not have had the patience to see the project through. I have only used it three times, and each time for a specific purpose. I have no interest in money except for how it can help others."

The priest believed him for the obvious reason that Jacob had been for several months living in a small room with no heat, and cleaning himself with cold water he scooped out of a plastic bucket.

"If I wanted to expand the community, small at first, would that be possible?"

"Yes. I don't think that would be a problem."

"If I started something, I would want the assurance it would be seen through. You understand my concern?"

"Yes. You don't want to be left without funds. I understand that."

They paused as the waitress brought their food, and after the priest blessed the food, he asked Jacob how he should proceed.

"Give me a plan of what you want to do and how much you think it might cost over five years. Then we can talk about specifics."

Father Rodrigo knew they would end up talking about hundreds of thousands of dollars; an amount of money that was beyond his experience. What that amount of money was doing in the hands of such a young man he could only guess. He was now ready to ask Jacob about his life in the orphanage, and for the next hour Jacob told his story to the priest. He left out only one detail; there was no way Jacob was going to tell the priest about his anomaly. It was his, and since Sister Flavia had died and Noah was living in a psychiatric hospital, and his alone. The priest listened patiently as Jacob talked, and only interrupted to ask questions that made things clearer for him. When Jacob related to the priest his encounter with the Bishop, the priest nodded his head in agreement. He understood about power from his time in the military, how it could corrupt even the best of men.

Later that evening, when everyone else was asleep, Jacob was typing an email he had been thinking about for months. There was no way the orphanage would ever come close to spending all the money his trading accounts were generating. He had not yet shut down his foundation, and in his email he included legal forms that would transfer ownership to the recipient. Assuming the recipient was willing to take over the duties from Jacob, the money could again be used for its intended purpose. He included a modest salary, recognizing there would be time involved in finding needy people to distribute the money to. Jacob transferred the money to an account he had opened in Zurich, Switzerland, in order to cover his tracks. The email was routed through several severs scattered around the world in order to mask his location. He didn't want anyone to come looking for him; he was just beginning to work his way into the world of the orphanage. Jacob was afraid of being distracted from his purpose, which was still the defining piece of his life. Holding his hand over the send button, he went back over everything he had done, trying to make sure his location would not be compromised. When he was sure he had covered his tracks, he sent the email to Megan, telling her that there was $500,000 in the foundation, with more to come. The email account he had created would not accept replies; he would be able to tell if she accepted his proposal if she used the money in the next 90 days. Then he closed his computer, and trying not to think about the past, lay on his bed waiting for daylight and thinking about the day to come.

9

Megan looked over the email, and for a few minutes was lost in remembrance. Jacob had been gone for months, and had made no effort to contact her. For weeks, she had tried to find out what had happened to him, all without success. There was no family, no employer, no friends, and though she suspected that Father Stephen knew something, he was not forthcoming. When the committee that oversaw the distribution of charitable funds was dissolved a few weeks after Jacob disappeared, she wondered if somehow the two were connected. The most Father Stephen would say was that the Foundation had changed its mind, and had decided to go in another direction. This seemed odd, given the amount of money involved, and the fact that the committee had barely had a chance to begin its work. It was strange, but it wasn't the only strange thing happening in her life.

Her father had become short with the family, which was totally out of character for him. Normally an attentive and even doting father to his children, he seemed preoccupied and distracted, worried about something that he was keeping to himself. As the oldest child, Megan had always been close to her father, now he would pass her in the home and not notice that she was there. When he found from an offhand remark by Megan that Jacob had seemingly vanished without a trace, he took the news without comment, and immediately went to his study, shutting the door behind him. He called the Bishop, who told him he already knew about Jacob, and that he needed to drop the matter.

So Jacob was out there somewhere, though the email gave no indication of where he might be living. She had a friend at the newspaper try and find where the email originated, but he gave up after realizing that Jacob had covered his tracks so well he doubted anyone would find out the location of the computer used in sending the email. He told Megan that even if they did find out where it came from there was no guarantee Jacob was still there. It was a dead end, plain and simple.

Then there was the matter of the Foundation. Since she now knew where the money came from that flowed into St. John's, she was even more confused. He had attached to the email two months of information on his trading accounts so she could see how the Foundation received its funds. It wasn't the amount of money in the trading accounts that impressed her, but the fact that Jacob lived as simply as he did given the amount of money he had access to. Any other young man she knew would have flaunted that amount of wealth, and would not have lived in a small apartment and driven a ten-year old car. Finally, there was the question of what she should do about the Foundation. There was no way to get in touch with Jacob to get answers to her questions, indeed, every instinct she had told her to leave the money untouched and walk away.

And yet. He was trusting her with vast amounts of money, money he had originally planned to distribute through the church. In the back of her mind she could not get rid of the thought that there was a connection between the church and his disappearance, but it would be years before she would know the truth. However, because Jacob had made such a profound impact on her through his obvious devotion to those in need, and his commitment to values and beliefs she shared, she decided to accept the responsibility. Over the next several years she would give away millions of dollars, and although she had no contact with Jacob, he was a hidden presence in the back of her mind, surfacing every month when she received a fresh infusion of money into the Foundation.

10

It was when they finished the new addition to the orphanage, converting the vacant warehouse into a dormitory, bathroom and kitchen, that Jacob's life took a new direction. He had been at the orphanage for over two years, and was now an integral part of the community. His time was divided between teaching the children English and computer skills, overseeing the remodeling of the warehouse, and occasionally going with the priest on his morning forays into the community. It would be fair to say that Jacob was happy, because for him happiness flowed from serving, though the priest recognized that the motives behind Jacob's service were mixed, and perhaps even contradictory. But he was patient with the young man, letting him find his own way. Then one morning on their way into Ensenada he asked Jacob why he never participated in the Mass, even though he attended chapel and church with the rest of the community.

The question came out of nowhere, and caught Jacob off guard. He always sat in the back of the chapel during the service, and it was obvious to everyone in their small community that Jacob abstained from Mass, even though he participated in every other function of the orphanage.

"Do we have to talk about this now?"

"We have the time. You have been with us over two years, we've never talked about your journey."

"What journey?"

"Everyone is on a journey. When you came here you said your journey had brought you to us. You have helped us in many ways. I wonder if we have helped you?"

Jacob hated talking about himself, and looked out the window of the truck as they drove north on the highway to Ensenada.

"I don't need any help. But thanks for asking."

"May I again ask why you don't take the Mass? You are very committed to serving, but I still wonder why you serve. It seems you take comfort in the church, but not in God. I wonder why that is?"

There was an answer to the question, and as Jacob looked at the priest sitting next to him
he thought about Sister Margaret. She had known about the anomaly that he and Sister Flavia shared, but had never said anything nor had it apparently changed how she viewed them. There wasn't a day that went by where Jacob didn't realize that he was different from everyone else. Though the thought had not yet broken through to his consciousness, he was tired of hiding in plain sight.

"If you want to talk about this, come by my room at three in the morning. Then I'll tell you anything you want to know."

The priest nodded his head, and did not ask why Jacob had chosen to talk so early in the morning. He decided to change the topic of conversation, and asked Jacob how he was progressing in hiring staff for the expanded orphanage. They would begin accepting new children in a week, the remodeled warehouse would allow 25 more children to join the community. Jacob was in charge of hiring two more cooks, two people to do laundry and other cleaning, and, finally, another teacher. Father Rodrigo would find the children; Jacob would make sure the orphanage was ready to receive them.

"We're ready to go, except for the teacher. It's been harder than I thought finding someone who will fit in. I want a person who can speak English, and knows something about computers. I'm talking to someone on Skype later today, a young woman who lives in Mexico City."

"Okay. Keep me informed. The first children will be arriving next week."

Later that afternoon, after they had returned from buying furniture and other supplies needed for the new children, Jacob waited in his room for his Skype call.

Precisely at 3 p.m., the time they agreed to talk, his computer came to life, and in moments he was looking at Maria Vega Alvarado. She had just graduated from a Catholic university in Mexico City with a degree in teaching, and was fluent in English. Jacob told her about the orphanage, the recent expansion, and what they were looking for in a teacher. He spoke for about 15 minutes, and then asked her if she had any questions.

179

"How does an orphanage afford to pay more than I would make working in the public sector? I'm just curious."

"We have people who support us with generous gifts. If you are concerned about your salary, we could pay you the first six months up front, if you like."

"Thank you. Also, would it be possible to live in the town, instead of the orphanage?"

"I suppose so, if you chose to. We built a room for our next teacher, it is the only room in the community with a private bath. But it's your choice."

"You live at the orphanage?"

"Yes. For two years."

The conversation paused while Maria considered her options. She could teach in the public school system, but it paid little and did not offer the opportunity to work with the less fortunate, which was important to her. If she lived in the orphanage she could save most of what she earned, which was also attractive. She came from a modest family, and the thought of being able to help her parents or siblings if needed was appealing to her.

"When would you want me to start?"

"Next week. We would send you money to fly from Mexico City to Tijuana."

"I'll take the job. I'd like to live at the orphanage, at least to start."

"I'll send you money via Western Union. Let us know about your flight."

He didn't mean to be abrupt, it was just like Jacob to move on to the next thing he had to do. When he ended the call, he could have never foreseen that in two years he would ask her to marry him.

11

The priest knocked lightly on Jacob's door at exactly three o'clock. Jacob motioned him inside, and the priest sat down on the one chair in the room. Jacob sat on the bed, and the priest noticed he was in the same clothes he had worn all day. Jacob was the first to speak.

"You look tired."

"I am tired. It's three o'clock in the morning. That's early even for me."

Then Father Rodrigo noticed that Jacob didn't look tired, not in the least.

"Have you not slept?"

"No. Never."

"What do you mean, never?"

"I mean that I've never slept in my life. I can't fall asleep. It's as simple as that."

The priest did not know how to respond to something so impossible, and wondered why Jacob would say something so foolish. It certainly did not fit with what he knew about the young man from the last two years.

"Why would you say such a thing? Who would believe you?"

"I only say it because it is true. If you understood, really understood, what it's like to be me, I think you would understand part of my journey."

Jacob spoke with a sadness that the priest had never seen in him before. Because the priest was at heart a rational, logical thinker, he was forced to consider that there were only three options open to him. The first was that for reasons that he could not fathom, Jacob was concocting a lie, but to what end he could not see. The second was that Jacob was suffering from some sort of nervous or psychological breakdown. That seemed implausible due to the fact that Jacob showed no signs of a breakdown or mental crisis. The third, that Jacob was telling the truth, was too fantastic to consider, or was it?

Father Rodrigo thought back over the two years he had known Jacob, and as he reflected over those two years a chill came over him. There were many times he had walked by Jacob's room on the second floor on his way to the storeroom very early in the morning and the light would be shining from under the door. How many times had he noticed Jacob wearing the same clothes the next morning at breakfast? He had assumed Jacob had just fallen asleep in his clothes and been in too much of a hurry the next morning to change. Finally, Jacob never seemed to be tired, never went to bed early, and was always willing to work late into the night when needed. He recalled that when he remarked on this to Jacob, he had always replied that he didn't need much sleep.

"This is true?"

Jacob nodded, and in that instant Father Rodrigo knew the enormity of the secret that Jacob carried, and shaking his head slowly from side to side, he said,

"I'm so sorry."

Jacob spent the next hour telling the priest about the anomaly, and about how it had defined and shaped his life. He told about arriving on the doorstep of perhaps the one person in the world who shared what he was, and how he would not have survived without her protection. The endless hours reading when everyone else was asleep, the accumulation of vast amounts of information, the ability to see life in terms of puzzles, and the growing capacity to put the pieces of those puzzles together.

He told the priest about the one person who had discovered what he was, and how tragically that had ended. The death of Sister Flavia had caused him to go out on his own, and how everything he did was because of the values she had embodied. The ability to make vast amounts of money was only to fulfill that purpose, and though it had ended badly in San Diego, he felt that in El Bajo he had found a place where his purpose was being fulfilled. He did not talk about Megan, and he said nothing about his father.

The priest was left with more than enough to ponder, but thought the better of asking Jacob the questions that filled his mind. He did, however, come back to what had brought them together so early that morning.

"Why don't you take the Mass, Jacob? Does it have something to do with your condition?"

"Sister Flavia called it a gift. And I get that, I really do. But it's also a curse. There isn't anyone else like me in the world, can you understand that? I've read thousands of books, and have two degrees from Harvard, but I've never had a girlfriend. I'm afraid that one day someone will find out what I am, and that my life will be over. "The Man Who Never Sleeps." Can you imagine what that would be like? I don't mean to complain, but why did God give this to me?"

"You do mean to complain, and it's okay. God is big enough to hear your complaint."

With that said, Jacob did something he had never done before in his life. He broke down and wept, his tears falling on the concrete floor, the years of guarding what he was flowing out of him in a torrent of emotion that he did not know he possessed. The priest got up from his chair and sat next to Jacob on the small bed. He put his arm around the young man, and said,

"God cursed His own Son, Jacob. And good came from that, nor did the curse last forever. You have brought good here through what you are. If you will let me, I would like to help you learn to live with what God has given you."

Jacob could only nod in assent to the priest's request, he had heard what Father Rodrigo had said, but was experiencing the relief that often accompanies the release of a secret that has been held for too long. His life would not change immediately, but in the next few years Jacob would slowly accept the counsel the priest offered. He began to see that instead of building his life around the memory of Sister Flavia, and the values and beliefs that defined her, he learned from the priest that those values and beliefs flowed from her relationship with God. He would not reveal what he was to anyone else until much later, and then with consequences that he could not have imagined. But the faith he would develop would sustain him during that time, though he would be stretched to the breaking point.

12

The priest thought it ironic that that night he could not fall asleep. After working all day with the workers who were finishing the remodeling on the new building, and then part of the evening setting up the furniture and beds that would be occupied the next week, he was sure he would be able to fall asleep. He had not gone back to bed after talking with Jacob early that morning, and though he was physically tired, his mind would not let go of what he had learned that day.

Jacob would be in his room, and Father Rodrigo tried to imagine what he was doing. There was always a pile of books stacked neatly in the corner, and, of course, his ever-present computer. The priest was not especially good at math, but as he lay on his bed thinking about Jacob he figured the young man had spent at least 8 years awake in the middle of the night; alone and awake. How many books could you read? How much time could you spend on a computer? What would you think about? What would keep you from going mad?

Then there was the social isolation that came from feeling you were alone in the world. After the death of Sister Flavia, there was no one else. Father Rodrigo knew the feeling of being alone in the world; after the death of his family he was cut off, adrift, and it was only his faith that enabled him to survive. Jacob had kept God at a distance, and the priest marveled at the commitment of will it took for Jacob to maintain any sense of sanity, let alone pursue what he believed was his calling in life. What a person Sister Flavia must have been, he thought. That she could impart to Jacob the values and beliefs she held, and have them guide him for years; he wished he could have known her.

Why God would have made Jacob the way He did, Father Rodrigo would never understand. There were too many mysteries in life that could not be explained, and the priest was content with that. The bigger question, the one that now confronted him as the leader of the small community that Jacob now called home was this: what was he to do with someone who possessed boundless knowledge, the ability to work around the clock, and almost limitless funds available at his disposal? Father Rodrigo knew that even though they had spent several hundred thousand dollars since Jacob had arrived, it was perhaps only a fraction of what was available to Jacob. What the priest could do with unlimited funds he could only imagine. If God didn't want him to use the money that Jacob possessed, he thought, then why send him to the orphanage?

Then, in a moment of clarity, Father Rodrigo knew that the money wasn't his to use. Jacob could have become a millionaire, living the type of hedonistic life that most young men can only dream about, but he had chosen to use the money only for good. It was now obvious to the priest that though it was a good thing to expand the community, the time had come to consolidate what they had done. He would need to help Jacob see that the fulfillment of his purpose might not mean spending millions of dollars in a quest to fix every tragedy, need or saving every lost child in the world. Jacob was unknowingly trying to fix everyone he could, because he could not fix himself.

13

Two days later Jacob was waiting at the Tijuana airport, looking at the passengers coming into the baggage claim area, scanning their faces for Maria. They had agreed to meet there since she would need to get her luggage. In the two days since he had unburdened himself to the priest, though he was not aware of it, there was a change in his demeanor and behavior. It became obvious the next day that Father Rodrigo was not going to treat him any differently, and though they worked together most of the day in the new building, he never brought up what he had learned that night. Jacob's greatest fear was being found out, and the rejection he was sure would follow. There was no doubt his fear was rooted in being abandoned by his parents, especially by his mother. Because Jacob was not introspective in the least, he didn't understand the connection between the fear he lived with and his past, though he did understand how his past had led him to the orphanage. If the priest could accept what he was, Jacob thought, then perhaps there were others, those who would not view him as some kind of aberration.

He saw her walking down the stairs into the large room crowded with other passengers, and began to move toward her. She was taller than he expected, almost as tall as he was, and after a moment she saw him walking towards her. She smiled in greeting, and said,

"Thank you for coming to get me. I hope you haven't had to wait long."

"No, not long. Let's find your bag, then we can get out of here. The traffic will be worse on the drive back."

They found the carousel for her flight, and then waited for her bag to appear. Maria was a naturally outgoing person, and found it awkward waiting in silence with Jacob for her luggage to arrive.

"Where did you learn Spanish? You speak almost without an accent."

"I lived in Miami for two years. I spent a lot of time walking around the city. Most of the people there speak Spanish first, then English."

"And you've been here for two years? At the orphanage?"

"Yes, two years. A lot has changed in two years. At the orphanage, I mean."

Maria could sense that Jacob wasn't as outgoing as she was, and wondered if she should keep the conversation going. Then she thought, I'm going to be working with him every day, I might as well find out what I can about him. However, before she could speak, her suitcase rounded the bend of the carousel, and she pointed it out to him. He maneuvered between some people, and then grabbed it quickly, and then said to Maria,

"I'm parked across the street. Follow me."

Minutes later they were paying the parking fee, and then they were out of the airport driving south through the city to Highway 1. Maria had never been close to the border before, and had never been in the United States.

"The border is close?"

"It's about five miles north from here. Lots of Americans come to Tijuana. Mainly to buy things cheaper than in the U.S."

He left unsaid the other reasons people crossed the border into Tijuana, and the fact that Father Rodrigo would be returning to Tijuana in a few days to bring several children to the orphanage, children that were now in state-run care, which was similar to being in prison. The government had little resources to help orphans, and gave them the most rudimentary care. They were more than willing to give these waifs to private institutions, relieving the state of a service they were hardly prepared to handle.

"We don't come to Tijuana very often. Most everything we need we can get in Ensenada."

It was an attempt by Jacob to keep the conversation going. He wanted to make Maria feel welcome, he just wasn't the best person at carrying a conversation. Maria, however, was much more extroverted, and said in reply,

"You said that the children would be arriving soon. Where are they coming from?"

"Father Rodrigo knows people in the government. The government takes children they find on the street, mainly children who are sick, and shelter them until they are better. They are not equipped to care for them, and are glad when we take them. It's not a problem finding children."

186

"You told me you have been at the orphanage two years. What did you do before that?"

Jacob looked out his window at the passing scenery; they had left the city proper and driving along the part of Highway 1 that overlooked the ocean. Maria's flight had arrived at noon, and Jacob asked her if she wanted to stop for lunch.

"Yes. If it's not any trouble."

"I know a vendor on this side of Ensenada. He sells shark tacos. He's a friend of Father Rodrigo."

"Shark? I've never had shark before."

"Only certain fisherman are allowed to fish for shark, so there's not many places that have it. It tastes a little different. I think you'll like it."

She noticed that he didn't answer her question, and hoped she hadn't been presumptuous in asking about Jacob's personal life.

They pulled off the road just before entering Ensenada, parking across the street from the vendor, who was busy serving other customers. Then Jacob did something that surprised Maria; he took her hand as he watched the traffic go by, and when he thought it was safe he gently guided her across the busy highway. He thought nothing of it, he was only concerned about her safety, but Maria had not held a man's hand in many months. Though it only lasted a few moments, it brought a flood of memories, both good and bad. When he let go, he said,

"It's a busy highway, you have to be careful."

She nodded, and then they walked up to the vendor, who greeted Jacob with a wave of his hand and asked how many tacos they wanted.

"Six, and two sodas."

He motioned to Maria to follow him to a table, and then they sat down and waited while the vendor cooked their food.

"I lived in San Diego before I came here."

"I'm sorry?"

"You asked me what I did before I came here. I lived in San Diego."

She had forgotten the question she had asked him, and because Jacob's answer was so general, she went a little farther.

"What did you do there?"

187

"I manage money for people. I still do, but it doesn't take all my time. I grew up in a Catholic orphanage in the United States."

She had only known Jacob for two hours, but could already see that he wasn't the most gifted conversationalist. Since they would be working together, she decided not to ask any more questions about Jacob's life. Jacob, however, since confessing his secret to the priest, was just a little more open than he would have been just two days earlier.

"You'll like working with Father Rodrigo. He's been at the orphanage for many years, and knows everyone in the town. He's also the pastor of the church."

The vendor got Jacob's attention by waving his hand, and Jacob went over to get their food. He came back with two paper plates, each having three shark tacos. He sat their sodas down on the table.

"If you want to put anything on your food, there's sauce and other stuff by the grill."

They both returned to the cart and added sauce, onions and peppers to their food. Maria noticed that the vendor smiled at Jacob, and then nodded in her direction. She immediately understood the meaning of the gesture, though Jacob had no visible reaction.

They ate in silence, watching as cars and trucks drove by on Highway 1. When they were finished, they tossed their trash in a can, and waited again to cross the street. Jacob again took her hand, and because the traffic was heavier than when they arrived, it took almost 30 seconds until they could cross safely. When they were back in the truck, Maria said,

"Thank you. You must come here often for the vendor to know you."

"We come to Ensenada at least once a week, either Father Rodrigo or me. Most of what we use at the community we get here. The next time I have to come back on the weekend, I'll bring you, if you want. I'm kind of busy during the week."

It was a throwaway line, and Jacob meant nothing by it, as Maria would come to learn. She was already sensing that Jacob was not like the other young men she had known in her short life, something that another young woman had also noticed about him.

14

They arrived at the orphanage late in the afternoon, and after parking the truck in the lot next to the church, he took her and her suitcase in through the front of the church.

"We use the church for chapel twice a day, once in the morning and again in the evening after dinner. It's not part of your job to attend, but it shows the children that we're willing to give up our time to be with them."

Maria was a Catholic, but did not consider herself especially devout. She had attended church with her family, mostly out of duty and not from a sense of devotion to the church. During her years at university, even though it was a Catholic university, like many of the students, she seldom attended any of the chapel services and often missed church as well. Like many young people, she was drawn to the opportunity of helping the less fortunate, in this case orphans. However, her decision was also based on the higher salary, the fact that she would be able to save much of what she earned, and, unknown to Jacob and Father Rodrigo, a desire to move away from her former boyfriend.

He took her through the courtyard, and then through the new door into the remodeled warehouse. There were five sections to the new part of the community; a kitchen, two sleeping areas, the classroom, two bathrooms, and a large community room for the children where they could play together. Maria was impressed by how new everything was, and said to Jacob,

"This is much better than where I went to school."

She did not say what she was really thinking, that it must have cost thousands of dollars to convert the warehouse into the new facility.

"Your room is this way."

Jacob took her through the community room, and then down a small hallway that was built into the corner of the building. They had constructed a room with a bath as far away from the other rooms as possible to give it some privacy. It wasn't large, but it had one advantage the other rooms did not have; it had an air-conditioner installed on an outside window to help with the summer heat.

He put her suitcase on the bed, hoping she would find the room acceptable. It was nicer than anything she could afford in the town, something that she understood. Her only concern was that she would be living and working in the same place, and asked Jacob if he ever spent time away from the orphanage.

"I sometimes go with Father Rodrigo in the mornings to visit people who are sick. I get into Ensenada at least once a week. We can find ways to get you some time away from the community, if that's what you want."

"Thanks. I think it would be helpful to have some personal time."

It was now almost guaranteed that Jacob and Maria would be spending time together outside of work. Jacob was already thinking how he might adjust his schedule to make sure she could accompany him on his trips to Ensenada. It was purely to accommodate her desire to not be confined to the orphanage, but over time it would change the nature of their relationship.

15

At dinner that evening Father Rodrigo introduced her to the children, staff and the three Sisters. She met with the priest after dinner in his office to go over her responsibilities, and during their conversation Father Rodrigo asked if she thought she could fit into life at the orphanage. She thought for a moment, and though she could have just said "Yes", and moved on, instead she answered by saying,

"I think so. It's not what I had in mind for my first job after university, but I wanted to be on my own. This is about as far from Mexico City as I could go."

The priest smiled, thinking there might be something or someone in Mexico City she needed to get away from. He appreciated her honesty, and was not surprised when she added that the salary, and the opportunity to save money, was a factor in her decision.

"We have generous donors, so we are able to pay a little more than the public schools. But then, sometimes the children can be difficult to teach. It will require patience and understanding; some of them have never been to school before, and some of them carry scars from tragedies they have endured. But you will learn."

"Jacob seems to know how to relate to the children. Was it hard for him at first?"

She was going to find out about Jacob eventually, so the priest decided to tell her about how Jacob arrived at the orphanage.

"I don't know what he has told you, but he came here two years ago and has helped us expand the community. Did he tell you he was raised in a Catholic orphanage?"

"Yes. In the United States."

"It seems that the Sisters who raised him did a good job of instilling in him compassion and hard work. Two characteristics you don't often see in young men."

She thought, certainly not in the young men she had known.

"When will I begin? Or maybe I should ask when the new children will arrive?"

"You can begin tomorrow by helping the Sisters and Jacob. You can watch what they do and how the children respond to them. The government is slow with completing the paperwork necessary to transfer children they are holding to us. They will call us when it is done. It might be tomorrow. You never know."

Father Rodrigo paused, looking at the young woman sitting across from him. He had wanted to find more Sisters to educate the children, but that proved to be nearly impossible. Jacob had persuaded him that they needed someone who understood computers, spoke English and possessed a college degree, and now Maria was sitting before him. He sensed that she was a sincere person, and refreshingly honest. Whether she would fit into the community was in his mind an open question.

The priest was going out the next day to the slums on the outskirts of Ensenada to look for some children he had been told were abandoned by their parents when they left looking for work across the border. They were living in a park, and going through the trash cans of a bakery that occasionally donated food to the orphanage.

"I have to make a trip into Ensenada tomorrow after breakfast. Perhaps you would like to go with me."

"Of course."

"There are some things I need to pick up. You might be able to help me."

They heard the children coming into the church for evening chapel, so they got up and walked out into the sanctuary. The children sat in the front, with a Sister on the end of each row. Jacob sat in the back, and she walked to the rear and sat next to him. When the children were seated and somewhat calm, the priest told them the story of the Prodigal Son. He emphasized the love that the father had for the son, and how much God is like the father in the story. It was short, simple, and heartfelt. He dismissed them with a short prayer, and they went to the new community room to play until bedtime.

"I'm going into Ensenada with Father Rodrigo tomorrow. I guess he needs to pick up some things."

Jacob knew why the priest was going into Ensenada, and wondered why the priest decided to take Maria with him.

"I'm sure you'll be a help to him."

It was early, but it had been a long day for her, and she excused herself and went to her room. She put her things away, and lay down on the bed, wondering what she had gotten herself into.

16

They left after breakfast, which was the usual cereal, tortillas and fruit. Maria sat with the children, and they peppered her with questions. Where was she from? What was her family like? How long was she going to stay? Jacob watched from the other end of the long table, admiring her patience in answering each question and asking each child their name and to tell her something about them. When breakfast was over, Jacob headed over to the schoolroom, nodding at her as he left the dining room.

Father Rodrigo, as usual, was not at breakfast, and returned from his morning foray into the village to find Maria waiting on the steps of the church. He had a child with him, and after dismissing the child to school, sat down next to her.

"One of the Sisters told me to wait for you here."

"We'll leave in a few moments. I want to tell you why we are going to Ensenada. I have friends there who sometimes donate to the orphanage that have noticed several children living in a park across from his restaurant. They look through his trash cans for food, and though he chases them away, they are persistent. He believes they have been abandoned by their parents who probably crossed the border looking for work. They have been there over a week, so I believe he is correct."

Maria had come from a loving, close family, and the thought that parents would abandon their children was incomprehensible. She wasn't naïve about poverty and tragedy in Mexico, it was impossible due to the drug war among the cartels and the government which left orphans, widows and suffering across the land. The priest read the bewilderment on her face.

"It may be that their parents told them they would come back for them, and they may not come with us. We will see."

"The parents won't be coming back, will they?"

"Probably not. Let's go, and see what the day will bring."

They stopped at a market on the main highway and bought enough food to feed the children, food that Father Rodrigo hoped would let them talk to the children. The priest usually took one of the Sisters with him on occasions like this, the presence of a woman helped to disarm the fear the children had of strangers.

They parked across the street from the park, and left the truck to talk to the owner of the small restaurant. He had seen them that morning when he arrived, but as they looked across the street, the park was empty. He told the priest to wait, they were probably looking for food someplace else but would be back to occupy a table under a large tree they had taken over for themselves. The priest thanked him for his concern, and took Maria back to the truck to wait.

"It's early, we'll wait and see what happens. We may also hear from the government today."

"What will you say to the children if they show up?"

"It's very difficult, you cannot tell them they have been abandoned. We merely tell them we want to get them off the streets, and bring them someplace safe. When there is a group of children, one of them will be the leader, usually the oldest. The others will follow what the leader does."

"Jacob told me you have been at the orphanage many years. You must have done this many times."

"Many times, yes. There are always children waiting to be saved. We cannot save them all, but we do what we can."

"You must think of the children as your family."

Before, he had a chance to respond, he pointed out the window of the truck at a group of five children coming into the park from the other side. There were two girls and three boys; the oldest boy looked about 12, and was carrying a bag that he sat down on the table under the large tree. The priest opened his door, and said to Maria,

"Let's go. Walk slowly and smile. Let me speak to them first."

When they were about twenty feet from the tree, Father Rodrigo stopped and called out to the children.

"May we share the table with you? We brought our breakfast with us, and we would gladly share it with you."

The children stood up as a group, tempted by the offer of food, and the priest waited to see what they would do. The older boy spoke first.

"What do you have?"

"Pastries, tortillas, milk, and some candy. May we sit with you?"

It was the moment of truth, and the hunger of the boy overcame whatever caution he had about trusting an adult, though it helped that Rodrigo was a priest. He nodded his head in response, and Father Rodrigo and Maria sat down at the table, and began slowly taking the food out of a large plastic bag. The children hurriedly took the food and began stuffing it in their mouths, glancing up at the priest and Maria as they ate.

"Please take your time. There is more in the truck. My friend who owns the restaurant across the street says you have been here for a while."

No one answered, but the priest could see the truth of his words not only in their eyes, but in the filthiness of their clothing and the dirt that covered their arms and legs. The priest knew he would not get any answers from the children, they were merely trying to survive from day to day, hoping that whoever had left them there would soon return. That hope died a little every day, and the priest could see the small group was on the verge of becoming lost in the slums of the city. There was only one way he was going to find out if they would come with him, so he turned to the oldest boy.

"I have a place you all can stay for a few days, if you want. We will give you food, clothes, a bed, and you can rest and see what happens. It's not far, and if you want to leave after you have rested and eaten, you may."

There was no way the boy was going to say no, the week they had spent on the streets had been harrowing for all of them. The thought of sleeping in a bed, with the safety that implied, was too much to resist. In addition, because Rodrigo was a priest, the boy felt a measure of trust that would not have been extended to another adult.

"When you have finished the food, we will go to the truck. There is no rush."

Maria was silent while the priest spoke, and waited patiently as the children ate all the food they had brought. She smiled as she sat at the table, though inwardly she was thinking there was going to be more than just teaching these children. There would be other people to help her, Jacob had hired staff to help manage the new children, but it would be her responsibility to teach them. She would have to find out what she could about each child, and then come up with a plan that would work for that child. Maria would find that she was equal to the task, and would over time gain the trust of both the children and the priest. Though they saw each other every day, and would spend time outside of the community together, Jacob and Maria's relationship would take time to develop.

17

It was after Maria had been at the orphanage for three months that Father Rodrigo brought up what was becoming obvious to everyone at the community. He and Jacob met at least once a week to plan, talk about the needs of the children and, most importantly from Father Rodrigo's perspective, what was happening in Jacob's life.

Since he had opened up to the priest about what they now referred to as his "condition", Jacob had become more social and outgoing. He was still the hardest working person at the community, seldom taking a day off and taking over more of the day to day operations of the orphanage, freeing Father Rodrigo from responsibilities he had shouldered for nearly 25 years. The priest was feeling his age, and was glad to let Jacob slowly become the face of the community.

They were sitting in his office late in the evening, it was the only time that they could be sure of having any privacy. Father Rodrigo was tired after a long day. Jacob, who experienced fatigue but not the accompanying sense of weariness that led to sleep, waited as usual for the priest to begin the conversation. Jacob wasn't prepared for how the priest began the conversation.

"Maria has been here three months. You work with her every day. I wonder why you have never spent any personal time with her?"

Jacob didn't know how to answer Father Rodrigo, and wondered where the priest was going with his question?

"Are you asking me why I haven't asked her out on a date?"

"Yes. Something like that."

Jacob had spent much of the last three months thinking about Maria. She had settled into the community, and worked well with the children, staff and the Sisters. She and Jacob spent time together nearly every day, but always in the context of work. He would occasionally take her into Ensenada to get supplies, but these trips were always work oriented. He was keeping his distance from her for two reasons. First, he had never really had to begin any type of relationship with a girl before, and though he sensed there might be the possibility of a relationship between the two of them, he was afraid of changing the dynamic of their working relationship. For Jacob, the children would always come first, and the thought of doing something that might jeopardize the teaching they were receiving was acting like a brake on Jacob's emotions.

Second, if he did develop a relationship with Maria, would he have to eventually tell her about his "condition"? He had told the priest; but the priest was a mature, spiritual person who could not only keep a secret, but understood in some way how Jacob's life was impacted by the secret he carried. Jacob did not want to live alone his entire life; if he wanted to have a normal life, with a wife and family, he would eventually have to trust someone. His thoughts were interrupted when the priest said,

196

"You have a life to live, a life that is outside of community. Whether you stay here forever, or eventually leave, you are entitled to happiness. You don't have to give all of yourself to the children."

"I'm just doing what you're doing. I don't see the difference."

It was a lame excuse, and they both knew it. Father Rodrigo smiled, and said,

"You're not a priest or a sister. God has not called you to live a life set apart as He has called us. I believe God admires your devotion, Jacob, but I also believe He wants you to be happy. You have been part of a family much of your life; first at the orphanage you grew up in and now here. It's time you thought about having a family of your own someday."

Jacob knew the priest was right, and again thought about Maria. She was obviously devoted to the children, and shared with Jacob a desire to help those less fortunate. He had found that during the times they drove into Ensenada on supply runs they conversed easily, and he thought that if he began to take the relationship in a different direction, she might be open to that change.

He was right, but only partly. Maria had spent three months working with Jacob, and though he was obviously smart, dedicated and could at times be disarming in an offhand way, she had no interest in pursuing any type of relationship with him. His devotion to the children and the work of the orphanage was almost all consuming, and she thought he would never have any time to develop a relationship outside of his work at the community. She was wrong.

18

A week later, on a Saturday, Jacob took Maria with him into Ensenada on a typical supply run. They would pick up food, clothes and some other staples that the community needed, and then return early in the afternoon. When they had loaded everything into truck, Jacob asked her if she would like to spend the afternoon at a beach just south of the city. It was a warm day, and as usual they had both worked long hours that week. She was surprised at the offer, and said she would like going to the beach to relax for a few hours. They picked up some food at a small store, and then drove south of the city to a beach that was just off the highway. Jacob had taken the children to the beach on occasion, renting a small bus to accommodate all of them. It was a public beach, and there were a few other people enjoying the sunshine. The waves were small that day and a few children were splashing around in the water. Jacob and Maria brought their food to a table close to the parking lot so they could keep an eye on the truck. The bed of the truck was covered by a canopy that locked, but it wouldn't take much to break into the truck and steal the cargo.

They had worked together for three months, but they knew little about each other. Jacob spent time telling her about growing up in the orphanage, and how it was different from the orphanage they worked in every day. Maria had many questions about the United States which Jacob tried to answer as best he could. She was intrigued by the abundance of consumer goods and the safety that was found in most places in America. Things that Jacob took for granted, she found fascinating. When she asked why Jacob had left the United States to come to Mexico, he thought for a moment.

"There wasn't the need like there is here. I wanted to work in a place where my efforts would have the greatest impact. I think it's what Sister Flavia would have wanted."

Jacob had spoken about the impact Sister Flavia had on him, and Maria again thought that Jacob was unlike any other young man she had known. At this point she wasn't sure if that was something she found attractive, but he had a refreshing honesty and simplicity that could not be denied. There was also, in the back of her mind, the fact that Jacob was a citizen of the United States, something that could be of benefit to her. She had no idea if there would ever be any sort of relationship between them, but for the first time since they had known each other they were doing something other than working together.

They spent three hours at the beach, leaving when the sun began to set into the ocean. She had told him about her family, her time at the university, and briefly mentioned that she had had boyfriends in the past. Jacob got the sense that one of the reasons she had come to the orphanage was to escape something from her past, just as he had. He didn't pry, and listened patiently to what she was comfortable telling him about her life. When he asked her how long she might stay at the orphanage, she was noncommittal, saying that while she was happy working with the children and especially with the opportunity to save money, she did not know what the future held for her.

A pattern would develop over the next year that would change the relationship between Jacob and Maria. They would find time every week to be together; either at the beach, shopping in Ensenada or going to the movies. Jacob was slowly becoming aware that he was thinking more and more about what a life with Maria would be like. They had not talked about a future together, but unless something dramatic happened, it was likely that at some point they were going to have a serious talk about their relationship. What Jacob didn't know was that Maria had decided that Jacob was not her future, though she enjoyed the time she spent with him. Because he showed no inclination to ever leave the orphanage, and had no apparent desire to return to the U.S., she figured she would enjoy his company as long as possible, either until she had to tell him she was not serious about him or she left the orphanage. She had saved nearly all her salary, and thought she might work one more year and then move back to Mexico City to be near her family and resume her life. Maria's plan came to an abrupt halt one morning when she had to go to the storeroom next to Jacob's room, and found his door slightly ajar.

She had never been in Jacob's room before, and as she opened the door to look inside she was surprised by how small it was. There was a bed, table, dresser and a small chair. Under the table was a box full of file folders; it was the only thing that caught her attention. Jacob was out with Father Rodrigo on a supply run to Ensenada, and though there was no chance of her being discovered, she hesitated for just a moment. Like many people who are basically honest and have values that would prohibit any type of pilfering or stealing, when faced with temptation, they will sometimes give way. Maria wasn't going to steal anything, there was nothing of value except for Jacob's computer, but she did close the door behind her and quickly bent down to look through the files. If she had to give a reason why she was going through the files, it would have been to find out more about who Jacob was, which seemed to her innocent enough.

What she found astounded her, and would alter the course of her life, and that of Jacob. The files were mainly related to the orphanage; accounts with vendors, receipts for large ticket items they had bought like the truck and generator, but there was one file that was completely different from the rest. It had to do with Jacob's business, which she had completely forgotten about since he had mentioned it to her the first day they had met. Though she didn't completely understand what she was reading, she did understand the amounts of money listed in column after column, page after page. If what she was seeing was true, then Jacob was worth millions of dollars; money that he seemed to make in the stock market in the United States. When she was done looking through his trading accounts, she carefully put the files back in the box and quietly opened the door. No one had seen her enter, and no one would see her leave. She went next door to the storeroom, and after she had closed the door behind her, thought about what she had just seen.

Now she understood who the "generous donors" were that Father Rodrigo had talked about when she first arrived. If there were other donors, they were dwarfed by the amount of money Jacob had to give to the community. Maria was smart enough to know that there was no way the orphanage could spend that much money, and incorrectly assumed that Jacob was letting it accumulate someplace in the United States. She wondered why he would choose to live in an out of the way orphanage in Mexico when he could apparently live any way and any place that he wanted. The only thing she could think of was that he was working off some kind of guilt for a mistake he had made earlier in his life. What that mistake might be, she had no idea. Jacob hardly seemed like the kind of person to do anything bad, certainly nothing that would require some type of penance like working in an orphanage. Because she could not reconcile the wealth she had glimpsed with the person she knew, she would never reach the correct conclusion: that Jacob had a set of values and core beliefs that she did not share. Maria was a genuinely decent person, but her decency and morality came mostly from riding the coattails of her parents faith, and not through personal belief or choice. And when the time of temptation arrived, she fell, though not without the little bell of conscience ringing in her mind.

19

Maria knew she would never love Jacob, but how much of life, she thought, was about love? Her parents loved each other, she was sure of that, but their love seemed based more on the responsibility each carried for the family. Their children were everything, and as she grew older Maria noticed they had little time or affection for each other. It seemed to Maria that they had carved out for themselves a good life, though not one that she would have chosen for herself. Until now.

She had been in love once, or thought she had been in love, during her time at the university. It had ended badly, the young man she was ready to give herself to, and had given herself to, had left her when he graduated and moved to the south of Mexico. She told him she would drop out of university and follow him, but he only laughed at the dramatics of it all. When Maria graduated several months later, she took the first opportunity that came her way to leave Mexico City and the memories that still plagued her.

That evening, after her duties were done for the day and she was lying on her bed with the air conditioning slowly humming in the background, she sat awake rationalizing her new feelings for Jacob. She would not kid herself that she would ever love him, but he was kind, patient to a fault, would never do anything to displease or hurt anyone, and had shown a newfound interest in her over the last year. Maria knew that if she reciprocated the feelings Jacob had for her, he would be hers. It took time, but eventually she came to the place where she could rationalize changing how she behaved toward him. She was only giving him what he wanted, she thought. What could be more selfless than that?

The fact that she hoped Jacob would one day return to the U.S., and the obvious fact that he was rich, she had buried deep in her subconscious. When those thoughts occasionally arose in her mind, she quickly blocked them and again told herself she was doing something worthy; bringing a happiness into Jacob's life that had not been there before.

As the year went out, and Maria began to respond to Jacob in a different, more personal manner, Jacob became a much different person. For the first time in his life he had someone who was his, someone who filled a void he had carried all his life. The change in his life was noticed by everyone at the community, especially by the priest. Father Rodrigo had not been feeling well for much of the last year, and had let Jacob take over most of the day to day operations of the community. Because Jacob could work when everyone else was asleep, the added duties did not bring any extra burden to him, nor did it take away from the time he carved out to spend with Maria. Father Rodrigo could see where the relationship was headed, and, finally, during one of their weekly meetings to discuss the business of the community, he brought the subject up with Jacob.

"Maria has now been with us two years, Jacob. You have seen her every day for those two years. We have all noticed that the two of you have become much closer during the last year."

Jacob knew where the priest wanted to go with the conversation, and as was typical for him got directly to the place Father Rodrigo wanted to go.

"I'm going to ask her to marry me."

"I suspected as much, and I'm happy for you."

The priest was a perceptive man, and though Jacob could usually read people well, he had missed what the priest had seen in Maria. As they say, love is blind.

"What do you think she will say to this proposal?"

Jacob assumed, like most young men who are about to propose, that Maria would say "yes". The thought that she might refuse to marry him had not occurred to him. They had become close during the last year, and there was no reason he could think of that she would not marry him.

"I think she'll say yes. Why do you ask?"

"I also believe she will agree to marry you. You have not told her about your condition, yes?"

It was always the elephant in the room. Jacob had conveniently blocked from his mind the idea that he would either have to tell her about what he was or find a way to conceal it from her if they married, which he knew would be almost impossible.

"No. I have not told her."

The priest nodded, and the two men sat in silence while they thought about the options open to Jacob, and the possible outcome.

"You believe she loves you?"

"Yes, I do."

"And her love is without conditions?"

"You were the one who said I deserved to be happy. She makes me happy. Why are we even talking about this?"

It was totally out of character for Jacob to be short with anyone, especially Father Rodrigo. His avoidance of the priest's question, and the implications that flowed from the question, showed that he was not at all sure Maria would be able to deal with his "condition".

"You deserve to be happy, Jacob. But as we have talked about before, I believe your greatest happiness is found in God, not in human relationships."

"That's easy for you to say. You've never had a family."

The priest thought for a moment, lost in remembrance of years past.

"I did have a family. Before I became a priest. They were killed many years ago by a cartel."

Jacob was stunned by the admission, and did not know what to say. He had known the priest nearly five years, and he had never once mentioned having had a family. Father Rodrigo was still remembering when he said to Jacob,

"God took my grief, and showed me I still could have a life, a life centered on Him. Without Him I would have lost myself."

They had drifted, and though Jacob felt for the priest, he needed closure on the conversation they were having, and brought them back to the present.

"I'm sorry about your family. But I don't see how it relates to me."

He didn't mean to sound unsympathetic by bringing the conversation back to the topic at hand, and the priest understood that was just Jacob being Jacob. Always to the point, always waiting to get to the next thing.

"When she understands what you are, and the difference between the two of you that she will never feel or share, what will she think? Perhaps she can accept the gulf that will always exist in your relationship, but you do not know that. At least not yet."

In truth, Jacob had no idea what Maria would think about his "condition". In his entire life, only four people knew what he was, and three of them were devout Catholics who had given their lives to serve others. They had kept Jacob's secret, and let him live without the burden of having others know he was perhaps the only person on the planet who required no sleep. The one other person who had found out about Jacob, Noah, had literally been driven insane by the knowledge. What Maria would think, Jacob honestly had no idea. There was, however, one avenue left open to him.

"I can hide it from her. It won't be easy, but I have already told her I require little sleep. I can pretend to sleep if it comes to that. I've done it before."

Jacob thought back to the years at the orphanage, where as a young boy Sister Flavia had taught him how to lie still and wait until everyone else was asleep before he began reading late at night and into the morning hours. He may have been fooling himself that he could do the same thing in a completely different relationship like marriage, but he was desperate, and it seemed the only option left to him.

"I don't doubt that you have the discipline to do something like that, Jacob. But over the course of a lifetime together? And what will she think if she finds out on her own? How will she ever be able to trust you?"

There was one more thing that needed to be said, though the priest knew it might be the nail in the coffin of Jacob and Maria's relationship.

"If you do tell her, or she finds out, will she keep this knowledge to herself? How many people could keep that kind of secret?"

Jacob needed to think about what the priest had said, and excused himself, leaving Father Rodrigo regretting what he felt he needed to say. It would turn out, however, that there was one person who could keep Jacob's secret, though it would not be Maria.

20

Jacob spent the next few days just going through the motions with the children and the staff. He didn't avoid Maria, but it was obvious to her that something was bothering him. He lay on his bed at night thinking through his conversation with Father Rodrigo, slowly convincing himself that he could hide from Maria what he was, and even practiced pretending he was asleep. Lying in the dark, he kept his eyes closed and tried to let his mind drift in neutral, but memories from the orphanage kept flooding into his mind. His earliest memories of Sister Flavia teaching him how to survive as a young boy kept bringing him back to the same question: what would Sister Flavia have him do? She had always brought everything back to Jacob finding the purpose for his life. He had found it, he believed, in serving in the community and giving away large sums of money to the truly needy. Jacob knew what Sister Flavia would say if he asked her about Maria and his desire to marry her. Does she share your purpose? Does she share your beliefs and values? And, finally, will she guard your secret?

It was the last question that Jacob could not answer. He truly believed that Maria shared his values, purpose and beliefs, at least that was what he told himself. She had been at the orphanage two years, teaching the orphans and becoming a valued part of the community. How she would react if she learned about Jacob's "condition" he had no idea. So, he decided he would not tell her, believing he could keep his secret. In the end it would not matter, because Maria was not who Jacob thought she was, as he would soon find out.

Once he had made up his mind, Jacob's personality dictated he take action. A lifetime of moving from one thing to another, driven by goals, projects and objectives, Jacob wanted to move forward with Maria and decided to ask her to marry him that weekend. He decided to take her to the beach they had first visited two years ago, and made a trip to Ensenada Friday afternoon to find a ring.

Jacob knew that his proposal of marriage might take Maria by surprise. They had spent one afternoon a week together for the last year, yet he had never kissed her; the only physical contact he had with her was to hold her hand, and then only on occasion. This is not to say that he was inattentive to her; on the contrary, he was unfailingly courteous, solicitous of her needs, and always made sure they spent time doing things she enjoyed. She didn't seem put off by his apparent lack of affection, it was just who Jacob was.

It was sunny when they arrived at the beach, the morning clouds having just burned off. They sat at the same table they had two years ago, and talked about their week at the orphanage. Jacob had the ring in his pocket, and when the conversation lagged for a moment, he took the small box out and sat it on the top of the table. He looked at it for a moment, and having rehearsed the night before what he wanted to say, said,

"Would you marry me, Maria? I've known that I love you for some time, and I want to spend the rest of my life with you."

She had waited a year to hear those words, and despite the fact that she had in some ways manipulated Jacob into the proposal by changing how she behaved toward him, she was genuinely surprised. She knew what her answer would be, but she wanted to make sure that she got what she wanted from the marriage, and thought for a moment how to answer Jacob.

"I'm not surprised that you asked me, Jacob. It seems we've been moving toward this the last year. I do love you, and want to marry you. I do have some questions about what our life would be like, if that's okay."

Jacob had heard what he wanted, and thought that any question she might ask would be about their future together. He was correct, but the questions she was going to ask were not what he expected.

"You've never told me much about your business, Jacob. What exactly is it that you do?"

Jacob thought for a moment, trying to remember when he had ever talked to her about his "business". Then he recalled when he first met her he had mentioned in an offhand remark that he managed money for people. That was two years ago, and he wondered why she would bring it up just after he asked her to marry him.

"I manage money for people. I use the Internet, and it doesn't take much of my time. I don't make much money from it. It's something I did before I came here."

He stuttered as he spoke the words, something that was unusual for him. It was obvious that he didn't want to talk about it, but Maria persisted.

"Do you think you'll ever want to do it again? I mean as a job?"

"I haven't thought about it. Why do you want to know?"

"If we are going to have a family, I'd like to know about how we are going to support ourselves. We can't live at the orphanage forever."

It had never occurred to Jacob that he would ever leave the orphanage. She was right in thinking that they could not live at the orphanage, but that could be easily solved by buying a house in either El Bajo or Ensenada. But that wasn't what Maria was thinking.

"We can live in the town or in Ensenada. I make enough money for us to do that."

He could see the questioning in her face, and a moment of doubt ran through Jacob's mind. What was she thinking, he thought? Typical for Jacob, he got right to the point.

"What are you thinking?"

"I wonder how long we are going to work at the orphanage, Jacob? You have given almost five years to them. Maybe it's time to think about having a normal life, especially when you are getting married and then beginning a family."

The only word that registered in Jacob's mind was "them". She had called the community that he had given himself to "them", an indication that she looked at the orphanage as a job, and a temporary one at that. And then came the question that ended their relationship.

"Don't you want to move back to the U.S. someday?"

He saw in a moment how he had been played, and felt a profound sadness. Jacob had seen in Maria what he wanted to see, thinking that the subtle change in her behavior over the last year was an indication of her affection for him, not a calculated ploy based on what she had discovered about Jacob's apparent wealth. Maria had genuine feelings for Jacob, but they fell well short of love and affection. Jacob didn't totally misread her, he just didn't know the motives behind those feelings. Nor would he ever find out. One dilemma, however, had been resolved. He would not have to worry about telling her about his "condition". Now that he knew where they stood, it was time to face reality.

"I don't ever plan on leaving the orphanage. I thought you knew that. Everything that I believe about life is found in being a part of that community. I guess we're not as compatible as I thought. I'm sorry."

He took the small box off the table, and put it back in his pocket. Maria had totally misjudged him, realizing too late that Jacob wasn't the person she thought he was. Part of her was relieved, she had just enough common sense to know that it would be difficult to live with a person she didn't love. She would leave the orphanage during the Christmas break, which gave Jacob two months to find another teacher. He threw himself back into the work of the community, and though everyone knew Jacob and Maria had ended their relationship, the Sisters and staff were careful to not intrude on their privacy. It was Father Rodrigo who would help Jacob find his way through his grief and loss.

21

It wasn't until after she left the community that Father Rodrigo thought it appropriate to talk with Jacob about Maria. In their meetings together they had avoided the subject, with Maria still living at the orphanage it just wasn't the time. Father Rodrigo drove her to the Tijuana airport a week before Christmas, and though he had much he wanted to say to her, they drove mostly in silence. The priest would never find out that Maria had discovered Jacob's trading accounts, but he knew she did not love him. He pulled up to the curb at the airport to drop her off, and after getting her luggage out of the back of the truck, took an envelope out of his pocket and gave it to her.

"I want to thank you for your work with the children. They are very sorry to see you leave. I hope you find what you are looking for."

She put the envelope in her pocket and did not open it until she had passed through security and was waiting at the gate for her plane to board for Mexico City. Inside was a note from Jacob. It read: "I'm not who you thought I was, but I think you know that now. I hope this helps you make a fresh start with your life." The money order was for $10,000, but instead of feeling grateful, all she could think about was what might have been.

Later that night, there was a soft knock on Father Rodrigo's door. He opened it, and motioned for Jacob to enter. Jacob sat on the chair while the priest leaned back against the wall in his bed. Father Rodrigo had a dry sense of humor, which showed itself when he said,

"Couldn't sleep?"

"That would be funny if it wasn't true. I suppose it's time we talked about it."

"Right to the point as usual. I gave her the envelope, but she didn't open it in my presence. I wonder what she thought?"

"I don't suppose we'll ever know. I hope it helps her in some way. Though I think we both know that money doesn't bring happiness."

"Many things don't bring happiness, Jacob. Money is only one of them. It's been two months now, how are you feeling?"

"I asked her to marry me."

This was news to the priest. He had no idea why their relationship had ended, and waited for Jacob to tell him more.

"She said yes, but then she started asking questions about what I did for a living, and where we would live, and when I thought I might go back to the U.S."

Jacob was reliving the moment at the beach two months ago, and the confusion was evident on his face.

"All of a sudden it came to me that she was only interested in what I could do for her, not who I was or what I believed. I can't believe I misjudged her."

"Perhaps you didn't totally misjudge her, Jacob. I believe she had feelings for you, but those feelings were mixed with other motives, motives that finally surfaced when you asked her to marry you."

Jacob didn't really hear what the priest had said, his mind was lost in grief and loss. Not so much for Maria, but for the opportunity he felt he had lost in having what he thought might be a normal life. For someone who had lived apart from the rest of humanity all his life, it now looked to him that he would never have a wife or family of his own.

"It's not fair."

"What's not fair, Jacob?"

"Everything."

"Everything is a big word."

"You know what I mean."

"Yes, I think I do. You have given so much, and you do not have the one thing you desire. You want your own family, because you believe that will make you whole. You want what you had with Sister Flavia. She made you feel whole, am I right?"

"Yes, she did. I haven't felt right since she died."

"You were younger then. It's normal to look to our parents for security. When she died you lost the one person who completely understood and accepted you."

"Yes. And I'll never find anyone else like her. Never."

There was no way the priest was going to talk Jacob out of his pain, so he remained silent as each man pursued his own thoughts. The priest had known pain and loss as well, and it had taken time for him to find his way up from the bottom of the pit he found himself in after his family was taken from him. Jacob was standing on the edge of that pit, and Father Rodrigo saw how easy it would be for the young man to fall headlong into thinking his life was over. As he continued to think about Jacob, he knew there was one thing he could do, though if he told Jacob he knew it would not bring him any comfort. He would ask God to show mercy on the young man, and bring him the happiness he sought. God would answer the prayer, but in a way that priest could have never envisioned.

22

On the first of each month Jacob transferred money to the foundation. In the years she had been running the foundation Jacob had sent her nearly six million dollars. Megan had recruited a team of people to help her distribute the money, and because Jacob had included a salary for her as head of the foundation, she quit her job at the newspaper and focused on her blog. It was widely read, and she was in the process of becoming a minor celebrity in the San Diego area. She thought of Jacob each time she received notice that the funds had been transferred into the foundation's account. It had been five years, and though she had known him for just a short time, she could not shake the impression he had made on her. Megan had dated a few times in those five years, but few of the men she met shared her faith, values or beliefs. Although she was just twenty-six years old, she often wondered if she would meet someone that she might share her life with. And then she got sick.

It had been several years since Jacob had read Megan's blog, and he would never know why he chose to bring it up on his computer that first week in January. He was still at loose ends after ending his relationship with Maria, and didn't feel like reading any of the books in his room in the long evening hours. It was after three a.m. when he read the entry for that day, which was short and to the point. Megan wrote: "I finally gave in and let the doctor admit me to the hospital. I haven't felt good for weeks. If I don't post for a while that's the reason."

He closed his computer, and thought for a few moments. Jacob hadn't seen Megan in almost five years, and knew that the thoughts he was having might be triggered by the loss of Maria. He had no idea if Megan had a boyfriend, was married, really anything about her current life. It was here that Jacob decided, for once, to be spontaneous. He thought, what was the worst that could happen? She had not mentioned what hospital she was in, but he could find that out from Father Stephen. He got up from his desk, walked out to the hallway, and went to the storeroom to get a suitcase. Jacob packed a few clothes, his computer, and lay down on his bed, waiting until he knew Father Rodrigo would be awake. His actions were so out of character that he was actually nervous, and spent the next few hours worrying about what might happen when he crossed the border back into the U.S. Finally, knowing that worry was not going to accomplish anything, he picked up a book, began reading, and waited for dawn.

The light was on in Father Rodrigo's room, shining from under the door. He was an early riser, usually getting started on the day before the sun was up. He had not been feeling well lately, though, and had been sleeping in a little later each morning. Jacob was mildly surprised to see him up so early, and after knocking on the door, went into the small room after the priest said to enter.

He was still in bed, reading a book, his glasses perched on the end of his nose. He motioned to the chair, and Jacob sat down, closing the door behind him.

"What brings you to my room this early? Though I know it's not early for you."

"I'm going to take a few days off, if that's okay. I have a friend who is sick in San Diego."

"You have a sick friend in San Diego? You haven't been to San Diego in five years. Who is this friend?"

"Someone I knew before I came here. She manages the foundation I set up. She's in the hospital. It sounds like she's really sick."

"I think we can manage without you for a few days. Is there anything else I can do for you?"

"I don't think so, but thanks. I'll call you when I know what's happening."

The priest merely nodded in response, and it was then that Jacob noticed that Father Rodrigo looked not only tired, but weak as well. In the two months since ending his relationship with Maria, Jacob had been working around the clock, and had not noticed until now how frail the priest had become.

"Have you been to the doctor? You don't look so good."

"Yes, as a matter of fact I have."

"And?"

"I'm old and tired. That's about it."

"Well, get some rest. I'll see you when I get back."

23

It took only two hours to get to the border, but the line to cross was long, and Jacob waited another hour to get back into the U.S. He got off the freeway and stopped for coffee, and then called St. Joseph's church. When no one answered, he hung up, deciding not to leave a message. He thought for a moment, and then decided to drive to the church in the hope that by the time he arrived the priest, or someone else, would be there and could tell him which hospital Megan was in.

It was another hour through mid-morning San Diego traffic to the church, and as he pulled into the parking lot he didn't see the priest's car. The church looked exactly as it had when he left, erasing the passage of five years and bringing back memories of his short stay in the city. He walked into the sanctuary, and then turned down the hallway to the priest's office. The door was open, and Jacob looked in to see if the priest was there.

The priest was there, but it wasn't Father Stephen. He was an older man, someone unknown to Jacob. The priest looked up from his desk, somewhat startled to see a young man he didn't know standing in his doorway. Jacob spoke first.

"I'm sorry if I startled you, Father. I'm looking for Father Stephen."

"Father Stephen isn't here any longer. I'm Father John. What can I do for you?"

"What happened to Father Stephen?"

"He was reassigned several years ago. He lives in New Mexico now."

Jacob hoped that the "reassignment" had nothing to do with him, but he doubted it. The Bishop was a vindictive and proud man, and probably needed a scapegoat when Jacob disappeared with his money. Because Father Stephen could not get Jacob to get in line with the wishes of the Bishop, he had been sent to run a rehab facility for lapsed priests.

Jacob wanted to know more about Father Stephen, but decided that could wait.

"I'm looking for Megan Lee. I heard she was in the hospital, but I don't know which one. I'd like to visit her. Can you tell me where she is?"

"And what was your name?"

"Jacob. I'm a friend of hers. I've been away for several years and read on her blog that she's ill and in the hospital."

"She's at Scripps Hospital. I saw her yesterday. She's very sick."

"Thanks."

Jacob didn't mean to be short with the priest, but once he had the information he needed he was out the door. The priest had no idea who Jacob was, but decided he should call Megan's father and tell him about the young man who unexpectedly showed up at his door asking about his daughter. After all, the man was one of the biggest donors to the church.

It was a short drive to the hospital, and after Jacob found out which room Megan was in from the information desk, he took a minute in the lobby waiting area to compose himself. It had been less than twelve hours since he had found out she was sick, and now he was about to reenter her life after five years. He had no idea what was going to happen, nor what he wanted to accomplish. He did know, however, that is was the right thing to do. It was what Sister Flavia would have done, he knew that, and that was enough.

He got off the elevator at the fourth floor and turned right, walking slowly down the hallway toward her room. The door was closed, so Jacob went to the nurses' station and waited for a moment until a nurse came to help him.

"I'm here to see Megan Lee, but I noticed the door is closed. Can she have visitors?"

"I think she's having a treatment, but let me check."

She left Jacob standing at the counter, and returned shortly to tell him he would have to wait a while. Jacob asked her to come and get him in the waiting area outside the ward, and then walked away, glancing at the closed door to her room as he passed.

Jacob had spent much of his life waiting; he had passed thousands of hours either reading, working on his computer or just lying on his bed looking up at the ceiling giving his mind a rest. He settled into a seat and looked out through a window to the south, which gave him a panoramic view of the San Diego coastline. In all his life, Jacob had never been in a hospital, and he idly wondered what they would do with him if they knew he had never slept in his life. What tests would they do to find out what was wrong with him? How would they explain someone who had never slept? Was it possible that they could find out why he was different and fix him? Was there some pill that would make him sleep? When Jacob was at Harvard, he had tried sleeping pills, but they had no effect on him. He knew there must be some kind of drug that would knock him out, or was there? He would have gone farther down that road, but just then the nurse touched him lightly on the shoulder.

"You can see her now."

She escorted him to Megan's room, and he hesitated for just a moment before he walked in. Megan was sitting up in the bed, propped up by several pillows. There was a moment of confusion on her face, and then recognition. Jacob walked to the side of her bed.

"I read on your blog that you were sick. I hope you don't mind that I came to visit."

She shook her head slowly from side to side, tears coming to her eyes. It took a moment for her to get her composure back.

"Where have you been? What happened?"

"That's a long story. The short version is that I've been working at an orphanage near Ensenada. The second part would take longer to explain. What's wrong with you?"

She took a moment to speak, the shock of seeing Jacob after so many years was still weighing on her mind and emotions.

"They don't know. I've been getting weak for almost a month. My arms and legs are weak and it's getting hard to breath. They might have to put me on a ventilator."

Jacob had never gone to medical school, but over the years he had read hundreds of books related to medicine. He took out his phone and hit the button to activate the voice recorder.

"Tell me everything you remember about how you became sick."

Megan spoke slowly for about half an hour, and then was exhausted. Jacob told her he would let her sleep and return later that day. His last words to her were,

"Don't worry. We'll figure out what's wrong with you."

Jacob left the room and went back to the nurses' station. He waited again until someone came to help him. He asked if he might have a moment to speak to her doctor, making sure the nurse understood he just wanted to ask a few simple questions. Jacob was told to wait out by the elevator, and she would send the doctor out to him when he was available.

Jacob had already moved into his puzzle solving mode, thinking about everything Megan had told him about her illness. He needed more information, and waited patiently for the doctor. An hour later, the doctor found him, and asked Jacob what questions he had about Megan. Jacob asked three questions, and then thanked the doctor for his time. The doctor was puzzled by what Jacob asked him, but didn't have the chance to follow up with him as Jacob headed off to the elevator.

He got his computer from his car, and went to the information desk to get the Wi-Fi password for the hospital. Jacob settled down in the lobby waiting area and began searching different websites to solve the puzzle that lay before him. Armed with only what Megan had told him, and the answers to the three questions he had asked the doctor, three hours later Jacob was pretty sure he had narrowed down Megan's illness to one of three possibilities. He was confident he knew which possibility was afflicting her, and hoped the doctor would take him seriously. If he was correct, Megan was the victim of an illness that only affected 1 in 100,000 people, and could present itself differently in each patient. He closed his computer and was about to head back to the fourth floor, hoping one of her doctors would have the time to talk with him.

Just as he was getting out of his chair, Megan's father came through the lobby doors, looking straight ahead, a man on a mission. Jacob was only a few feet from him, but the man didn't look in his direction. Jacob sat back down, and decided to wait until Megan's father finished his visit. An hour later, he left the hospital, and again didn't notice Jacob sitting in the lobby looking at his computer.

As before, he waited in the area outside the patient's rooms. Finally, around dinner time, a different doctor found him, and sat down across from Jacob. He had thought about how to approach the doctor with what he believed, and after Jacob thanked him for taking the time to speak with him, he said,

"I know you must be skeptical when friends or relatives give you opinions on medical matters, but I want to just give you an idea that you might not have considered."

In normal circumstances, the doctor would have politely declined Jacob's offer, and gone back to work. But there was something in Jacob's manner that gave him pause, and he told Jacob to go ahead.

"I think she may have Guillain-Barre Syndrome. It's pretty rare, but it fits all her symptoms."

The doctor had heard of Guillain-Barre Syndrome, but had never seen a patient who had the disease. He thought for a moment about what he knew about the Syndrome, and asked Jacob how he arrived at that conclusion. All Jacob said was,

"I'm good at solving puzzles."

The doctor left, and gathering several other physicians, they came to the same conclusion after again going over everything they knew about Megan's case. They knew that with Guillain-Barre she would eventually recover, but it was likely she would get worse before she turned the corner. Jacob waited until the doctor returned and told him they were going to treat her for Guillain-Barre Syndrome, and he could see Megan, but only for a few minutes. They were close to putting her on a ventilator, which would make it impossible for her to speak.

The doctor took him back to Megan's room, and stood aside to let Jacob in. Jacob was relieved to see that she had a smile on her face, though she was still having difficulty breathing.

"The doctor told me I have something called Guillain-Barre Syndrome. They say I'll eventually get better, but I might have to go on a ventilator first."

She had to stop for a moment to catch her breath.

"The doctor told me you figured out what I have. Is that true?"

"They would have figured it out. It's not a big deal."

She was again reminded of Jacob's humility and lack of any type of pretension. He had just done something her doctor had not been able to do, and was downplaying it to avoid taking any type of credit.

"Can you stay for a while? It's difficult for me to talk, but I'd like to know why you left so suddenly. And why you never contacted me. What happened?"

"Let's wait until tomorrow. You won't like some of it."

"You'll still be here?"

"I'll have to go back to the orphanage, but I'll stay through tomorrow. When you get out of the hospital I'll come back and we can have coffee at the café on the boardwalk."

"I'd like that."

He left her room and headed back to the elevator, thinking about what he was going to do next. It was getting late into the evening, and Jacob thought about getting something to eat. The hospital cafeteria was on the third floor, so he waited for an elevator. When it opened, the doctor Jacob had talked with was standing alone in the back, and when Jacob got in and the doors closed the doctor said that Jacob was correct in his diagnosis. He told Jacob that Megan would recover, but he had no idea how long it would be.

"Will I be able to see her while she recovers?"

"We usually don't let anyone but family see patients who go on a ventilator. But I think in your case we might make an exception. I'll tell the nurses you're allowed to visit. Why don't you come tomorrow morning? I think the family is coming around 10. That might be a good time."

"Thanks."

Jacob got off at the third floor and headed toward the cafeteria, thinking if he should be there when the family was in the room with Megan. It had been five years, and he wondered how her father would react to seeing him again. There was only way to find out, and as Jacob ate his meal he hoped the man could put the past behind him and concentrate on what was best for his daughter.

He found a hotel close to the hospital and watched TV into the early morning, trying to keep his mind from processing everything that had happened in the last twenty-four hours. Despite the passage of five years, Megan hadn't forgotten him, and if he was reading her correctly, she was more than glad to see him. What she might think after he told her why he had suddenly left for Mexico, he had no idea. But he was going to tell her the truth, no matter what the consequences.

Jacob thought it best to give the family some private time with Megan before he showed up, so he walked into the hospital around 10.30 that morning. He stopped at the nurse's station to ask how she was doing before going to the room, and found that she had improved slightly and might not have to go on a ventilator. Jacob stood just outside the door listening to the conversation, waiting for a pause before he entered. Instead, her doctor showed up right after he did, and said,

"You can go in. She seems to have improved overnight. She's still has weakness in her arms and legs, but her oxygen levels have stabilized. She might not have to go on a respirator."

The family heard the doctor speaking with Jacob, and turned around to see who he might be talking to. They both came into the room at the same time, and Megan's father stiffened when he saw Jacob. Jacob nodded at the family, and then smiled at Megan. Megan returned his smile, and then said,

"Mom and Dad, this is Jacob."

Jacob shook the mother's hand, and then turned to face her father.

"Pleasure to meet you both."

"Jacob used to attend St. Joseph's, and then his work took him out of the country until now. He heard I was sick and came to visit."

Megan's father could not take his eyes off Jacob, he was like a ghost that had come back to haunt him. The last time they had spoken had left him with a moral hangover that took months to dissipate. Jacob's presence reminded him of a time in his life that he had tried hard to forget. Pleased that Megan was doing better, and realizing that his presence was making her father uncomfortable, Jacob said,

"The doctor tells me you're doing better. I'll let you visit with your family. I'll come back later this afternoon."

Jacob nodded at Megan, and then smiled to let her know she was in his thoughts. He turned to leave the room, and then Megan's father said,

"Excuse me for a moment, Megan."

He followed Jacob out of the room and walked with him until they left the ICU and were in the waiting area by the elevators. Jacob turned to face him, and told him he was glad Megan was feeling better. He waited for a response, and then Megan's father said,

"She says you figured out what was wrong with her. How did you do that?"

"They would have eventually figured it out. It's not a big deal."

There was a pause, and Jacob noticed the man was looking down at the floor, without a trace of belligerence in him.

"I'm not the same man I was five years ago. I want you to know that."

Where did that come from, Jacob thought? He didn't know how to respond, and there was a moment of awkward silence between them.

"I just wanted you to know that."

"Sure. Thanks. I'm sure I'll see you again."

Jacob pushed the elevator button and waited for the doors to open. Megan's father turned and headed back to her room, leaving Jacob wondering what had happened in the man's life, and why he would mention it to him.

24

Jacob checked out of the hotel where he had spent the night, intending to go back to the orphanage later that evening. He returned to the hospital just after lunchtime, and walked into Megan's room, where she was leaning against the pillows on the bed with her eyes closed. Jacob quietly sat down in a chair, and thought about what he wanted to say to her. He was sure that if he had stayed in San Diego he and Megan would have eventually become serious about each other. Where it would have lead, he had no idea, because he would have eventually had to tell about what he was. He had thought with Maria he might have been able to hide his "condition", but he now knew that was wishful thinking. He was who he was, and if he had any type of future with Megan, he would have to tell her.

Megan eventually opened her eyes, and smiled at Jacob when she saw him sitting next to the bed.

"How are you feeling?"

"I had something to eat, and then fell asleep for a while. I'm tired, but I think I'm getting some feeling back in my arms and legs."

"I'm glad to hear that. The prognosis for Guillain-Barre is good. It may take some time before you're back to normal, but you'll be out of here before you know it."

"Are you going to tell me what happened to you? I haven't been able to think about anything else since you showed up yesterday. And what's up between you and my dad?"

"You noticed that?"

"He went rigid when you came into the room this morning. What did you talk about when you left?"

"I told you yesterday you might not like what I have to tell you about why I left. Some of it has to do with your father."

"He did something wrong, didn't he? Back then."

"What makes you say that?"

"He wasn't the same after you left. He was distracted, and he didn't pay as much attention to the family. He seemed depressed, which isn't him at all. Then he got better, but he never said what was wrong."

Jacob spent the next hour telling her everything he could remember about the foundation, the Bishop, her father, the bribe, and his decision to leave and find another avenue to use his gifts and fulfill his purpose. He told her about the orphanage, Father Rodrigo, and, finally, about Maria. When he finished, all Megan could say was,

"I'm sorry."

There was one more thing he needed to say to her, and he knew this would be the time to do it. It would give her time to process what he was going to tell her, and her response would determine if they had a future together.

"There's something else I need to tell you. It's something you might not understand, but I think you need to know this about me."

He paused for a moment, and then got right to the point.

"I don't sleep. I've never slept. Not ever."

She reacted like he expected, with a frown of confusion and doubt about what she had just heard.

"What do you mean, you don't sleep?"

"When you go to sleep at night, I read books or work on my computer. Sometimes I watch TV, sometimes I just lay in bed and look at the ceiling. It's why I'm an orphan. My mother couldn't handle it, and my father dropped me off at the orphanage to try and save her. I think it was driving her crazy. Watching me lie in my crib all night without going to sleep."

When Megan didn't immediately respond, Jacob continued.

"It's how I could get two degrees from Harvard in two years. I studied all night, every night. It's how I could come up with the algorithm to beat the market. It took me two years working almost every night to come up with the program. It probably wouldn't take me that long now. I was only ten at the time."

It was a small attempt at humor, but it was lost on Megan. She still hadn't spoken, so Jacob asked her what she was thinking.

"I don't think you could make something like this up. And I don't think you would lie to me. It's a lot to take in."

"I wouldn't lie to you, and you're right, it's not something anyone would ever think to make up."

"Does anyone else know?"

"Father Rodrigo. And my father. One other person. And now you."

Then she said something that revealed her character, the depth of her compassion, and reminded Jacob of something Sister Flavia might say.

"I can't imagine what your life has been like."

"It's gotten easier over the years, but I still feel alone most of the time."

"I could help with that."

Jacob didn't know what to say, and looked out the window toward the ocean. There was no way she could fully grasp what she had just learned, so Jacob said,

"I need to get back to the orphanage today. It's a lot to take in, I know. But I want you to think about this. For the last five years, every time you went to bed and fell asleep, I was alone, usually in my room, waiting for the night to be over so I could rejoin the real world. I'd like a chance at a normal life, but not at someone else's expense."

Jacob hoped she understood the meaning of his words. He wasn't a project, or someone who needed to be fixed. He would in some way always live apart from everyone else on the planet, but he hoped that didn't mean he couldn't find someone who would understand that, and be content to live with what he was. It was time for him to leave, and as he rose from the chair he took her hand.

"Call me when you need to, and when you're released. I'll come back up and we'll go to the café."

Megan would call Jacob every day, mostly just to hear his voice. She had thought long and hard about what he had told her, yet it didn't make a bit of difference to her. Much like Sister Flavia, she looked on Jacob's "condition" as a blessing, not a curse, and thought about all the good they could accomplish together.

25

As Jacob rode the elevator down to the lobby he had one persistent thought he could not get out of his mind. It was too easy, picking up where they had left off five years ago. Was it possible Megan would accept what Jacob was and want to make a life with him? He got off the elevator and was heading out the lobby to his car, when he heard his name called from behind, and then he turned to see who it was.

Jacob had only seen him twice, once by Skype and then at Sister Flavia's funeral. It took Jacob a moment to recognize him.

"How did you find me?"

"Why don't we sit down so we can talk for a bit?"

He motioned him to a sofa in the lobby waiting area, and Jacob reluctantly sat down, wondering what was going to happen. His mind was already running through various scenarios of why his father would seek him out, and none of them were good. To say the least, the situation was awkward, but Jacob's father wasted no time in getting the conversation going.

"You're a hard person to find."

"Why would you even want to find me? It's been five years."

And then in a flash he figured out why his father had been searching for him. But first he wanted to know how his father had found him.

"My law firm has a security company on retainer. When you came back over the border, your passport was entered into the Immigration system. We have access to that information."

"This is about money, isn't it?"

"Yes, Jacob, this is about money. A lot of money."

"Tell me what you want."

His father was in his mid-fifties, but looked much older. There had been much stress in his life in the last few years, and it showed on his face. When he answered Jacob's question he looked past him, and spoke softly, with a touch of regret.

"The years you ran your stock scheme were good years for me. I made a lot of money. I waited to make sure it worked, and then I bought the stocks your program picked."

"It wasn't a scheme. It was an algorithm I developed over several years."

"Yes, I know that, but that's not the point."

"What is the point?"

"I put the money I made in some bad investments, and lost nearly all of it. We're talking millions of dollars, Jacob. This happened over several years, and then I did something really stupid. I went back over the transactions your program made over those years. It looked to me that if I bought the same stocks again, I could get the same kind of return."

"It doesn't work like that. It's much more complicated."

"Well, it didn't look that complicated at the time. I borrowed money from some of my clients after showing them how much money I had made in the past buying and selling stocks."

"You lost their money, and now you want me to bail you out. Is that right?"

"Yes, that's right."

"How much money?"

"Three million dollars. I know you can get it. I know the program is up and running. You've been giving it to her to give away for the last five years. It wasn't hard to put everything together once you lead me to her."

"I don't have three million dollars."

"But you can get it. I've assured my clients that you have the ability to get the money. These are not men that you want to disappoint."

"What do you mean?"

"My firm represents clients that have legitimate businesses in the United States. They also have businesses in other parts of the world that aren't so legitimate. Much of their business is done in Mexico, which is where you now live. You do not want these men as your enemy."

Jacob's world was in danger of falling apart, and he knew it. He also knew that if he gave his father the three million dollars, which he could, though it would take time, they would certainly come back and ask for more.

"If I give you three million dollars, they'll just come back for more, you know that. What did you tell them about me?"

"I told them you're a genius at picking stocks. That you were never in it for the money. I told them you gave all the money away. They were quite impressed."

"But they're not going to leave me alone until they get their money? And you have no other way to get it?"

"I wish I did. I'm sorry."

There was no point in getting angry at this father, Jacob's only thought was in trying to find a way out for him and Megan.

"I have to go back to Mexico tonight. Give me your phone number. I'll call you tomorrow."

Jacob had one final thought, and asked his father one more question.

"What's the name of your client? I think I have a right to know."

"They are brothers, Manuel and Victor Cordillero. Not that it will do you any good."

Jacob got up to leave, but his father caught him by the arm, and sat him back down on the couch.

"They'll come after you, after they're done with me. I have a family, Jacob."

Jacob pulled himself free.

"I'll call you tomorrow."

On the four-hour drive back to El Bajo, Jacob could not think of any way to extricate himself from the predicament his father had put him in. He could get the money, but he knew he would then be looked upon as a cash machine that the Cordillero brothers would continue to use. He could run, but what would that accomplish? It left his father's family in jeopardy, and perhaps Megan as well. If his father told the brothers about Jacob visiting Megan, and how she distributed his money, they might threaten her to get to him. Just when it seemed there might be the possibility of a normal life for Jacob, it was on the verge of tragedy.

It would help to talk to the priest, and as Jacob pulled up to the orphanage early in the evening, he walked through the chapel to the office, and knocked on the door. When there was no answer, Jacob went out the back through the courtyard, looking for the priest. Instead, he found one of the sisters, who called to him from the kitchen. He crossed the courtyard, and was told that Father Rodrigo had been taken to the hospital that afternoon. It didn't seem to be serious. He had fainted in his office, and as a precaution the doctor wanted to do some tests. Jacob thanked the Sister, and went back out to his car. Thirty minutes later was walking into a hospital for the second time that day.

The hospital in Ensenada wasn't anything like Scripps Memorial, but it was as good as any hospital in Mexico, a reflection of the relative prosperity of the Ensenada community. Jacob found Father Rodrigo resting in a room with four other patients. He sat down in a chair by the bed, and as usual got right to the point.

"How are you feeling? What's wrong with you?"

"I'm tired and old. They tell me my heart isn't as strong as it should be. They are giving me some medication that should help. I'll probably be out tomorrow. How is your friend?"

"She is going to be fine, but might not get out of the hospital for a while."

He paused for a moment, and then said,

"I saw my father today. At the hospital."

The priest sat up in his bed, and looked closely at Jacob.

"After all these years? What did he want?"

"Do you know who the Cordillero brothers are?"

"What? What do you mean by asking me that?"

"Do you know who they are?"

"Yes. I do. They are drug dealers."

Jacob spent the next hour telling the priest about the meeting with his father, the demand for money, and the implied threats that his father hoped would pry the money lose from Jacob. When Jacob was finished, the priest said,

"These are dangerous men, Jacob. I don't think the police would be of much use. Certainly not police here in Mexico."

"I can't figure a way out of this. I don't know what to do."

"If you give them the money, they will want you to work for them. They are always looking for ways to make money legitimately so they can launder their drug profits."

For almost five hours Jacob had been thinking of how to solve this puzzle, but for literally for the first time in his life, there was nothing. It was going to end his newfound relationship with Megan, and may even put her in danger. How would he explain that to her, he had no idea.

"I don't know what to do. I'm stuck in this mess because I thought I was doing something good. If I hadn't saved the orphanage years ago, I would have never needed my father to buy the stocks for me."

And then he said something he had said to the priest before.

"It's not fair."

"You have said that before, Jacob. I believe it is possible for God to solve this situation. I don't know how. But I will pray He has mercy on you, and gives you a way out."

Jacob wanted to believe the priest, but the reality staring him in the face was bigger than any faith he possessed. He nodded in respect to the priest, but had almost resigned himself to calling his father and telling him he would work on getting the money. His only thought was to spare Megan, and he wondered how he was going to tell her they could not be together. He got up from the chair, and said to the priest,

"I need to go. I've got to figure out how long it's going to take me to make three million dollars. Call me when you're released, and I'll come and get you."

With that, Jacob left the room, and went in search of the cafeteria. He had not eaten for hours, and when he found the cafeteria, it was nearly empty. Jacob bought a sandwich, some fruit, a soda, and then sat down at a table off to the side of the large room. There was a TV mounted on the wall, and as he slowly ate his food, he idly looked up at the screen. The sound was off, but across the bottom of the screen was scrolling the narration. The TV was on a news channel, and as Jacob watched what was unfolding before him, he lost all interest in his food.

The camera was obviously some type of GoPro, mounted on the helmet of a soldier. There were other soldiers coming in and out of the picture, and it was clear there had been some type of pitched battled. Bodies were lying on the ground, and several soldiers could be seen pointing at two bodies in particular. They were lying against a wall, riddled with bullets. The narration at the bottom of the screen read: "Victor and Manuel Cordillero shot dead by forces of the Mexican government. The raid took place in Hermosillo, the center of their drug operations. The government says this signals the end of the Hermosillo cartel."

There was more, but Jacob had seen enough. He grabbed his food, and left the hospital, heading back to the orphanage. Everyone was asleep when he arrived, and as he made his way to his room he had two thoughts running swiftly through his mind. The first was that the dilemma he could not solve had just been solved for him by Mexican Special forces. Second, and almost more important, was this: Did God just answer Father Rodrigo's prayer?

It was after midnight, but he called his father anyway. It rang several times before he answered. Before he could say anything other than hello, Jacob said,

"You need to get to a computer."

"Jacob? Why are you calling me so late?"

"I told you I would call you tomorrow. It's tomorrow. Now get to a computer."

"Alright. It will take a minute."

Jacob waited while his father went to his study, turned on his computer, and then said,

"What do I do now?"

"Go to Google and type in the names Victor and Manuel Cordillero."

"What are you talking about?"

"Just do it."

There was silence for a moment, and then Jacob heard a gasp, followed by the words,

"Holy hell."

"I think you can assume your debt to them no longer exists."

His father was still taking in the implications of the image on his computer; the Cordillero brothers slain just hours ago. He had heard Jacob speak, but the words did not register.

"What? What did you say?"

"I assume your debt to them no longer exists."

"It would seem that way."

"I'm going to be back in San Diego soon. I'll call you then. I'll have something for you."

His father was like a man who had just been told his cancer was in full remission, and he was only thinking about the weight that had been taken from him. His response to his son was short and to the point.

"Fine. Whatever you want."

Jacob spent the rest of the evening lying in bed, thinking through the last 24 hours, and the roller coaster of emotions he had gone through. He had failed to solve the biggest puzzle of his life, and then in a flash, it was solved for him. He had just found his way back into Megan's life, and then it seemed she would be gone again, perhaps forever. The feeling that everything had been resolved without him was humbling, and as he lay on his bed and let the hours pass until morning, he could not shake the knowledge that God had intervened to save him. It could be coincidental, but Jacob was at his core a logical, rational person, and the odds were just too long in light of everything that had happened.

If God did exist, which Jacob firmly believed, then it followed he might intervene in the lives of His followers. Sister Flavia certainly believed that, Father Rodrigo certainly believed that, and he was certain Megan believed that. For the second time in his life, Jacob took a step closer to God when he said,

"Thank you."

26

Father Rodrigo called Jacob at noon, telling him that he was being released from the hospital. Jacob left the orphanage soon after, and before he reached the hospital, stopped at a small market and bought a cup of coffee. He also bought a newspaper for the priest, thinking that the priest might not have heard the news about the Cordillero brothers.

Father Rodrigo was dressed and sitting up in his bed, waiting for Jacob to arrive. Jacob stopped at the foot of the bed and tossed the newspaper to the priest. The cover had a photo of the two brothers leaning against the wall, bodies riddled with bullets. The priest looked intently at the photo, and there was a touch of sadness in his voice when he said,

"So much death."

He tossed the newspaper on the chair, and rose from the bed, ready to leave.

"It seems that your problem has been solved. You must be relieved."

"Yes. It seems God heard your prayer. About giving me a way out."

"I think the brothers were killed hours before we talked. But it's an interesting thought."

"You know there's a verse in the Bible that says God answers before we ask."

They were walking out of the room, and continued the conversation as they waited for the elevator.

"I would not try to overthink this. However, I do believe it is proper to thank God for the outcome. It may just be that the Cordillero brothers were victims of the life they chose. When you have time later today, I need to talk with you. We will need to get my medicine at the pharmacy on the first floor."

They were mostly silent on the drive back, each man content with his own thoughts. It wasn't until later that evening that Jacob found his way to the priest's office. Father Rodrigo was propped up in his bed, reading a book. Jacob sat down across from him, and waited for him to speak. The priest wasn't in any hurry, and read for several minutes until he finished the chapter that was occupying him.

"I know it's hard for you to wait, but I wanted to finish this part of the book. Now, let's talk about the future, now that we know you have one."

Jacob had known the priest for five years, and was familiar with his dry sense of humor.

"It wasn't that funny at the time."

"Yes, please forgive me."

He paused, and then said,

"I want you to think about becoming the leader here at the community. You've been doing most of the work anyway, I think it's time it became official."

"Does this have to do with your health?"

"Not really. The doctor says I have to slow down, or I'll meet my maker sooner rather than later. I will remain the pastor of the church, but I'd like you to lead the orphanage."

The news didn't come as a surprise; Jacob knew the priest's health had been declining for some time. It made sense on many levels, and if the priest had asked him a week earlier he would have had no problem agreeing to take over the leadership of the community. But things had changed in the last week, and Jacob could not give an answer until he went back to San Diego and had two conversations: one with his father and one with Megan.

"A week ago, I would have said yes. I love working here, but things have changed. I won't be able to give you an answer until my friend is released from the hospital. And I need to talk to my father, but that's not about the community."

"You have never told me her name, this friend of yours."

"Her name is Megan. I told her about my condition. She says it doesn't matter to her, but I needed to give her time to think about it."

"She must be more than a friend if you told her."

"That's what we're going to find out. I don't know what she would think about moving to Mexico and working at the orphanage."

The priest frowned, and asked Jacob if he thought he might be moving too fast with Megan since they had not seen each other for five years.

"Maybe, but I don't think so. We'll find out soon."

There wasn't anything left to say, so Jacob went back to the school, and spent the rest of the day catching up with the children. He found time to call Megan, who was slowly recovering, gaining more strength every day. There was still no timetable for her release, and though he wanted to tell her about becoming the leader of the orphanage, he knew that news would be best delivered in person.

Three weeks later, Megan called him and said she would be released in two days. Jacob promised to be there, and reminded her he wanted to take her to the café where they could talk. Then he called his father and told him to meet him the next evening in the lobby of the hospital.

Jacob spent that evening going through his trading accounts. He had not transferred any money into the foundation since Megan had been in the hospital, and as such there was nearly $500,000 available in the accounts. There was also money for the community he had been setting aside for five years in a local bank. He figured it would be enough for what he had in mind, and then he spent an hour or so updating the program that generated all that money. He put a copy of the program on a flash drive, and put it in his pocket. Thinking for a moment about what he was going to do next, he hit the "delete" button and erased the program from his computer. He had divorced himself from the money-making business, and would never go back.

The next morning, he found the priest before breakfast, and told him he would be leaving that afternoon for San Diego. He hoped to be back later in the week with his future resolved, one way or the other. There was one other thing he needed to say to the priest.

"I shut down the program last night. I'm not in the money-making business anymore. I thought you should know."

Father Rodrigo was genuinely surprised, and said so. Jacob reminded the priest of what he had told him years earlier.

"I remember when you said you couldn't save every child. I can't make enough money to save everyone, and though the money has accomplished a lot of good, it almost destroyed whatever my future might be."

"Go to San Diego, and find out what your future is. I'll be praying for you."

It was another small attempt at humor, given what happened the last time the priest prayed for Jacob.

"Great."

He left after lunch, and crossed the border several hours later. Jacob checked in at the same hotel, and then walked across the street to the hospital to wait for his father. He showed up right on time, and took a seat next to Jacob. He was obviously relieved by the deaths of the Cordillero brothers, and even managed a smile when he saw his son. The irony that he might have been responsible for wrecking Jacob's life was apparently lost on him, but not on Jacob. He didn't want the conversation to last any longer than necessary, so Jacob got right to the point.

"I don't want to see or hear from you again. I wanted you to know I'm out of the market. I deleted the program from my computer, and I don't have any way to get it back."

He reached into his pocket, and took out the flash drive, handing it to his father.

"This is a copy. I want you to have it, to help you get back on your feet. I hope you use it to provide for your family in the future, but that's your choice. There's one thing I should tell you. It's only good for three months, after that it will self-delete. If you try to change the program, it will self-delete. You should be able to make enough to provide for your future. Good luck."

Annoyed at how Jacob talked to him, he said,

"I'm the only father you'll ever have. You should think about that."

"That's not really true, but I expect you wouldn't understand."

His father didn't understand, and Jacob would never hear from him again, nor would he ever know what his father did with the program. Jacob went back to the hotel, resisting the urge to go up and see Megan in her room. He would wait until the next morning when she was released, and then take her back to Pacific Beach and the café they had first visited over five years ago.

27

Not much had changed in Pacific City; the church, his old apartment, and the café were all there. Megan walked slowly from the street where they parked to the boardwalk, where they rested for a moment, and then farther on to the café. She would never fully recover, there would be periods of fatigue that would plague her for the rest of her life, but on the whole she would find that she could do about anything she wanted, within limits.

They sat down at a table, and waited until they had ordered coffee to begin their conversation. They both knew what they wanted to hear from the other, and both knew that their future together would be decided that day. Jacob, who usually got right to the point, was hesitant to begin. In one sense, he had been waiting his entire life for this moment; the moment he would begin to end his aloneness. Megan had been waiting as well; waiting for someone who shared her values and beliefs, though her experience of being alone could not be compared to Jacob's. She had wondered if the day would come when she found someone she could share her life with, and she spoke first.

"You look nervous. I've never seen you nervous before."

"I need to tell you some things, and then ask you a question."

She nodded in response, and then Jacob said,

"Father Rodrigo has asked me to take over the orphanage. He's getting older and doesn't have the energy he used to. I told him I would give him an answer when I returned."

"You mean you needed to talk with me about it?"

"Yes. That's what I mean."

"You want to know if I'll come back with you to Mexico? To work in the orphanage?"

"Yes."

"Are you going to ask me?"

"I'm sorry?"

"Are you going to ask me to marry you, Jacob?"

"I need to tell you something else first, if that's okay."

"Take all the time you need."

"I'm going to close down the foundation. There won't be any more money. I deleted the program from my computer. I'm out of the money-making business."

It was here that Jacob knew she might balk. He knew she might ask questions like: How will we live? What will we do for money? Why would you stop giving away money to those in need? Instead, Megan said,

"I think that's a good idea. You've done a lot of good in your life for people you don't even know. You can't save everyone, Jacob, but I guess you've figured that out."

"The priest told me the same thing years ago. It just took me a while to figure it out on my own."

Jacob was reliving the last month in his mind, going through all the events that had brought him to this place. He needed the moment to get his mind clear of the past, and concentrate on the future before him.

"Can I ask you now?"

"Yes, Jacob, you can ask me now."

"Will you marry me?"

"Yes, Jacob, I will."

And for the first time in his life Jacob kissed a girl.

Epilogue

They were married three months later in the chapel by Father Rodrigo. Megan's family came down for the ceremony, and though Megan had assured her mother and father that she wasn't rushing into marriage with Jacob, her mother had her concerns. When she told them that they would be living in El Bajo, and working at the orphanage, Megan's mother expressed her disappointment that she would essentially be living in another country, and wasting her education and gifts at the orphanage. Her father, however, had no issues with the union, no doubt being influenced by knowing Jacob's depth of character.

Jacob found them a large house up the street from the community, and during the three months before the marriage, went over it in detail, adding some comforts, such as hot water and air-conditioning. They spent their honeymoon in Cabo San Lucas, the first vacation Jacob had ever taken. It was awkward with nothing for him to do but enjoy himself, but after a few days he began to relax. When they returned to El Bajo, Jacob resumed his duties at the orphanage, while Megan spent her mornings taking Spanish lessons at a school in Ensenada. She would return to the orphanage in the afternoon and help out wherever she was needed. This would be the pattern of their lives until the birth of their first child, which occurred two years into the marriage. Father Rodrigo did not live to see the event; he died peacefully in his sleep several months after Jacob and Megan were married. The sisters, Jacob, and the staff met together and decided not to replace the priest, and closed the doors to the church soon after.

Jacob's trading accounts had enough money to keep the orphanage funded for many years, but Jacob knew the money would not last forever. Thinking how he might establish a secure source of funding for the community, he began a medical transcription service for doctors in northern Mexico. The older children at the orphanage spent part of each day working in a separate room, generating income for the community and developing skills they could use when they left after turning eighteen.

Finally, Jacob adapted himself to life as a married man, and did his best to accommodate his wife. He went to bed the same time she did, and would wait until she was fast asleep, and then would quietly slip out of the bed. Most of the time he would read or take care of community business. Occasionally, however, he would walk into his son's room, looking down at the child, making sure he was asleep.

Made in the USA
San Bernardino, CA
28 November 2018